HOPLITE

ALIEN WAR TRILOGY

BOOK ONE

IRIDIUM

PUBLISHING

A DIVISION OF

HOOKE
PUBLICATIONS

BOOKS BY ISAAC HOOKE

Military Science Fiction

Alien War Trilogy
Hoplite
Zeus
Titan

The ATLAS Series
ATLAS
ATLAS 2
ATLAS 3

A Captain's Crucible Series
Flagship
Test of Mettle
Cradle of War

Science Fiction

The Forever Gate Series
The Dream
A Second Chance
The Mirror Breaks
They Have Wakened Death
I Have Seen Forever
Rebirth
Walls of Steel
The Pendulum Swings
The Last Stand

Thrillers

The Ethan Galaal Series
Clandestine
A Cold Day In Mosul
Terminal Phase

HOPLITE

ALIEN WAR TRILOGY

BOOK ONE

Isaac Hooke

Text copyright © Isaac Hooke 2016
Published October 2016. All rights reserved.

www.IsaacHooke.com

ISBN-13: 978-0-9951955-6-1
ISBN-10: 0-9951955-6-0

Cover design by Isaac Hooke
Cover image by Shookooboo

contents

ONE 1
TWO 9
THREE 15
FOUR 19
FIVE 27
SIX 32
SEVEN 39
EIGHT 49
NINE 55
TEN 65
ELEVEN 75
TWELVE 83
THIRTEEN 92
FOURTEEN 101
FIFTEEN 111
SIXTEEN 118
SEVENTEEN 127
EIGHTEEN 138
NINETEEN 145
TWENTY 151
TWENTY-ONE 157
TWENTY-TWO 167
TWENTY-THREE 174
TWENTY-FOUR 179
TWENTY-FIVE 185
TWENTY-SIX 193
TWENTY-SEVEN 202
TWENTY-EIGHT 206
ACKNOWLEDGMENTS 213

*To my father, mother, brothers, and
most devoted fans.*

one

The badly damaged ATLAS mech toppled to the sand, the grit-clogged servomotors of the machine no longer able to bear its own weight. The motive elements hummed in complaint for several moments as the unit struggled to stand, but then the machine ceased all movement and simply lay there in a toppled, useless heap. No noise pierced the lonely desert air. No birds. No insects.

No servomotors.

And then the cockpit hatch opened a crack, the reverberations echoing loudly along the outer hull. The breach widened. A gloved hand abruptly gripped the rim of the hatch from inside and forced it open entirely.

A figure emerged into the merciless sun. A soldier whose face and body were wrapped in a military-grade exoskeleton: a strength-enhancing jumpsuit with a dented jetpack.

The individual took a few hesitant steps before collapsing onto the sand.

The soldier reached up and removed his helmet, revealing a broad, tanned face. It was all bony angles, a testament to his low body fat percentage. His eyes were weary, yet hard. While he was relatively young, those eyes seemed out of place, belonging to a much older man, or to someone who had witnessed far too much for his age. They also had an oddly glassy quality to them, as was common to those whose eyes had been replaced by the bioprinted varieties.

The man had a thick beard. So he was not an ordinary soldier, then, but special forces—regular soldiers were required to shave.

The man hauled himself back to the mech and then sat against it so that he was shaded from the sun.

He checked the PASS device. His cockpit had been breached during the battle, and the Personal Alert Safety System he wore at his belt had taken a hit. He tried to activate the distress beacon for several moments but the device appeared to be damaged beyond repair.

He spoke into the empty air. "This is LPO Rade 'Rage' Galaal, Alpha Platoon, MOTH Team Seven. I have been cut off from my unit. Repeat, cut off from my unit. Requesting immediate evac."

His Implant had the strength to transmit the communication to any nearby repeaters, but the signal wasn't powerful enough to travel very far on its own. As such, unsurprisingly no answer came.

"It would appear we're still out of range, sir," came a voice from the fallen mech.

"Don't call me sir," Rade said reflexively. "I work for a living."

"My apologies," the mech answered innocently. "I had forgotten."

"Really," Rade said. "A machine. Forgetting."

"I took major damage in the attack..." the mech replied.

Rade frowned. "According to the damage report, your core was fully intact."

"All right," the mech admitted. "You caught me. I was being facinorous."

"*Facinorous?*" Rade shook his head. "Damn AIs with their damn verbal vomit. Is that even a word?"

"It is," the mech told him. "It means, 'extremely wicked.'"

"Remind me to dial down your sense of humor sometime," Rade said.

"Actually, that one came from my sarcasm setting," the mech replied.

"Really. Well let's set that to zero."

"As you wish, LPO Galaal," the mech intoned.

"And call me by my callsign," Rade said. "I am a MOTH, you know."

"Yes, Rage."

MOTH. MObile Tactical Human. An elite force within the navy specializing in direct action missions, mostly guerrilla warfare and counterinsurgency. They were trained to operate on land, sea, air and space. Advanced weaponry, jetpacks, mechs—MOTHs were trained to use them all, and often employed multiple advanced technologies during deployments. Rade had a jetpack attached to his exoskeleton at that very moment, for example; it might have actually proven useful if he hadn't siphoned all the fuel from it into the mech's jumpjets during the battle.

Rade crawled away from the mech, moving into the sun.

"Try to stand again," he told the machine.

The ATLAS hummed, and its arms and legs gyrated up and down, but otherwise the mech remained on its side.

"All right all right, that's good enough." Rade returned to the machine again to rest in its shade. "How easy is it going to be to clean the grit from your servomotors?"

"Because of the damage, the sand has gotten into all of the actuators," the mech explained. "You'd have to take them apart and clean each unit individually. Needless to say, it is not something you can do without the necessary tools."

"Wonderful," Rade said. "And what about the power situation?"

"I have enough deuterium to last for at least one hundred years," the mech replied. "If I idle my processor, I should be able to extend that to a thousand years, at minimum."

"That doesn't really help me, does it?" Rade said.

"No, it does not," the mech replied. "Unless of course, you find some water for me to purify. Or meat to cook."

Rade examined the dreary dunes around him. "Don't think I'll be getting my hands on either of those any time soon." He studied the position of the sun in the sky. "How long until nightfall?"

"Approximately three hours."

"Wake me when it's dark." Rade shut his eyes and soon fell into an exhausted sleep.

RADE PROCEEDED ON foot in the dark. He had chosen to travel by night, because in theory the desert wouldn't be so hot. But he still sweated immensely, no thanks to the exoskeleton. His liquid-cooling undergarments were soaked, and obviously not functioning very well. He would have abandoned the jumpsuit entirely, but he was so weak from lack of food and water that the strength-enhancing suit was the only thing carrying him forward at the moment. He held his helmet in one arm, the headlamp turned on and pointed forward to light the way. He had tried wearing that helmet earlier, for the theoretical improvement in thermoregulation, but it hadn't helped.

He used the compass in his Implant to make his way back toward the general direction of the base. There were no positioning system satellites in orbit above the planet, so he had no actual coordinates to guide him.

He had broken away from the others to pursue one of the privateers who had tried to escape into the desert. Rade had been ambushed, and in the ensuing combat was driven even farther from his unit. He eventually managed to drive off his attackers, exhausting his jumpjet fuel in the process, but by then the privateer had escaped. Rade's mech had taken severe damage in the battle, and its comm node was offline. So he had begun the long trek back. It hadn't been long after that when his mech collapsed.

He momentarily shut off the helmet lamp and glanced at the night sky. So many stars out there, forming constellations unlike anything he had grown up with. The frigate *Granada* would be up there, disguised as a Sino-Korean merchant trader, looking for him. There would be a few Raptors, too—high altitude recon drones. And his platoon mates, of course.

Sometimes he wondered at the wisdom of the career he had chosen. Enlisting in the space navy so that he could leave Earth behind and travel to faraway places. The lure of the navy was the lure of a better life. He was an immigrant recruit, a temporary resident of the United Countries, his full citizenship dependent on the completion of his twelve year service term.

Well, even if he wasn't yet a full citizen, he *did* have a better life, that much was certain. His current circumstances notwithstanding...

"Rage, are you out there?" a voice came over the comm, courtesy of his Implant.

"Chief Facehopper?" Rade said.

"There you are," Facehopper returned. "I thought we'd lost you."

Rade saw the searchlight up ahead, sourced from a fast-moving shuttle, and he nearly wept in relief.

4

AFTER THE PREREQUISITE rehydration session with the surgical robots, known as Weavers, Rade had his debriefing in sick bay with Chief Facehopper, who explained that the main high value targets had been terminated.

"Strike two more Sino-Korean privateers from the kill list," the blue-eyed, red-faced Brit said. That accent of his, matched to his roguish charm, had often attracted women by the dozen on shore leave. Not that he joined the platoon on such occasions much anymore, not since becoming chief. Still, Facehopper was always willing to lend an ear, or a helping hand, and the men loved him for it.

"But is it really going to make a difference?" Rade said. "Take down two, four more pop up somewhere else."

"True enough," Facehopper admitted. "On the bright side, we'll be gainfully employed for years to come, mate."

"You'd think after all the help we gave the Sino-Koreans in Tau Ceti, they would at least relax their foreign policy a bit, and cancel their privateer initiative. Stop harrying our commercial ships. As a favor. You know?"

"Well, I suppose it's an essential part of their economy by now," Facehopper said. "Hard for them to stop."

Rade sighed. "I suppose so."

"You shouldn't have gone off on your own," Facehopper said. "Especially now that you're LPO. You have to lead by example, Mr. Galaal."

When the chief called one of his men by surname instead of callsign, Rade knew a chewing out was on the way.

"You're right of course, I just—" Rade hesitated. He hated admitting he was wrong. "I don't have an excuse. It was a lapse in judgement. It won't happen again."

"I certainly hope it does not," Facehopper replied.

"I accept full responsibility for what I did. If you have to punish me, then so be it."

"You're going to have to explain what you did back there to the platoon," Facehopper said. "That's your punishment right there."

Rade nodded wearily. "I suppose so."

"We almost lost you," Facehopper said. "The lieutenant commander was about ready to recall the platoon. Every minute we wasted on the planet looking for you was another minute we risked discovery. And the LC will be first to cite the extra cost per day of keeping the platoon deployed, along with all the support craft and personnel, not to mention the disguised frigate at the ready in orbit. It's somewhere in the tens of millions. Our commanding officer is going to take some hell for this, I assure you. I would advise you to avoid him for the next little while, if you know what's good for you."

Rade lowered his gaze. "Yes, Chief."

"Shit, mate, I'm going to take hell for this. If you weren't waylaid here in sick bay, I'd probably have you pumping out pushups as we speak. In fact, hell with it. Drop, you bloody bloke."

Rade boosted himself over the edge of the bed and dropped to the deck. The IV line trailed from the top of his palm to the drip above him.

"Give me fifty," Facehopper said.

Rade began pumping them out. He worked through a sudden dizziness, and blinked the phosphenes from his vision.

"You do realize, if we had to leave you behind there would be no coming back," Facehopper said. "Not ever. You know that, don't you?"

"I do," Rade said between reps.

He heard the sick bay hatch open, and deduced from the way Facehopper had tucked in his heels beside him that Lieutenant Commander Braggs had entered. Rade was careful not to look up from the deck. He knew his chewing out was about to get worse.

"Is that the son of a bitch?" Braggs said. His voice was stern, cavernous.

The LC knew exactly what Rade looked like, but apparently that day he had decided to forget.

"Yes, sir," Facehopper said. "That is him."

Rade continued pumping out the reps, aware of both their eyes upon him. When he finished his fifty, he started to lie down on one side.

"Another fifty," Facehopper said.

Rade was careful not to show any emotion as he assumed the starting position once again. He knew that Facehopper's punishment would be much more lenient compared to what the LC would mete out. Facehopper likely realized that, too—it was a small mercy on the chief's part. Rade suspected Facehopper had advance warning that the LC was coming, which was why he made him begin the pushups in the first place.

Rade pumped out the reps, his arms on fire. His pace was roughly half of what it was for the first fifty.

"Mr. Galaal," Lieutenant Commander Braggs said. "I'm disappointed in you."

Rade continued his pushups, not daring to glance up.

"Abandoning your brothers to chase an enemy on your own?" Braggs continued. "A leading petty officer. Abandoning his unit. Tell me again why we promoted you?"

Abandoning...

Rade felt a sudden swell of tears but he fought them back.

"You let your men down," Braggs said. "Left them without a leader. What would have happened if another attack had come when you were gone? Who would have led them, then?"

Braggs knew very well that any one of them was capable of taking charge, and would have. But he wanted Rade to feel terrible for what he had done. And rightly so.

"I need to set something straight, for the record," Braggs continued. "You think we saved you because you're our brother? You think we came back for you out of some sense of obligation? Because we were going to shed a tear at your absence? Because we're *friends?* No, Mr. Galaal. You see, it was in our best interest not to leave you behind. The navy pours millions of dollars into each and every spec-ops soldier. In terms of deployment costs, support costs... training, room, board. Add it all up, and you're five times more expensive than a mech. You hear me?"

"Yes, sir," Rade said, panting.

"You're a leading petty officer," Braggs said. "Now start acting like one, goddamnit. Before I put someone else in your shoes."

"Yes, sir," Rade repeated.

Unfortunately, Braggs took over his punishment at that point, making Rade complete another five hundred pushups, for a total of six hundred reps. When he was done, the LC simply walked from the compartment. Rade hadn't looked at him once.

Rade couldn't lift himself off the deck by himself so Facehopper had to help him back into the bed. Rade lay there, feeling absolutely winded, just gasping for air. He thought he was going to throw up any second.

"Check him," the chief told one of the nearby Weaver units.

The robot whirred to life. "Extreme glycogen depletion in the muscle cells. Hydration levels below minimum. Initiating electrolyte- and glucose-dense fluid transfer."

Rade continued to pant raggedly, his throat completely dry. He tried to swallow, but the act only set off a coughing fit.

After several moments his breathing began to calm and it felt like he wasn't about to die anymore. He was still slightly nauseous.

"His body is returning to homeostasis," the Weaver said in its masculine voice. "He will recover."

"Good," Facehopper said. "You got yourself a valuable piece of navy property here, *machine*. Make sure his recovery is swift."

"Affirmative," the Weaver answered.

Still panting slightly, Rade glanced at Facehopper and said: "Thanks."

"For what?" Facehopper said. "I told the LC I would handle your punishment and chewing out. Guess he decided he wanted to get his hands dirty, too. Teach the new LPO his boundaries."

"No, I deserved it," Rade said. "I'm lucky he didn't give my position to someone else. Then again, maybe that wouldn't be so bad." He forced a weak smile.

The chief's eyes became distant, and he nodded ever so faintly. "The burden of command."

"By the way," Rade said. "Were you able to retrieve my ATLAS unit?"

"We were," Facehopper said. "We followed the trail you left in the sand. Led us right to it."

"Good, I hate to lose an AI."

Facehopper pursed his lips. "You know, about that. We mostly recovered the mech so that it wouldn't fall into enemy hands. It's scheduled to be decommissioned."

"Oh."

Facehopper rested a hand on his shoulder. "Don't worry, mate. We've got some new mech classes in the pipeline. Big, bad beasts of machines that'll make you forget the ATLAS units ever existed. And, well, I can't say much about it now, but we have a mission coming up. A big one. Get some rest. And try to stay on the LC's good side, if you wouldn't mind?"

"I'll try," Rade said. "No guarantees."

two

The next morning Rade felt well enough to join the rest of his platoon in the *Granada's* gym. The frigate was Trakehner class, designed to travel fast and light, meaning that the gym was relatively small, but the MOTHs made do. Though the vessel was outfitted with several external attachments as part of its Sino-Korean merchant trader guise, the inner layout was unchanged. Probably a good thing. He didn't think he could stand to be aboard a ship without a gym. Calisthenics, while a great warmup, could only take one so far in terms of sheer muscle mass.

Rade took over his leading petty officer duties, and led the platoon through a series of pushup and ab exercises. When they finished their main sets, the men split into three groups, with the first congregating around the bench press, the second the squat rack, and the third the pull-up bar. The gym aboard the *Granada* utilized real weights in the form of thick metal plates, not the tiny "gravity inducers" found on some of the smaller vessels.

Rade approached the bench press. The newest member of the platoon, Keelhaul, was currently attempting to press four plates per side. Keelhaul was a seasoned sniper reassigned from MOTH Team Eight. Grappler was the second new member, also from Team Eight, where he had served as a mech specialist and heavy gunner, though so far in Team Seven he had only been recognized for the latter role. He was one of Keelhaul's spotters on the press.

"Come on, push it!" Tahoe said. He was spotting Keelhaul on the other side. "Push that pussy!"

Tahoe's callsign was actually Cyclone, but Rade knew him from since before the Teams and mentally referred to him by his real name, unlike the others. Tahoe was a Navajo, with a wife and two children back home. His official position was that of heavy gunner. He certainly had the build for it.

Keelhaul shoved the bar upward, completing a rep.

"Three!" Grappler announced.

Keelhaul began to lower the bar.

"He's going for another!" Bender said. The well-muscled black man barely fit his T-shirt, and his upper chest was covered in heavy chains. His front teeth were capped in gold, big hoops hung from both ears, piercings tipped each eyebrow, a labret studded the skin under his lower lip, and several rings decorated each finger. All of that jewelry—chains, hoops, labrets—was made of gold. He usually didn't wear most of it during actual combat operations, but while on base, or aboard a starship, he flaunted it. Rade had figured out that the jewelry served the same purpose as the beard the others grew—a sign of their elite status.

Bender was the lead drone operator, meaning he issued orders to the combat robots and drones that supported the platoon.

Keelhaul touched the bar to his chest and pushed. The weight didn't move. He tried again, the vein in his forehead bulging. No good.

Tahoe and Grappler helped Keelhaul lift and rerack the weight.

"Good try," Grappler said.

"You call that a good try?" Tahoe said. "I felt like I was curling the damn weight for him."

Snakeoil stepped forward. The short man was one of the comm officers. He was built like a tank, most likely due to hauling around all that heavy comm equipment.

Snakeoil interlocked his palms, cracked his knuckles, and then made a dismissive, almost contemptuous sweeping gesture toward the bench press.

Keelhaul immediately vacated it and Snakeoil took his place.

"Five plates per side, please," Snakeoil said.

"Oh ho," Bender said. "He's going to embarrass himself again."

Snakeoil ignored him. He shook out his muscles, as if trying to get rid of knots. It was his way of limbering up. "I said five per side."

As Tahoe and Grappler added an extra plate to either end of the barbell, Fret came over from the pull-up area to watch.

"This is going to be good." Fret was also a comm officer, yet unlike Snakeoil, he was completely opposite build-wise, coming in at very tall and lanky. The comm equipment he carried was just as heavy as Snakeoil's, but he likely offloaded most of the weight to his exoskeleton during operations.

Snakeoil spread chalk over his hands and then lay back on the bench. "Help me unrack it," he instructed the spotters. "After that, don't intervene unless I say."

Other members of the platoon wandered over to watch.

"He's attempting five again?" someone asked.

"Yup," Rade answered.

Snakeoil stared at the racked barbell above him. He took several deep breathes, then punched his chest with a fist three times in rapid succession, grunting loudly each time.

"Love how he psychs himself up," someone said.

Snakeoil's arms shot up and he wrapped both hands around the bar as fast as he could, as if he was afraid his body would change its mind. "Go!"

His muscles flexed.

Tahoe and Grappler quickly lifted either end of the bar off the rack and then released their grip so that Snakeoil held it above his body on his own. The two spotters kept their arms near the bar in case it proved necessary to catch the weight.

Rade touched Bender on the arm to get his attention, and then pointed at the rack. Bender nodded, quickly taking up a position behind the bench near Snakeoil's head so that he was ready to offer assistance from that quarter as well.

Snakeoil slowly lowered the bar. The metal bent slightly beneath the burden of the five plates weighing down either end, two hundred twenty five pounds per side. Including the bar, the whole thing weighed four hundred and ninety five pounds.

When the barbell reached his chest, the muscles in Snakeoil's neck and arms corded, and it became obvious he was pushing with everything he had.

But the bar refused to move.

Bender smirked. "That's right, baby. Come on. Call mommy for help."

Rade shot Bender a dirty look. That wasn't a light weight. Rade had hoped to quell any sarcasm from him by assigning Bender the topmost spotter position. It hadn't worked, apparently.

When Bender noticed Rade's disapproval, his smirk instantly evaporated.

Tahoe and Grappler touched either end, obviously intending to render assistance.

"Get back!" Snakeoil snarled.

Tahoe and Grappler exchanged worried looks, then released their grips, though they kept their hands close. Bender, too, was ready to grab the center portion of the bar.

Snakeoil sucked in his belly and pushed again. His back arched dangerously, and Rade worried the comm officer was about to throw a disk. The muscles in his neck stood out even greater than before, adding several millimeters of thickness.

The bar slowly rose. One centimeter. Three. Five. But there it froze, five centimeters from his chest, and several more from the top of the rack, his elbows bent at an eighty-degree angle.

"Help," Snakeoil squeaked.

Tahoe, Grappler, and Bender all interceded, and in moments Snakeoil racked the weight.

The squat comm officer lay there on the bench, panting for several moments.

Bender was snickering. He tried to cover his mouth when he caught Rade's eye, and he ended up turning around as his shoulders rolled with barely restrained laughter.

"How's your lower back?" Tahoe asked the question that was foremost on Rade's mind.

Snakeoil kicked his legs out to the side and sat up. "Never better."

"Next time wear a belt," Grappler said.

Snakeoil sniffed. "Belts are for pussies." He abruptly stiffened, grimacing as if feeling a jolt in his back. Then he slumped again, and smiled wryly. "Just kidding."

"Good job." Rade patted him on the shoulder.

Bender turned around. He wore the biggest smirk. "Yeah, good job man," he said sarcastically.

Rade ignored him, and ran his gaze across his fellow warriors, his eyes lingering upon the newest members of the team, Keelhaul and Grappler.

"You see what just happened here?" Rade continued. "Snakeoil displayed the qualities of a true MOTH. A man who refused to give up so very easily, but who also knew when it was time to enlist the aid of his friends. Because not giving up is one thing, but being needlessly stubborn, at the expense of one's own life, or one's platoon... well, let's just say there's no place for behavior like that in the platoon."

"Are you talking about your own behavior in the last battle?" Trace piped in. He was East Indian. Bengali. And like Rade, his specialty was sniping.

"I wasn't being stubborn," Rade said. "Or putting the platoon at risk. I saw one of the enemy trying to get away. I was the closest, so I intercepted."

"But when you were ambushed, you should have let him go," Trace said.

"I would have," Rade agreed. "Except that they had me trapped."

"But you didn't even radio for help!"

"I tried," Rade said. "But my comm node was damaged."

Trace remained silent.

Rade remembered what Facehopper had told him.

You're going to have to explain what you did back there to the platoon. That will be your punishment.

Punishment indeed.

"You're right," Rade admitted. "I should have taken someone else with me. There's a reason why we use the buddy system. We're brothers here, not lone wolves. I let you guys down. I'm sorry. It won't happen again. As your LPO, you deserve better than this." He pursed his lips, and lowered his gaze. "Because of my actions, you were forced to scour the desert for me for two days. You were probably worried sick."

"Nah, not really," Bender joked. He punched Rade on the shoulder. "Glad to have you back, boss."

Rade smiled slightly. "I'm glad you'll have me."

He noticed TJ, the second drone operator, scowling from the squat rack. Rivets and servomotors were tattooed along the bulging muscles of his left arm, while military robots decorated his right side. An Atlas moth inked his neck, its wings reaching toward his chest before vanishing under the low collar that showcased the deep divide between his upper pectorals.

The tattooed Italian had vehemently opposed Rade's promotion, and was likely still jealous Rade had been the one promoted to leading petty officer over him. Rade would just have to prove to TJ that he was worthy of the position.

Nothing's ever easy.

three

R̲ade sat in the small briefing area aboard the *Granada* with Alpha platoon.

The officer in charge of Alpha and Bravo platoons, MOTH Team Seven, stood at the lectern and towered over them all. Lieutenant Commander Braggs was in his late thirties, though he looked older because of the deep lines graven into the angular planes of his face. Those lines were partially balanced out by his body, which had the look of a hardened athlete.

Rade met the officer's gaze steadily, remembering well the chewing out he had received from him a few days before. Braggs caught his eye, and Rade inclined his head slightly. The lieutenant commander nodded in return.

"Members of Alpha Platoon," Braggs began. "We're going to rendezvous with Task Group 68.2 in three weeks time. We will proceed with the task group to the Arcturus system at the periphery of UC territory. There, we will travel through the outgoing Gate to the unexplored 11-Aquarii system, one-hundred lightyears from Arcturus, to determine why two Builder ships, and the warship sent to escort them, have gone missing. Alpha Platoon has been called upon to act in a reserve capacity."

"A reserve capacity?" Bender said. "As in, we're just going to sit on the sidelines?"

"That is correct," the lieutenant commander responded coolly. "We will act when called upon. But until then, we are merely bystanders. Maybe we won't even be utilized at all."

"Can I ask the name of the missing warship?" Lui asked. He was the resident Asian American, and was one of the official mech pilots of Alpha Platoon: when access to mechs proved limited, he was one of the three usually assigned a machine.

"The *John A. McDonald*," Braggs answered.

"*John A. McDonald*..." Lui tapped his lower lip. His eyes defocused, and it was obvious he was accessing data via his Implant. "A Decatur class supercarrier. One of the most powerful starships ever made, with three times the armaments and twice the starfighter capacity of the Rickover class. Hell of a ship to go missing."

"Yes," Braggs agreed.

"Obviously we don't think the Sino-Koreans are involved," Tahoe said. "Otherwise you wouldn't have told us even half of what you just did, Lieutenant Commander. Operational security, fear of moles, and whatnot. You would have said, 'we're going to Arcturus, boys,' and that's it. Then again, maybe the moles have already leaked the information."

"You're absolutely right, on all accounts," the LC said. "The Special Collection Service does not believe the Sino-Koreans are involved. And the SKs know about our mission already, thanks to their moles. In any case, I am authorized to show you something. I must warn you though, the following video is highly classified, and is not to be shared outside of this room."

A retinal video feed filled Rade's vision. He floated above a G-type main-sequence star at relatively close range. It was white, the same color as Earth's sun, Sol. He tried to remember why Sol appeared yellow from Earth. Something about Rayleigh scattering... he would have to look it up on his Implant later.

Instinctively, Rade tried to save the video stream, but he realized that not only was the feed tagged as unrecordable, but Braggs had disabled video recording in his Implant entirely.

"This is the only image we have from 11-Aquarii, a year after the arrival of the *John A. McDonald*. We acquired it from a civilian, who deployed an experimental telescope that used the Slipstream to 11-Aquarii itself as a gravitational lens."

Slipstreams were the holes in spacetime that connected different systems together in that region of space. They could only be traversed by means of human-made Gates, massive, ring-like structures that encircled the Slipstreams and balanced out the gravitational forces.

"Observe," Braggs continued.

In front of the white star, the contour of what looked like a UC supercarrier moved in front of the sun. Several moments passed, until behind it another object slowly crept into view, silhouetted against the bright surface—a black dodecahedron, about twice as big as the supercarrier.

The Lieutenant Commander paused the video and skipped forward some frames. He zoomed in.

Upon the uppermost edge of the supercarrier was a slight discoloration set against the sun. As the LC advanced the video, that discoloration bloomed. Like an explosion.

"Some of the scientists believe what we're looking at is a coronal discharge from the sun," Braggs said. "That the supercarrier just so happened to superimpose as it flew past. However most of the senior command believe it's an explosion, caused by the pursuing vessel."

"That ship design isn't in any of our databases," Lui said. "Are we talking a new race of alien beings here? A first contact scenario?"

"That's the operating assumption, yes," Braggs said.

"Have we sent any advance drones to scout the system?" Bomb asked. He was the second black man in the platoon after Bender, though he wasn't nearly as muscular. He shaved his head on either side in a fade pattern, so that a dark mohawk sprouted from the centerline. Like Lui, he was a mech pilot.

"The Special Collection Service has determined that no return Gate exists on the other side of the Slipstream," the LC answered. "So even if we did send drones, none could return to transmit their discoveries. There will of course be a Builder accompanying Task Group 68.2, which will begin work on the return Gate while the remaining ships investigate the system."

"So we're traveling into an uncharted system," Bomb said. "One potentially owned by an alien race. And we'll be trapped there until the Builder creates a return Gate."

"That is correct," Braggs replied.

"Wait a second," Lui interjected. "We're bringing a fleet of destroyers into a potentially alien jurisdiction. Wouldn't that be considered an act of war from the point of view of the alien party?"

"I have to emphasize that this is an *exploratory* mission," Braggs replied. "The warships are present only for our protection."

"Lui's right," Manic said. "If a similar situation happened in a UC controlled system, with invading warships arriving from a remote Slipstream, the UC would consider it an act of war."

17

It seemed the mech pilots were teaming up that day, because Manic, like Lui and Bomb, was another official pilot of the war machines. A port-wine stain above his eye vaguely resembled a moth—the insect. Manic claimed the stain was the whole reason he had joined the service in the first place. "I was destined to become a MOTH," he often said.

"It's an act of war only if the arriving ships initiate aggressive action," the LC stated.

"Well sure," Manic said. "But does anyone else see how this could quickly spiral out of control? We're going to have a second alien war on our hands. And we barely won the first, I'd like to remind you all."

"If you don't like it," Braggs told him. "Feel free to request a transfer to a different Team via Master Chief Bourbonjack. Though he'll probably turn it down. As will I."

"Don't get me wrong," Manic said. "There really is nowhere else I'd rather be. I signed up for action. I'm just saying, we have to look at the bigger picture."

"You're not paid to look at the bigger picture," the lieutenant commander responded. "Nor to overthink. You're here to do what you're told. And that's precisely what you're going to do. Don't get your hopes up about seeing any action, because as I already said you might not be employed at all. The most action you might see is from your quarters, where you'll sit, helplessly cooped up while the encounter unfolds. And if the enemy decides to open fire, and you find yourselves aboard a sinking ship, you'll spend the subsequent weeks in a jettisoned lifepod waiting for retrieval."

It was certainly a bleak picture the lieutenant commander had painted. But come what may, the platoon members would follow their orders, Rade knew.

"Any other questions?" Braggs asked. "No? Good."

"We'll do what needs to be done," Rade said.

"Damn right you will. Dismissed."

four

Affter rendezvousing with Task Group 68.2 and transferring to the *Rhodes*, a destroyer in said group, Rade was forced to take on an unexpected new team member.

Chief Facehopper marched into the berthing area leading a shy-looking young man who appeared extremely out of his element. He wore tight-fitting fatigues, just as if he were part of the *Rhodes'* regular crew. He was extremely skinny, almost gaunt. His eyes seemed friendly, but there was something slightly off about them. They didn't seem to reflect the light properly, like natural eyes would. Sort of like Rade's own, he supposed.

"The Navy is performing an experiment," Facehopper announced. "Introducing Artificials into the ranks of every rating, the MOTHs included. I guess they're trying to determine the viability of allowing permanent combat robots into our collective midsts. Anyway, meet your new caterpillar."

The humanlike robot extended a hand. "I am Bradley."

No one made a move toward the Artificial.

Bradley cocked its head slightly, seeming confused. "I'm Bradley?"

Rade sighed mentally.

Lead by example.

He stepped forward and grabbed the Artificial's hand. The grip was surprisingly soft, as if the Artificial was trying very hard not to injure him.

Rade forced a smile. "Welcome aboard, caterpillar."

"Thank you, LPO!" the Artificial beamed.

"Bradley?" Bomb said. "Did you just call yourself Bradley? Like the ancient tank?"

"If you are referring to the Bradley Fighting Vehicle," the Artificial replied. "It was not a tank, but a combination of armored personnel carrier and tank *killer*. And yes, I called myself Bradley. It has no meaning—it is simply my name."

"You named yourself after an outdated tank." Bomb shook his head.

The Artificial glanced at Rade. It seemed confused. "My name is Bradley?"

"Actually, about that," Rade said. "We already have a Bender and a Bomb. Too many B's as it is. In the heat of combat, you definitely don't want to be getting people's names mixed up. It's something we're going to fix right now. From this moment forward, you're Harlequin. At least until you earn yourself a proper callsign."

"He ain't ever going to earn that," Bomb stated.

"*Harlequin?*" the Artificial said. "But—"

"As I said, it's not a callsign," Rade persisted. "Just a name. Don't read too much into it."

"But you can't call me Harlequin. That won't match the data in my embedded ID. When someone views my profile—"

"Then update that data if it makes you feel better," Rade said. "Because we're calling you Harlequin."

"Harlequin," the Artificial said. Its eyes became distant, as if it were looking up the word in its dictionary. "A mute character in a Roman mime, typically masked. Dressed in a diamond-patterned costume."

"Sounds about right," Rade said. "I recommend, for the first little while at least, that you behave the same way." Grinning slightly, he added: "The mute part, I mean. The costume is optional."

Bomb had folded his arms, and he was huffing and puffing as if he was struggling to hold back some rant.

"Something on your mind, Bomb?" Facehopper said.

"An experiment," Bomb said. "You called it an experiment, Chief? I ain't going to let the navy replace me. And I ain't going to treat no machine like a brother." He spat at Harlequin's feet. "I'm going to personally ensure this *experiment* ends in failure."

"But AIs are sentient," Facehopper said. He glanced at Rade, as if hoping he would back him up.

Rade nodded. "They are." He wasn't sure what else the chief wanted him to say.

"And they're fully capable," Facehopper continued. "I'm not asking you to treat Harlequin like a brother. All I'm asking is that you trust him. You've trusted combat robots with your lives before after all."

"We have," TJ agreed. "But this is no combat robot."

"I'm running the same realtime operating system as a Centurion class combat robot," Harlequin said. "And I've downloaded the complete combat algorithms, along with algorithms dealing with a myriad of intricate tasks. I think you will find I am far more versatile than your usual assault robot, able to assume many roles. I hope one day to prove myself to you all, and be worthy of a callsign."

It sounded like something the Artificial had prepared precisely for that moment.

"Like I said, you'll never be worthy of a callsign, bitch." Bomb attempted to shove past the Artificial, but his shoulder slammed against Harlequin's unyielding chest with a loud thud.

"Gah!" Bomb stepped back to rub his shoulder.

Harlequin smiled sheepishly. "Sorry." The Artificial slid to one side, almost stepping on other members of the platoon.

"Stay away from me," Skullcracker said heatedly. He had the tattoo of a realistic-looking skull inked onto his face. He kept mostly to himself, and could usually be found in the berthing area slumped over a desk as he relived memories on his Implant. On the rare occasion when the soft-spoken MOTH talked, people listened. He, too, was a heavy gunner, though one would have never guessed it from his relatively slight build.

Harlequin moved again, giving both Bomb and Skullcracker a wide berth.

"I'm not fighting alongside no machines," Skullcracker told the chief.

"Facehopper's right, we've done it before..." Bender said.

"You mean before they turned on us?" Skullcracker replied. "No thanks, Drone Operator. After everything we've been through, I'm surprised any of you would be fixing to fight alongside a machine."

"I see our southern accents are finally rubbing off on y'all," Snakeoil said. "Fixing to fight. We done good, Lui."

Skullcracker gave him a withering glare in reply, and the smile quickly fled Snakeoil's face. No one liked to be stared at like that by a death's head.

"The problems we've had with the robots are behind us," the chief said. "We've built extra security measures into all the units, and placed shielding into the AI cores of the starships. We have to start trusting the machines again, one way or another. You don't seem to have any problems with piloting mechs into battle, after all."

"That's only because we're in complete control of them," Skullcracker said.

Manic spoke up. "I have to agree with the general sentiment here. I'm not liking this, not one bit. So we introduce one combat robot into a platoon as a full time member. That's just a small thing, right? But what's next? Entire platoons manned by them? Machines already run our lives. And now we're going to let them fight our battles, too? Seems like a step backward, not forward." The port-wine stain above his right eye seemed particularly bright and angry that day.

"All right, that's about enough," Rade said. "Set aside your personal feelings and take the high road, people." He turned toward the Artificial. "Welcome aboard, Harlequin. It's good to have you, previous comments notwithstanding. Cyclone, find a bed for him."

"Can we haze him, first?" Tahoe asked, responding immediately to his callsign.

"*Haze?*" the Artificial said, eyes widening in trepidation.

"What a fine idea!" Bender grinned broadly, his golden front teeth gleaming malevolently in the light. He put his arm around the Artificial. "Yes, welcome aboard, Harlequin. Cyclone and I will show you to your bed."

With a happy skip to his step, Bender proceeded to lead the Artificial deeper into the berthing area. Harlequin looked over his shoulder at Facehopper helplessly.

"Do what you can to integrate him," the chief said when everyone had vacated to the adjoining head, presumably to begin Harlequin's hazing.

"I'll do my best," Rade said. "But I have to admit, it's going to be a hard sell. Especially since I share the same feelings about allowing an AI into our midst. I'm not sure how much I can rely upon the thing, let alone trust it."

"You seem to trust the AIs of your mechs," Facehopper said.

"That's different," Rade replied. "As Skullcracker said, we're always in complete control. We can easily override the AIs and take full command. But an embedded Artificial? I don't know..."

"We've always worked with embedded combat robots," Facehopper said.

"We have," Rade agreed slowly. "But we've always treated them as support units. Like the Raptor drones that provide air support, or the Equestrian tanks and artillery on the ground. But now we're calling a robot a MOTH? It doesn't sit well with me. Not at all. How can a robot that has never gone through Trial Week understand what it takes?"

"We've made the Artificial endure Trial Week," Facehopper said. "And it has undergone the full BSD/M training."

Rade cocked an eyebrow. "Really. Well then, have you made the Artificial do it with its battery running on near empty? With a missing arm, perhaps? Because you know as well as any of us that the training is all about mental fortitude, and overcoming the weaknesses of the body. A robot doesn't have those weaknesses."

"But a robot can be programmed to have mental fortitude," the chief said.

Rade heard a distinctly mechanical howl emanating from the head.

"Hm. Maybe not." Facehopper forced a smile. "Well, like I said, do what you can."

THAT EVENING RADE noticed that Harlequin had scuff marks on his right palm. Apparently the others had made him shove his hand down one of the toilets in the head—after Bender had filled it up with his excrement, of course—and they had flushed it repeatedly, so that by the time they were done a laser torch was required to cut out the feces-splattered Artificial.

Rade put the instigators of the deed, Bender and Tahoe, on half rations for the next three days. That was one of the recommended disciplinary actions, as listed in the handy LPO guide he had downloaded to his Implant. Facehopper had warned him not to rely too heavily on that guide, telling Rade to use his own judgment instead. Even so, half rations seemed like the perfect punishment for those two.

"I'm surprised at you, Tahoe," Rade scolded him. "Don't you remember the hazing you and I went through when we first joined the platoon? We swore we'd be better than that."

"You might have sworn it," Tahoe said. "I never did. Besides, I'm a firm believer that hazing builds character."

"If you say so," Rade told his friend.

"Half rations," Tahoe muttered. "That isn't so bad."

"Wait until the afternoon of the second day," Rade said. "When your stomach growls nonstop, and you can feel your muscles digesting themselves. Big man like you? You're definitely going to feel it."

Tahoe's face paled. "My muscles are going to shrink."

Rade shrugged. "Maybe you'll learn your lesson." Though he knew it wouldn't be that dramatic. If anything, Tahoe would probably lean out.

The Navajo didn't answer.

"Anyway, earlier you said you had a new message from Tepin?" Rade began, wanting to change the subject. He was Tahoe's friend first, his LPO second. "What's the news from the wife? More kids on the way?"

Tahoe laughed, his punishment completely forgotten. "If there are any more kids on the way, then I'm going to have to file for a divorce, because they're not from me."

"Come on," Rade said. "She didn't really withhold sex from you last time you were home? I thought you were joking."

Tahoe shook his head gravely. "She wouldn't let me lay a finger on her, let alone my dick. She's still mad about the former girlfriend incident from last year."

"A year later and she's still upset about that?" Rade said. "I thought you never actually caught up with your old girlfriend. And stopped messaging her cold turkey."

"Oh I did stop," Tahoe said. "I deleted all her contact info, and yes, I never met her. But Tepin, she's the jealous type. She had me install a message monitoring service so she could see everything I get or send. It only works on civilian messages, of course. But that's the crux of it. She thinks I'm using my encrypted military account to stay in touch with her instead. As if the lieutenant commander would tolerate that." He shook his head. "A guy never gets a break.

But you know what? I don't even care. When I'm home, I have my augmented reality porn stash, and my teledildonic stimulators. I get better sex from machines. Besides, she's so ugly now, I'm not sure I can get it up for her anymore anyway."

Rade smiled wistfully. "You don't mean that."

"I do," Tahoe said stubbornly.

"I don't believe you," Rade insisted.

"That's because you're a foolish romantic," Tahoe said.

"I know you love her."

"Oh I love her," Tahoe agreed. "But she's still ugly. My kids, though, they're something else. They're the beautiful ones. Must have gotten the genes from me."

"Right. So how's she taking the news of our upcoming mission?"

"Not well," Tahoe said. "Even though I forwarded her the official notice, she doesn't believe it. She told me, even if it's true, I'm just going to spend all my time and wages on strippers."

Rade furrowed his brow. "Strippers? How? We're not on shore leave here."

"Yeah," Tahoe said. "But her latest is that she's convinced all we do on deployment is spend our days in strip clubs. She actually believes the navy has installed strippers on the ships."

Rade looked at him incredulously and then burst out laughing. Tahoe joined him.

"Just be glad you're not married, Rade," Tahoe said. "Be very, very glad."

"I suppose so," Rade said, trying to hide the sadness those words inflicted upon him.

Apparently it hadn't worked, because Tahoe said: "Still miss Shaw?"

Rade nodded, but then quickly moved on to another topic. "I saw you spotting Facehopper on the bench press this morning. I'm glad to see you and he are getting along better."

Tahoe regarded him appraisingly for a moment, as if considering whether or not to grant Rade his latest change of subject. Apparently, he decided to allow it, because he said with a shrug: "We have to get along. He's chief now."

"You still don't like him, do you?"

Tahoe shrugged. "Something about Englishmen gets under my skin. But no one ever said I had to like my chief. In fact, back when

I lived on the reserve, I can't recall ever liking any of the chiefs. Anyway, regarding Facehopper... while I don't necessarily like him, I will obey him."

"I'm sure that's all he cares about," Rade said.

"I'm sure of that, too," Tahoe sniffed.

five

Rade retired to his bunk soon thereafter to check his inbox, and was disappointed to see no new messages from Shaw—his on again, off again girlfriend. The two of them were currently in one of their off phases, with both sides having agreed to a relationship break. It was a full-on sort of break, meaning that either party was allowed to pursue external relationships. So far Rade hadn't had the opportunity to avail himself of that allowance. And he wasn't sure he would, given the chance.

The two of them were so different from when they had originally joined, so long ago. They had been like children, then. So naive. Rade's training had hardened him, turned him into a killer, Shaw said. Unfortunately, when they had last fought together, she had become a killer, too. That hurt the most for him, seeing her like that, given the gentle person she once was. He felt responsible, somehow, and that guilt carried through into their relationship and soured it. The fact that they were serving different deployments on opposite sides of the galactic quadrant didn't help matters.

He wondered if he'd ever be able to maintain an ordinary relationship ever again. Or if he'd become like most of the other MOTHs—meeting girls on shore leave, or sneaking away with ensigns on the larger ships for one or two night stands, or relying on rented Artificials for pleasure. Tahoe was the only one of them who was married. None of them could understand how he could be on the Teams, and yet have a happy home life. Some of them envied him. Rade used to as well, until he learned just how rocky Tahoe's relationship with his wife was.

Ah, Shaw. Change was inevitable, he supposed. Eighty billion human cells died every day from apoptosis. Another eighty billion were birthed. Biologically, he wasn't the same person he was yesterday, and he'd be a different person the day after as well. Personality changed over time, too. People could become inflexible and rigid—hardening and crimping like a sponge left too long in the sun.

He resisted the urge to send Shaw a message, as that would have been his third unanswered communication in a row. He had learned that sending too many unanswered messages only made him look desperate and needy. So instead he closed the inbox, shutting down the interface with a few eye navigations.

His Implant was responsible for overlaying the necessary computer-generated imagery onto his vision. Everyone with a MOTH rating had one. Others in Big Navy had the option of wearing aReal goggles or contact lenses instead. aReal stood for augmented reality, and that was exactly what it did. With an aReal or Implant, one could access the InterGalNet anywhere, anytime. Aboard starships, that connection was facilitated by the Li-Fi v312 protocol of the overhead lights, which flickered imperceptibly fast, constantly transferring data at terabit per second speeds. A comm node aboard the vessel transmitted that data at much slower rates to 'node probes'—specialized drones that orbited near Gates and constantly passed in and out of them, transferring packets between solar systems. Delay-tolerant networking at its finest, as Tahoe once said.

A few days later the ship approached the Gate to 11-Aquarii. The lieutenant commander shared the external forward-facing video feed with Chief Facehopper, who in turn authorized the rest of the platoon to view it.

Rade stared at the broad, circular metal frame, twelve kilometers in diameter. Beyond it, space seemed completely normal, without the distortions one might expect from a wormhole.

Ordinarily there would have been a line up of merchant ships in front of a Gate, waiting to pass through. However, the only ships queued that day belonged to Task Group 68.2. No one else wanted to go to 11-Aquarii. Why would they? There was nothing there. No trade outposts. No luxury worlds. Only uncharted space. Not that the two destroyers perched on either side would allow any unauthorized vessels past the military embargo anyway.

"There she is, people," Rade said. "Our one way ticket to 11-Aquarii."

"Eleventh star in the constellation of the Water-carrier," Tahoe said. "Detected only in the last five hundred years, when telescopes became powerful enough to peer through the dense cloud of planetary nebulae surrounding the region."

"The Age of Aquarius," Manic mused.

"What's that?" Rade asked.

"Nothing," Manic replied. "Just an old saying from the 21st century. Humankind was apparently on the brink of entering a grand age of enlightenment. We're still waiting for it."

"Enlightenment," TJ said. "I think we've achieved it."

"Have we?" Tahoe said. "Then why do we still have wars?"

The lead ship in the queue passed into the ring and vanished.

"Never ceases to amaze me," Mauler said. "Slipstreams. A network of wormholes we can use for travel throughout our small region of the galaxy. Conveniently stable wormholes. But doesn't it ever bother anyone that these Slipstreams weren't made by us?"

Mauler was officially a heavy gunner, and he had joined the platoon to replace Big Dog. Rade hadn't trusted him at first, but he had proven himself many times over. He had lost both arms, but instead of choosing bioprinted replacements, he had elected for robotic limbs. They looked indistinguishable from ordinary arms, though when touched the texture wasn't quite right. Mauler had chosen to keep the aesthetics rather modest, aiming for a moderate muscular appearance. It was an illusion, of course, because those arms made him the strongest present—without a MOTH exoskeleton anyway. Definitely wasn't a man anyone would want to arm-wrestle with.

"Well whoever made them certainly isn't using them anymore," Bender said. "We might as well take advantage of the fact." He paused. "Did you know, the Slipstreams are slowly evolving over time? Getting larger. We have to keep resizing our Gates. And it takes longer to build new ones, because we have to make them bigger. At this rate, in seventy years, it's going to take six months to build a Gate, rather than the two it takes now."

"None of us will be around in seventy years time," Fret said.

"Don't be so dour," Manic said. "Of course we will."

"Not in the military, I mean," Fret clarified.

"Don't be so sure about that," Rade said.

"What, you plan to remain enlisted into your nineties?" Manic asked.

"Not necessarily," Rade said. "All I'm saying is, we don't know what the future holds."

"Wouldn't be so bad," Bender said. "We have free rejuvenation treatments, after all. The military will keep us young until we decide we've had enough."

"Those treatments don't work forever you know," Mauler countered.

"True," Bender agreed. He stared off into space. "I don't think I'm ever going to leave, to be honest. This shit is too addicting. And it's all I've ever known."

"You're crazy, Bender," Manic said.

"At least I'm not a pussy, like you."

"Bender..." Rade warned him.

"Just saying," Bender mumbled. He eyed Manic with disgust. "Skinny little runt."

"I'm just as skinny as Skullcracker," Manic said. "And you'd never tell that to him, would you?"

Bender glanced at Skullcracker, but didn't answer. The latter MOTH seemed disinterested in the conversation. Even when he was relaxed like that, his skull tattoo seemed menacing.

"That's what I thought," Manic said. "And how exactly am I a pussy? I've proven myself in every single battle we've ever fought. Hell, I saved your life on more than a few occasions, if I recall."

"That's why you're a pussy." Bender seemed like he was trying to keep a straight face, but he couldn't. He burst out laughing.

Manic, seeming angry at first, laughed along with him.

"Peace," Bender said, extending a hand.

Manic reached out to shake it.

At the last moment Bender formed a fist and punched Manic in the palm.

"Hey! You'll break my hand!" Manic grabbed Bender's fist and stepped forward, shoving the arm tight behind Bender's back.

Bender struggled against the painful grip, but couldn't break free. Rade was worried that his arm was about to snap, and he stepped forward to intervene.

Bender abruptly lifted his legs and pushed off from the bulkhead, forcing Manic backward. The two tumbled to the deck. Manic, apparently stunned, released his hold.

The instant he was free, Bender spun around; the black man was on top of him momentarily and assumed the mount position, wrapping his legs around Manic's chest. He squeezed tightly, robbing Manic of precious oxygen.

Manic tried to grab Bender's biceps to initiate an escape, but Bender was already attempting a collar chokehold with his hands, forcing Manic to repeatedly swat at his arms. Manic finally grabbed the biceps, and was about to break free when Bender slid to one side and used his sheer weight to turn Manic over. He resumed the mount position, this time on Manic's back, and bent one of his arms dangerously upward.

"Don't you try that crap on me," Bender said, panting.

"That's enough, Bender," Rade told him.

"Let them fight," TJ countered.

Rade glanced at TJ and narrowed his eyes. Not looking from TJ, Rade spoke again: "I said, that's enough."

Bender sighed, then released Manic and got up. "Sorry boss. Bitch pissed me off."

Manic stood, and dusted off his clothes. "I would have won," he said defiantly.

"I want a hundred push-ups from the both of you, right now," Rade said. "Drop."

The two dropped.

"TJ," Rade said. "Join them."

TJ flashed him a look of sheer scorn, and for a moment Rade thought he was going to disobey, but then he dropped and began pumping them out.

"Though I've studied you all my life," Harlequin said. "I don't think I'll ever understand you humans."

"Remember what I said about keeping mute?" Rade told the Artificial.

Harlequin looked like he was about to respond, then apparently thought better of it and kept his mouth shut.

General quarters sounded and everyone stopped what they were doing.

"Remember, it's just a precaution, people," Rade said. "Just in case there's a little surprise waiting for us on the other side. You three, continue pumping out the push-ups."

The *Rhodes'* turn at the Gate came and the destroyer passed through into 11-Aquarii.

six

The next several hours proved uneventful. The *Rhodes* remained under general quarters lockdown, and the MOTHs were confined to the berthing area waiting for news. They passed the time playing competitive war games on their Implants, and performing PT.

Finally the voice of the *Rhodes'* AI came over the main circuit and announced that general quarters had ended.

Rade unconsciously pulled up his inbox to check for new messages. There were none, of course. He reminded himself that he would only receive transmissions from local members of the task group going forward, because without a return Gate the fleet was cut off from the rest of the InterGalNet.

Rade was used to operating under similar scenarios, of course. Radio silence came with MOTH territory.

Facehopper arrived at the berthing area shortly thereafter.

"So, here's the deal," the chief said. "We've detected debris above the third planet in the system, a terrestrial with an unbreathable atmosphere. The fleet believes it's the wreckage of the *John A. McDonald*. Automated distress signals, of the kind present in lifepods, have been detected in profusion on the surface. So far we haven't received any other communications. Two destroyers are remaining behind to guard the Builder while it assembles our return Gate; the rest of the fleet is moving inward to investigate. Five days from now, when we reach the orbit of the third planet, Alpha Platoon will be making a drop. Our destination will be the largest cluster of distress signals detected on the surface. The first officer of the *Rhodes*, and her chief science officer, will be joining us. A platoon of Centurions will provide additional ground support. Two Raptors will give air support."

"So we see action after all," Bender said.

"We see action," Facehopper agreed.

"What about mechs?" Bomb said. "Will we be getting any?"

"You will," Facehopper answered. There was a strange twinkle in his eye. "I'll let you know more closer to the launch date. In the meantime, I've loaded a new program into the simulators for you. I recommend you and the others get in as much practice as you can until then."

THOSE FIVE DAYS passed extremely slowly. The anticipation was killing them. Rade called on his sniper training to help temper his own restlessness. The other snipers on the platoon, Trace and Keelhaul, exhibited similar detachment: if there was one thing to be said about snipers, it was that they were patient. The only distraction they had came from the war games of the simulator, where they spent four hours a day training with the new mech program that Facehopper had installed. It involved an unnamed class of mech they had never seen before: a smaller, nimbler class than the ATLAS.

Rade had to enact disciplinary action against Bomb and TJ, who had caused Harlequin to lose an arm in their latest hazing episode. Apparently the pair had hacked the hatch to the berthing area, and made it close on the unsuspecting Artificial after he had gone on an errand to fetch a nonexistent item for them. The arm was easy enough to replace, but Rade had the cost to repair the hatch and appendage docked from the pay of both individuals. Rade also limited their access to entertainment programs on their aReals. He considered halving their rations as he had done to Tahoe and Bender, but he didn't think that was a good idea after the resultant fiasco—Tahoe and Bender had proven extremely combative by the second day of their reduced food intake, and Rade had had to breakup three fights instigated by them over the following forty-eight hours, including the Manic/Bender incident.

Facehopper wore a knowing look when Rade reported the fights.

"I expected that would happen," the chief said. "Reducing rations is fine in bootcamp, when you got yourself a plump trainee who needs to shed some weight. But cutting the rations of seasoned MOTHs? Not something I'd recommend. Despite what the LPO guide might tell you."

"Then why didn't you warn me?" Rade asked.

Facehopper shrugged. "I told you to take the advice from the guide with a grain of salt."

"Yes," Rade said slowly. "But when I mentioned I planned to reduce their rations, you didn't say anything."

"Have you learned from your mistake?" Facehopper asked.

"I've certainly learned," Rade said. "Starvation and testosterone-fueled MOTHs do not good bedfellows make. I won't ever use rations to discipline someone again."

"There you go."

The fifth day proved the longest. The *Rhodes* and other members of the planetary task unit had achieved orbit above the third planet, and Rade was waiting for the order to report for deployment.

It didn't come.

One hour passed. Two. They distracted themselves by immersing themselves in the simulator. Rade performed poorly in the war games: his mind was distant, and he constantly found himself wondering about the mission that lay before them. He simply couldn't concentrate on the simulation objectives. Finally Rade excused himself and returned to the berthing area.

He was beginning to think their mission had been canceled when finally an incoming call came from Chief Facehopper.

Rade tapped in and Facehopper's hologram appeared before him.

"Hello Chief," Rade said. "What can I do for you?"

"Bring the boys to hangar bay three," Facehopper returned. "We got a mission to perform."

Rade gathered up the members of Alpha and led them through the tight corridors of the *Rhodes*. He was relatively unfamiliar with the layout of the destroyer, which was of the Nautilus class—heavy on armaments and hangar bays, light on crew space—so he had to use the blueprint overlay provided by his Implant.

Rade was the first to enter the airlock of the hangar bay, and when the inner hatch opened, he strode between two parabolic-winged MDVs—MOTH delivery vehicles—toward the Chief. Those MDVs blocked the remainder of the bay from view.

Facehopper was grinning widely; as Rade approached, the two drop ships fell away behind him, revealing the remainder of the bay.

His gaze was immediately drawn to the shiny black objects to his right.

"Tell me those are ours," Bomb said from behind him.

Facehopper's smile deepened. "Gentlemen," he said. "Meet your new toys."

Arrayed there in the hangar bay resided sixteen mechs, appearing nearly identical to the units the platoon had practiced with in the simulator. The units were nearly pure black, their camouflage features obviously inactive at the moment. Smaller than the ATLAS class, they had the usual two arms and legs. The head seemed integrated with the upper chest, with only a slight bulge emerging from the top of the torso. A red visor dominated the eye area, but the face was otherwise featureless. He could see the outline of the cockpit hatch against the bulky chest.

Though the armor was currently black, it was polished to a luster so that Rade could see the reflection of the other MOTHs, who gazed at the mechs with glee.

"Welcome to the Hoplite class," Facehopper said. "Smaller and more agile than an ATLAS, but packing a meaner punch. Let's see if you've done your homework. Bender, would you mind telling us all about them?"

"These fine bitches are the same class you programmed into the simulator?" Bender asked.

"They are," Facehopper said. "Don't you recognize them?"

"They seem bigger somehow, in the flesh." Bender stepped forward and ran his hand along the large leg of one of the units. "The jumpjets have twice the range of the ATLAS, and last three times as long. We have the usual Trench Coat anti-missile countermeasures. A retractable ballistic/laser shield in the left arm. The swivel mounts in each hand alternate between cobras"— infrared lasers—"and grenade launchers. There are four grenade types—frag, electromagnetic, smoke, and flashbang. Since these babies are designed to be fast and light, there are no incendiaries, or serpents, and we've done away with Gats. Why would you need Gats or missiles when you've got lasers, after all? The weight savings in ammunition alone are responsible for a fifty percent improvement in speed and agility over an ATLAS."

"Well done," Facehopper said.

Mauler stepped forward eagerly. "I count sixteen. We all get one for the planet-side operation?"

Facehopper nodded. "The mission parameters advocate a mech for each and every one of you, yes. Except for Harlequin, who'll be hitching a ride aboard Bender's mech. In the passenger section, of course."

"The *passenger* section?" Harlequin said. "On the outside?"

Bender flashed those golden teeth malevolently at Harlequin.

The Artificial took a step back.

"As usual," Harlequin said. "AIs and Artificials are treated like second class citizens."

"You'll be fully armed, Harlequin," Facehopper said. "With an exoskeleton specifically designed for your body, amplifying your already enhanced strength. You'll be like a mini mech out there. So I'll fully expect you to participant in any engagements."

"What about the other officers joining us?" Rade asked.

"I'll be carrying the first officer of the *Rhodes*, Commander Blaine Parnell, in my passenger section. And you, Rage, will transport Lieutenant Rebecca Vicks, the chief science officer. While they're going to be armed, both officers will be only wearing standard-issue jumpsuits, so it'll be our job to protect them."

"Where are they now?"

"They're in hangar bay five," Facehopper said. "They'll be taking one of the Dragonfly shuttles to the surface, joined by a platoon of Centurion class combat robots. Let's get suited up."

From a storage closet the platoon members retrieved cooling undergarments. After changing into those outfits, they attached the MOTH-grade exoskeletons, which they often referred to as jumpsuits. The suits fit to mount points embedded in their arms and legs, providing a seamless interface to the strength-enhancing electronics. When Rade put on the final component—the helmet— the suit injected an accelerant into the dorsal venous system of his right hand, vastly reducing the amount of time his body needed to acclimate to the inner environment.

From the armory, Rade selected a small laser blaster that he could carry with him in the cockpit, then he hauled himself into his designated Hoplite, readily identifiable because the word "Rage" hovered overtop, courtesy of his Implant.

The hatch closed, sealing him in darkness. Inner actuators pressed into his jumpsuit, cocooning his body and suspending him in the center of the unit. The view from the mech's external camera filled his vision, and he found himself looking down on the hangar bay from a height of three meters. Every movement he made was translated by the cocoon, which fired the associated servomotors and electrical circuits of the actual mech, mirroring him. The lag between his movements and that of the mech was in the microsecond range—essentially instantaneous. The Hoplite had an external microphone that transmitted sound to his helmet, so he was able to hear the loud clanks and whirs as the others moved around him.

"Welcome aboard, Rage," the Hoplite's AI addressed him by his callsign. "I'm Smith."

Rade pursed his lips. "Smith? That's a change. I'm used to mech names that have a bit more... I don't know, punch. Names like Yellowjacket. Wasp. Scorpion. Insect names."

"Yes," Smith said. "My first choice was actually Happy Butterfly, but the provisioners made me change it."

"Probably a good thing," Rade replied. "Hell, if you chose Happy Butterfly, *I'd* make you change it."

"That was a joke," Smith said.

"Ah yes," Rade commented. "I've noticed that trend lately. Mech AIs coming out of the box with a predilection for jokes and sarcasm. Not sure I'm okay with that. What we do here is a serious business."

"I can dial down my respective settings," Smith said. "If it pleases you."

"It does. Do it." Rade took a few tentative steps. He found himself slightly off balance at first, as the actual mech handled slightly differently from the simulator.

"Do you need assistance, Rage?" Smith asked.

"That's a negative," Rade answered. "I got this."

After a few wobbly steps he quickly acclimated. He flexed one hand, and rotated the cobra mount into his palm. "Just like in the simulators." The weapons couldn't be armed while aboard the *Rhodes*, unless overridden by the chief of course, but he quickly retracted the weapon anyway.

"Confirm loaded status, please," Facehopper said.

One by one the members of the platoon reported to Facehopper that they were aboard their respective mechs. The chief would have been able to determine as much via the status indicators his HUD—heads-up-display—overlaid onto his faceplate, but protocol demanded a manual check.

When the last of them had reported in, the chief said: "Harlequin, you strapped in?"

Rade glanced at Bender's Hoplite. Behind the mech's head, right above the jetpack, Harlequin sat in the seat specifically provided for a passenger.

"I'm ready," the Artificial returned.

"All right," Facehopper said. "Prepare to drop."

The air vent siren sounded, and a revolving yellow light shone from one corner of the compartment.

"Warning," came a female voice. "Depressurization commencing. Hangar atmosphere venting overboard. Warning."

In moments the hangar had depressurized and the bay doors opened. Below the curtain of stars resided the round dome of the planet.

A metal ramp extended from the edge of the hangar doors.

"Let's drop," the chief ordered.

One by one the mechs walked the plank, leaping from view.

Rade's turn came.

He steered Smith through the opening of the hangar bay, leaving behind the artificial gravity. The weightlessness of space momentarily disoriented him: Rade lost his sense of direction, and he could no longer tell which way was up or down.

The magnetized ramp prevented him from unintentionally floating away. He could feel the resistance as he lifted each mechanized foot.

He reached the edge and stared at the planet below. The surface was a motley of purple, black and white swaths.

As usual, at the last moment he found himself not wanting to make the leap. It was only natural: the body's innate inclination to avoid discomfort.

Now or never.

"Geronimo!" He stepped off.

seven

The *Rhodes* appeared to literally launch upward, and in moments the destroyer was a tiny dot, simply another star among billions.

Goodbye, civilization.

The world below seemed to remain the same size the whole time. It felt like Rade was merely floating in place. A dangerous illusion.

The gyroscopic thrusters of the Hoplite fired regularly, stabilizing his descent. Below him, the aeroshell heat shield deployed in preparation for atmospheric entry.

Flames bloomed at the edges of the heat shield, and in moments the external camera feed that fed his vision turned completely orange. Despite the cockpit cooling systems, he still sweated profusely inside his jumpsuit. The danger didn't help matters—all it would take was one small leak in that shield, and the air cushion underneath the shell would retract, enveloping the Hoplite in the heat from the compression shockwave. His entire mech would be reduced to a molten meteor. Yes, he had good reason to perspire.

The Gs picked up as the air friction decelerated the mech. Rade instinctively squeezed his abdominal and jaw muscles.

The flames abruptly receded and he was through. The depleted aeroshell fell away, revealing a layer of clouds.

He glanced up momentarily; in the sky above he saw glowing meteorites with bright white trails marking the descent of the remaining mechs.

In moments his vision was sheathed in white as he entered the clouds. He couldn't see a thing, so he activated the radar imagery.

The outline of another mech appeared in the mist, located about fifty meters below and to his left.

The cloud cover soon lifted, revealing a purple and black land mass below. It looked like he was approaching a giant bruise.

"Did anyone try zooming in?" Bomb's voice came over the comm. The moderate digital warping in his signal indicated he was some distance away. "That purple stuff looks like vegetation."

"Probably because it is," Manic answered.

"I thought the atmosphere was unbreathable?" Bomb complained.

"To humans," Manic replied.

"Wait a second," Tahoe said over the comm. "Plants use photosynthesis to turn carbon dioxide and water into a food source. Oxygen is generated as a byproduct. Eventually, that would result in a breathable environment. In fact, if I recall, preliminary readings pegged the oxygen content in the atmosphere at five percent."

"Did they?" Manic said. "Well it's too bad that the atmosphere is full of unbreathable hydrogen sulfide."

"That would kill the plants, too," Tahoe argued.

"Not necessarily," Manic said. "And since when did you become a biologist? I thought you had a background in astrophysics?"

"Keep the comms clear, people," Facehopper reminded them. "We're in the middle of a drop, here."

The surface came up fast.

"Uh, Smith?" Rade said to his local AI. "Are we going to activate the air brakes soon?"

"Yes," Smith replied.

The ground devoured everything around Rade by that point.

"Smith, now would be a good time..."

The Hoplite abruptly engaged its air brakes and the aerospike thrusters in the feet fired.

Rade hit hard. His body folded on impact, with his knees slamming into his chest. A dust shockwave traveled outward from the impact site.

Rade stood up and marched from the dust cloud. He rotated the powerful cobra laser into his right hand, the grenade launcher his left. He left the launcher at its default setting: frag. The outer hull of his mech changed color to imitate the surrounding terrain.

Above, the thumbnail-sized alien sun gave the landscape a washed-out look, imparting tones of cool blue to everything. When Rade glanced at the sky, the photochromatic filter of his camera instantly compensated, darkening the display.

"Gather at the muster point people!" Facehopper said over the comm.

On the overhead map overlaid in the upper right of his vision, Rade saw the blue dots that represented the positions of his platoon. Near them a larger, flashing yellow dot indicated the muster point, which overlapped with the shuttle containing the commander, the chief scientist, and the Centurions—the craft had already landed, apparently. Further south, purple dots indicated the booster payloads, one per mech, that had dropped with the party. The fuel in those rockets would allow the Hoplites to achieve escape velocity and return to orbit.

"TJ," Facehopper continued. "Deploy the Centurions in a defensive posture around the Dragonfly."

"Aye Chief." TJ had made his descent aboard the shuttle, while his mech had dropped on its own, operating under autopilot.

Rade rendezvoused with the closest Hoplite, piloted by Bomb, and proceeded toward the muster point. More mechs joined them en route until there were five of them. Similarly sized groups converged on the muster point from multiple directions, so that the whole platoon arrived at nearly the same time. The black and gray digital patterns on their hulls matched the surrounding terrain so that the Hoplites blended in.

The sixteen Centurions had formed a cigar shape around the shuttle. They were all lying flat on the rocky soil, their AR-51 plasma rifles scanning the surrounding terrain. TJ resided on the ground beside them, and he surveyed the terrain through his rifle scope with the best of them. The rear ramp of the shuttle remained open, touching the rock and dirt terra firma.

"Headcount?" Facehopper said.

"Mauler is missing," Rade said. He glanced at the overhead map and realized Mauler's mech was still located three kilometers to the east.

"Sorry Chief," Mauler's slightly garbled voice came over the comm. "Stupid autopilot landed me a bit farther from the site than expected."

"That's right, blame the autopilot," Bender taunted accusingly.

"That's fine, Mauler," Facehopper said. "But hurry it up, mate."

"Am I authorized to use jetpacks to make the muster faster?" Mauler asked.

"Absolutely not," Facehopper said. "Save the fuel for when you need it." He turned toward the only one of them who had not yet mounted his mech. "TJ, load up."

The unmanned Hoplite in the group crouched, and its cockpit hatch dropped open.

TJ approached. He placed his rifle in the weapon stowage compartment built into the leg of the mech and then clambered aboard.

"Bender, launch HS3s," Facehopper commanded.

Eight of the circular, fist-sized scouts emerged from the shuttle's rear ramp and sped off in different directions.

Though he couldn't see them, Rade knew that two MQ-91 Raptors were flying overhead, ready to provide air support. It was those Raptors that had recorded the locations of the nearest lifepods, which appeared as green dots on the overhead map.

As the scouts headed for different pods, Facehopper transmitted: "Muster site is secure, Commander."

Commander Blaine Parnell and Chief Scientist Rebecca Vicks stepped onto the down ramp and emerged from the shuttle.

"Chief," Commander Parnell's voice came over the comm. "Any answer to our contact requests?"

"Snakeoil," the chief said over the MOTH private line. "Have you been sending out communication pings?"

"I have," Snakeoil replied. "Got nothing in response so far."

"Keep trying." Over the general comm, Facehopper finished: "We haven't received any replies yet, Commander."

"All right," Parnell said.

"Your orders, sir?" Chief Facehopper asked.

"I'm waiting on the HS3s," the commander said.

"Yes sir."

Upon hearing the word, Rade mentally recited *don't call me sir...* Of course, as a commissioned officer, the commander wouldn't object to that form of address, and in fact would probably prefer it.

"HS3s are reporting in," Bender said over the general comm a few moments later. "No sign of life at any of the pods so far."

"Have them move on to the next pods, then," the commander said. "Meanwhile, let's send the Centurions in to have a look. We'll follow just behind, in traveling overwatch formation. If that works for you, Chief?"

"It does, sir," Chief Facehopper replied. Over the MOTH line: "Let's move out, people. Bender, have the combat robots lead the way."

The Centurions moved forward in two separate squads, performing their own embedded traveling overwatch during the advance.

The chief scientist approached. "If you don't mind, LPO?"

Rade knelt and she loaded into the passenger seat. Facehopper similarly allowed Parnell aboard.

"Are you buckled in?" Rade asked her.

"I am," she replied.

When the second squad of Centurions was away, Facehopper ordered the squad forward. "Single file line, people. Zig zag pattern. I want a separation of ten meters per mech."

"Bender, on point," Rade said.

Bender's Hoplite jogged forward.

"Manic, you're next," Rade said.

He continued to call out names until everyone was jogging in their mechs. The chief was at position five, while Rade was at tenth place in the line. Tahoe took the drag position.

Because of their spread out, zig-zag formation, all of them were able to keep both squads of Centurions in their sights. Rade pointed his right arm at the trailing squad and switched to autopilot before activating the point of view of the cobra. He zoomed in and scanned the terrain beyond the robots. The auto-stabilizing gyroscope of the scope ensured he had a steady shot. In the distance, a few kilometers beyond the mostly black terrain, a wall of purple blotted out the horizon. Rade increased the zoom, reaching the limits of the optics. He switched to digital zoom, and as the display pixelated, he realized that purple wall was some kind of alien jungle: white tree trunks with purple leaves; purple ferns; orange bushes.

"Psychedelic jungle," Manic commented.

"Look sharp people," Facehopper said. "Those trees are the perfect spot for an ambush."

Rade continued to survey the distant foliage, but saw nothing. "Looks dead out there." He returned his aim to the plains, and slid the scope westward across the landscape. He spotted towering rock formations, and searched them for signs of any attackers waiting in ambush.

"The first squad has reached a lifepod," Bender announced.

Rade momentarily tapped into the video feed of the Praetor unit in charge of that squad, and watched as it examined the inside. One of the seats had broken away, but everything else was otherwise intact. Deflated air bags covered the deck.

"The pod is empty," the Praetor reported over the comm.

"HS3s have found nothing else in the remaining pods so far," Bender continued. "No signs of life. Nor any bodies."

"Have the Centurions move on to the next pod," Commander Parnell said. "Meanwhile, let's continue forward until we reach the pod."

"How you doing back there, ma'am?" Rade asked his charge over a private line.

"Other than a splitting headache?" Vicks replied. "Just fine."

"Not used to traveling by mech, I take it?"

"That's not it at all," she said. After a moment's hesitation, she finished: "Our landing was a little rough in the shuttle."

"Ah." Rade had returned his point of view to that of the cobra's scope, and he continued to scan the rocks. "G forces will do that too you."

"Well, let's just say, the reentry qualifications during school were never my favorite."

"I didn't know officers from your rating school did reentry qualifications," Rade said. In place of rating school, he had almost said 'Big Navy,' but he had caught himself in time. It wouldn't do to start insulting the officer he was assigned to protect, as minor as the insult was. "Seems like something reserved for the infantry. And MOTHs, of course."

"You'd be surprised at what they make us do," Vicks said. "Just because I'm a scientist, doesn't mean I haven't endured the same bootcamp as everyone else."

"That's true." Rade aimed his targeting reticle over a particularly large rock outcropping. "Though some of us have to endure an even harder bootcamp when they start their rating schools. Not that I'm trying to brag, ma'am." When he was satisfied that the outcropping was innocuous, he moved his aim on to the next suspicious-looking formation.

"I think I could pass MOTH training," Vicks said.

It wasn't the words that irked Rade, but rather the way she had said it. Like it was the easiest training in the world. He decided it wasn't worth an answer, because if he spoke to her in that moment, he would definitely insult her, just as she had inadvertently done to him.

"Then again, maybe not," Vicks continued. "I've watched Trial Week videos on the InterGalNet. Some brutal stuff. And then when they spray you with OC-40—most concentrated pepper spray around—and shoot you in the arm, and still expect you to fight your instructors? Crazy."

"Actually," Rade said. "They shoot you in the arm *first*. Then spray you. As luck would have it, during that particular qualification, I was shot by a member of my own platoon here. Trace. I didn't know it at the time, but he's one of the best snipers on the Teams. A corpsman marked a small X on my forearm, and Trace hit it right in the center. The bullet passed clean through without hitting any bone."

"So they shoot you, then they OC you, and then you fight?" Vicks asked.

"Well, after you're shot in the arm, you fight your first instructor," Rade continued. "If you win that, *then* they spray you with OC-40, and you fight again. Bleeding away, unable to see through the burning tears. Definitely isn't for the faint of heart."

"No, I imagine it isn't," Vicks said.

"I actually enjoyed myself though."

"That's such a stereotypically MOTH thing to say," Vicks responded.

"I suppose it is. But that qualification is the one chance we have to get even with the instructors for the weeks of cruelty they've inflicted upon us. I enjoyed kicking the ass of one particularly mean bastard."

"While you were shot, and sprayed?" Vicks said, the disbelief obvious in her voice.

"Yes, ma'am," Rade replied.

"You MOTHs are even crazier than I thought," Vicks commented.

"Thank you, ma'am," Rade said.

The mech party reached the first life pod, and Rade had the Hoplites assume a defensive formation around it. He and

Facehopper moved closer to the pod, and knelt so that their passengers could disembark.

Harlequin clambered down from Bender's mech to join them.

"Harlequin!" Rade shouted. "Get back to your position, soldier!"

Harlequin hastily complied. Bender didn't bother to kneel his Hoplite, forcing Harlequin to climb. To his credit, his movements were quick and agile, and he was back in the passenger seat half a second later.

Parnell and Vicks entered the lifepod. The pair emerged a moment later. Parnell seemed troubled.

"These pods have been sitting out here for over a year," the commander said. "What are the chances we'll find any survivors? Their oxygen supplies would have run out in the first month. The food and water, gone by the second, if they rationed carefully. Assuming everyone survived the landing."

"If they're dead, then where are the bodies?" Trace asked.

"That's the mystery, isn't it?" Parnell replied.

"It's conceivable the survivors were able to create solar powered oxygen extractors, with equipment salvaged from the *John A. McDonald* before they jettisoned," Vicks said.

"And what about the food and water situation?"

"Same thing," Vicks explained. "Water reclaimers could have given them purified drinking water. And while the atmosphere and land aren't natively conducive to Terran plants, the soil does have some nutrients—the alien foliage we've witnessed in the distance is testament to that. With proper hydroponics, I see no reason why the survivors couldn't have grown food."

"Fine," Parnell said. "But tell me something then: if you were stranded on this world, where would you take shelter?"

Rade studied his overhead map. He had some ideas, but Vicks spoke before he could voice them.

"That alien jungle is one option," she said. "Though the more likely option is those rock formations, to the west. It would be far easier to set up an oxygen environment inside a closed cave system than in the middle of an open-air jungle. Besides, it would protect them from the elements, and any native inhabitants."

Facehopper had earlier warned the platoon that alien animal life had been detected on the surface: the shipboard telescopes had reported flocks of grazing animals, and the predators that hunted them, some of them very large. The hope was that, because of the mechs the platoon piloted, Rade and the others would be left alone by the native wildlife. No signs of any higher forms of life had been detected, however, nor anything else that would denote an advanced civilization.

Parnell turned toward Facehopper. "Chief, let's get half of the HS3s to perform an exploratory run on those formations. Let the others finish scouting the remaining pods."

"Aye sir," Facehopper said. "Bender, direct half of the HS3s toward the rock formations."

"On it," Bender replied.

A rumbling abruptly resonated through his helmet, as picked up by the Hoplite's external microphone. Rade's cockpit seemed to shake, too, as the inner actuators mimicked vibrations detected by the hull sensors.

"What the—"

His gaze was drawn toward the distant jungle. From it, two large missiles soared skyward.

"Spread out, people!" Rade said.

Rade scooped up Lieutenant Vicks and secured her in the passenger seat, then he dashed from the pod. On his overhead map, the blue dots of the other Hoplites scattered. Parnell was aboard Facehopper's mech once again.

"Bender," Facehopper said. "Have the Raptors triangulate the position of those launches, and return fire."

"Raptors are firing," Bender returned.

Rade glanced over his shoulder as he ran. He spotted smoke billowing from the jungle.

"Did we get them?" Facehopper asked.

"I believe so," Bender replied. "The targets appeared to be mobile silos of some kind."

When Rade had attained a distance of two hundred meters away from the pod, he dove to the rocky surface and spun around to face the jungle. He tracked the missiles with his scope. The objects continued skyward. He studied the computed trajectories his HUD provided.

"They're not targeting us," TJ said, coming to the same conclusion Rade just had. "But the Raptors."

"Have the Raptors blow those missiles from the sky," Facehopper said.

"The missiles just separated into eight individual units each," Bender replied. "The Raptors won't shoot them all down in time."

"Get as many of them as you can," Facehopper said.

Rade watched as four of the red dots that represented the missile pieces on his display winked out. The remaining four reached the Raptors, two each, and all the airborne dots vanished.

The Raptors would have launched chaff, and their own equivalents of the Trench Coats that the mechs possessed, but apparently it hadn't mattered. In place of the Raptors, two fiery meteors descended from the skies.

"We just lost our air support, people," Bender announced.

The earth began to tremble around Rade. He felt the vibrations far more keenly than those of the missile launch.

"Anyone else feeling that?" he asked over the comm.

"Feeling what?" Manic returned.

In his mad flight from the missile attack, Rade had unintentionally maneuvered closer to the purple jungle, so that he was about five hundred meters from its eaves. The trees along the periphery appeared to be swaying.

The rumbling grew more intense, and then from the edge of that purple foliage a long line of darkness burst forth. He zoomed in, and realized a herd of alien beasts had broken free; the creatures were either spooked by the missile launch and the subsequent attack against the silos, or the hidden assailants in the jungle had purposely dispatched the beasts.

Well, in that particular moment in time, the cause didn't really matter. Because Rade was directly in the path of a large portion of that herd.

eight

H ang tight, ma'am," Rade said.

He began running away from the jungle and the incoming herd. He checked his overhead map. The blue dots representing the rest of the team were spread out in front of him. He was the only one that close to the creatures.

"Smith, take over!" Rade said.

"Autopilot engaged," the Hoplite's AI responded.

"Switch my video feed to the rearmost camera," Rade said. "Let's see what we're dealing with."

"Done," Smith replied.

Rade found himself staring at the retreating jungle once again. He zoomed in on the dark mass flowing onto the plains. He began to make out individual entities in their midst. They ran on all fours, but given the size of their rear legs, he thought they also had the ability to walk upright. The incoming herd stretched from one side of the jungle to the other; the ranks flowed ceaselessly outward from the depths, seeming endless. It wasn't a herd, but a swarm.

"Retreat to the rock formation, people," Facehopper's urgent voice came over the comm.

Rade zoomed in further, focusing on one of the creatures. The head reminded him of a hammerhead shark, and the insectile body was vaguely reminiscent of a skinny Tyrannosaurus Rex—while it possessed the size and menace of the extinct carnivore, it lacked the girth. The tail was long and segmented, and covered in spikes; the sharp tip could be readily utilized as a weapon, Rade thought. The thin body was covered in a tough, spiky carapace. Closer to the head, from the shoulder region, a protective plate of long, bony horns formed a vague crest behind the broad head. A pair of small, gripping arms with fingertips capped by talons were located in the center of the torso, underneath the head. The front legs were bottomed by pads from which flashed the tips of sharp, retracted claws. From the head, a central mandible extended outward, locked in a perpetual snarl to showcase the rows of razor-sharp teeth harbored within.

"Chief, you getting this?" Rade asked over the comm.

"I am," Facehopper replied. "Retreat to the rock formation!"

Despite the vaunted speed and agility of the Hoplites, nature seemed to be winning out: the front line of aliens was slowly closing, and the nearest creatures were about fifty meters behind him by that point. Their shrinking proximity from him only seemed to spur them on. The rumbling had grown commensurately.

"But what about the booster rockets?" Manic asked. "Our trip home..."

"Too far to the south," the chief replied. "We won't make them in time."

"We're not going to make it to the rock formation either!" Rade said. More softly, he added: "I'm not, anyway."

He took a running leap and fired his jumpjets. Unfortunately, the activation proved a waste, because he covered the same amount of distance he would have on foot alone. Maybe even a little less.

The creatures in the forefront began to break away from the front ranks, converging into a line headed straight toward Rade's fleeing mech.

"Chief, request permission to open fire," Rade said.

Facehopper didn't answer.

The aliens grew closer.

"Chief..." Rade said.

"If they were spooked by the launch of those rockets," Trace said over the comm. "Then there's nothing we can do to stop them. Once a panicked herd runs toward a cliff, they're going to jump off that cliff, if only because of the pressure exerted by those coming behind them"

"What if they weren't spooked," Lui said, giving voice to Rade's earlier doubts. "What if they were *sent* by whoever launched those rockets?"

"Either way, I doubt we'll be able to scare them off," Trace said.

"If they were spooked," Rade transmitted. "Wouldn't they at least be *trying* to leave me some space? Even just a small berth? Instead of funneling directly toward me?"

"Hey, they're headed directly toward me, too, you know," Bender said.

Rade glanced southward, and from the horde he saw another long line breaking from the front ranks. Bender's Hoplite sprinted there, located only a little farther from them than Rade.

He glanced at the overhead map. Trace was the next closest, thirty meters ahead of them, followed by Tahoe. The remaining members of the platoon retreated from random positions beyond them. The rock formation was still a kilometer away from the closest member.

"Chief, I ask again, do I have permission to fire?" Rade pressed.

Facehopper didn't answer immediately. Finally:

"Bender and Rage, take out those nearest you," Facehopper returned. "Try to maim, not kill."

"Thank you," Rade said. To his local AI: "Keep running, Smith."

He switched to the forward camera and swiveled his torso all the way around while Smith maintained the Hoplite's current heading. Rade rotated his cobra mounts into place and aimed for the legs of the closest creature. He fired the infrared lasers.

The alien fell with a squeal that Rade found strangely gratifying.

Not unexpectedly, the others in behind merely trampled the body.

He unleashed the cobras again and again, hamstringing more of the creatures, but those in behind either leaped over the fallen or trod over them.

Rade rotated the grenade launcher into either hand and launched frags into the swarm. Aliens exploded in satisfying displays of gore, but the horde didn't slow. Flying body parts to the south alerted him to the fact that Bender had given up on his lasers and was using grenades as well.

"Ain't working," Bender said. "We're going to have to stand and fight. Rage and I, anyway."

"Bender," Rade said. "Rendezvous with me here. We'll buy the others as much time as we can."

He marked off a location on the overhead map, a position eighty meters ahead and halfway between both of them. Based on the estimates his Implant provided, the leading aliens of the swarm would overrun them shortly after they arrived.

"Will do," Bender returned.

"I never gave the order for anyone to stay behind," Facehopper said.

"Neither did I," Commander Parnell intoned.

"Don't think either of you have much of a choice, sirs," Rade said. He could imagine Facehopper bridling at being lumped in with the officer as a *sir*. "Bender and I are going to be overwhelmed." When no reply came, he sent a message to his charge. "Lieutenant, are you okay with this?"

"I'll fight from the passenger seat with my blaster," she replied. "For as long as I can."

"None of us will make the rock formation in time," Facehopper said. "You'll only delay part of the swarm, Rage. The rest of us are going to be overtaken not long after that. Look at them. The far edges of the front line are already curling inward. They intend to outflank us all. So no, Rage and Bender. We stand together. And we retreat together. It's the only way. Everyone, make for the coordinates Rage marked on the map."

Rade sighed, but he knew Facehopper was right. He and Bender might be able to delay a small portion of the horde, but there was no way two Hoplites would be able to stop the hundreds headed toward the remaining mechs.

He neared the rendezvous point and swung his torso forward to face his direction of travel.

"Smith, grant me full control," Rade said.

"Yes, Rage," the AI said. "Good luck, LPO."

"Luck has nothing to do with it," Rade said.

Bender's Hoplite reached the muster point first, and Bender turned around to fire at his pursuers.

Rade bounded several steps, took a running leap toward the rendezvous point, and then spun about in midair.

He launched an electromagnetic grenade before he landed.

As he slammed into the alien soil, the grenade landed. Electrical bolts traveled outward in all directions, disabling five of the hammerheads at once.

The following beasts hurled themselves forward, leaping at him and Bender. He managed to kill two more with his infrared laser, but one of the dead bodies struck Rade and he was thrown to the ground by its weight.

Others were quickly on him and claws dug runnels into his hull. He couldn't get up.

The rumbling around him was at thunderous levels by then.

"Vicks, are you all right?" Rade asked, worried that he had crushed her, or that an alien had gotten to her.

He thought she said something back, but he couldn't hear above the roar. He glanced at her vitals overlaid on his HUD. The data indicated she was fine, though her heart rate was through the roof, unsurprisingly.

"Smith," Rade said. "Can you filter that goddamn noise?"

Instantly the roaring thunder of the passing horde subsided. He heard only the continual scrapes and thuds as the alien claws worked on his mech.

"Done," Smith said.

"Vicks—"

"I'm fine," she said. Her voice sounded like it came from between gritted teeth.

An alien's head exploded beside him, and he realized she had shot it at point blank range with her blaster. She was still buckled in, apparently, though he understood it would be a tight fit back there, given her proximity to the ground.

Body parts exploded above him and Rade realized Bender had tossed a frag near the beasts pinning him down. The weight pressing into him vanished.

He grabbed one of the bodies and swung it in a wide arc as he scrambled to his feet, using it to cripple three more incoming creatures at the same time.

Another four raced toward him...

He tossed aside the body, bent his knees and activated the Hoplite's jumpjets as he unleashed the pent-up potential energy of the mechanical legs. Three of the horde leaped and managed to grab onto him before he could clear them.

Because of the added weight, the jump was far weaker than he had hoped, and he only rose three meters.

He managed to shake off two of the aliens and thrust again on the way down, boosting his mech to an altitude of five meters. The lone alien hanging onto him continued to whale on his cockpit.

Rade wrapped his hands around the creature and squeezed; some of the spikes on its carapace embedded in the arms of his Hoplite, but he managed to crush the thing. He tossed aside the still-squirming body and the spikes slid from his hull.

"Damage alert," Smith said. "Right arm actuators."

Rade test swung the arm and saw that its movement was jerky. The limb was still useable, however. For the moment anyway.

"Could use some help here, boss," Bender said.

From his vantage point in the air, Rade spotted Bender's Hoplite buried under a mass of the creatures.

Rade unleashed a frag at the aliens, setting the proximity fuse to detonate a few centimeters above them—he didn't want to damage Bender's mech.

The grenade exploded and alien pieces flew in every direction. Bender was on his feet a moment later, in fighting form.

Rade descended toward the seething ground and launched two frags to clear the area directly underneath him. He landed amidst flying alien body parts.

He grabbed one of the alien corpses and swung it like a bat, swatting aside the incoming horde members. After taking down around ten of them in that manner, the legs of his makeshift weapon abruptly tore away and he was left momentarily defenseless.

He rotated the cobras into either hand but before he could fire an alien dove into him. In seconds he was completely pinned; all he could hear was the scraping of claws and mandibles against his outer hull as the aliens strove to get at the good stuff inside. The metal moaned from the weight it had to bear.

"Bender..."

"I'm pinned too, little buddy," Bender replied. "We're just sardines in a tin can at this point. And it's mealtime."

Rade struggled against the weight above him, but he couldn't move his assailants. From that terrible sound of teeth gouging into metal, he was certain his cockpit was about to be pierced at any moment.

nine

S mith," Rade said. "Tell me you have something up your sleeve we can use here..."

"I don't have sleeves, Rage," Smith replied.

"Damn it," Rade said. "I mean something in reserve."

"I don't have anything in reserve."

Rade flexed his jaw in frustration. "Well some ideas, then!"

"I don't have any ideas."

"Useless AIs." Rade shook his head.

The alien bodies above him abruptly exploded.

Trace and Tahoe had arrived.

Rade leaped to his feet and waded through the dead to free Bender. "Form up, back to back!"

Trace and Tahoe rendezvoused with them, and the four of them formed the rod and spokes of a fighting wheel.

"Long time no see, boss," Trace said. "Did you miss me for the long time we were parted?"

"Trace, man." Rade let off a few shots from his infrared laser, then beat off the next opponent using his hand as a club. "Your arrival is a much wanted whiff of fresh air."

"You wouldn't be saying that if you slept next to him in the berth." Bender bashed in a hammerhead's proboscis. "And I'm not talking FAN, either." Feet. Ass. Nuts. "This guy gives new meaning to the phrase noxious fumes. I swear, he's sneaking Bangladeshi food back there. Smells the same going out as going in."

"Hey, Bangladeshi food smells good!" Trace chopped down with his shield, severing the lower limbs of an attacker. "And I eat the same fooking gruel as everybody else."

"Maybe that's the problem then," Bender said. "We got to wean you off the Western food, and put you back on your native diet."

Tahoe threw a frag. "You do that to him, bro, I have a feeling you're going to make the problem worse."

Trace blocked a blow, and accidentally elbowed Bender's mech in the chest.

"Hey, watch it," Bender said. "You sister fooker you." He had assumed Trace's accent for the latter bit.

Rade deployed the shield in his left arm, and continued to utilize his right arm alternately as a club and a laser. That close to the enemy, he was fully aware of the stature of these hammerheads. On all fours, they only reached to his chest area, but when they stood on their hind legs they were slightly taller than the Hoplites, and able to bite down on them from above with their sharp proboscises.

"You okay back there Lieutenant?" Rade asked.

In answer he heard the high-pitched keen of her blaster, and one of those hammerheads exploded nearby.

A wall of dead alien bodies was forming around them.

"Let's retreat a few paces, people," Rade said. "I don't want to get hemmed in by these bodies. Tahoe, start moving. Stop after five meters."

The four backed away as a group, wading through the dead.

Something crashed into the ground nearby, taking out a long swath of the creatures. At the end of the fresh ditch carved into the alien soil, Rade spotted a smoking wreckage. Rade realized it was the remains of one of the Raptors.

The other Hoplites began to arrive, one by one, easing off the pressure. Soon the entire platoon was present, and the mechs formed a bridgehead, making their stand out there on the plains. Rade glanced at the vital signs summarized on his HUD. So far, no one had sustained any life-threatening injuries.

Chief Facehopper's voice came over the general line.

"I want us to begin a controlled retreat toward the rock formation!" Facehopper said. "We move backward as a single cohesive unit."

The group slowly edged backward. They fought in a nested, twin-circle formation. Twelve mechs covered the outer circle, shields facing outward, free arms used as clubs, lasers, or grenade launchers. The remaining four resided in the center, aiming past the defenders, lobbing grenades or firing lasers to ensure that no one in the outer ranks was ever overwhelmed. Those on the rear outer edge pressed against the enemy with their shields; the retreat was slow, laborious.

The individual mechs took turns between the inner and outer formations, because staying too long in those outer ranks, swinging one's arm as a weapon and forcing the enemy back with one's shield, proved tiring. Rade was tempted to allow Smith to assume control of the mech on more than one occasion, though he knew staying in the outer rank for a prolonged period would only increase the probability his Hoplite would suffer an unlucky blow.

"Any chance we can get some new Raptors to replace the ones we lost?" Bender asked hopefully. "And maybe a gunship or two? Or an Equestrian?"

"Any luck, Snakeoil?" Facehopper's voice came in answer.

The communicator responded a moment later. "I'm still not getting anything, even though I've piggybacked with the comm node in the commander's Dragonfly. Maybe the repeaters in orbit have been shot down, and the fleet has moved to the far side of the planet."

"What are you saying," Grappler transmitted. "We can't communicate with the *Rhodes?*"

"That's exactly what I'm saying," Snakeoil answered. "Nor any other ship in orbit."

"What if the fleet hasn't moved to the far side of the planet?" Fret transmitted. "What if the fleet has been destroyed?"

"Fret," Facehopper said. "Positivity, my friend. Morale."

"Forget morale," Fret said. "I'm a realist, here."

"Got an answer," Snakeoil announced, gruffly. "Support won't be coming any time soon. Comm officer tells me they're 'occupied' at the moment."

"Cast your eyes skyward," Skullcracker sent. He was currently in the middle circle. "To these coords."

Rade accepted the coordinates Skullcracker transmitted to the platoon, and then he momentarily transferred control over to Smith. He zoomed in on the blue sky and saw white flashes but not much more. He resumed control of the Hoplite and fended off the next wave of claws.

"The fleet is under attack," Chief Facehopper said flatly.

"A big-time attack," Bender agreed. "They've been ambushed, just like us."

"Guess that rules out the cavalry," Manic said.

Rade gazed toward the distant jungle. The black ranks of the enemy spread away from the group, reaching all the way across the plains to the eaves of those alien trees. There was no end in sight. Best of all, the focal point of the horde was the platoon: there was now no doubt that their emergence from the jungle was a coordinated attack.

"They just keep coming," Keelhaul transmitted.

"They do indeed," Rade muttered.

"I'm out of frags and electromagnetics," Tahoe sent.

"Me too," Bender said.

"My cobra's beginning to overheat," Lui transmitted. "I'm going to have to retract my shield if I want to stay in this battle."

Rade had similar warnings on his HUD. One particular flashing message caught his eye:

Frag inventory low.

Rade was abruptly pulled from his place in the circle by a hammerhead that had evaded his notice. It threw him against a pile of dead bodies. Others surged forward, cutting him off from the platoon. Before he could clamber to his feet a particularly large specimen approached. It stood on its hind legs, and was roughly a meter taller than the rest. Rade thought it must be a lead unit of some kind, because the other aliens backed away to let it pass.

The creature cornered Rade against the pile of dead bodies, and the guttural, rumbling growls it made could best be described as that of an angry lion, though deeper, and amplified tenfold.

It opened is mouth and roared loudly. A thread of slime connected those long, razor-sharp upper fangs to the lower teeth.

Rade slammed his fist upward as he stood, catching the beast under its proboscis, and the entire head snapped backward. It staggered away, and Rade attempted to fire the laser in his right hand. Unfortunately the weapon chose that moment to overheat. There was no time to rotate the grenade launcher into place, nor to retract the shield on his left hand: the creature had already recovered, and it was running at him.

His cockpit reverberated under the force of the impact, and he was taken off his feet.

An instant later he found himself lying on the ground, with claws raking his metallic torso. He wrestled the creature, unsuccessfully trying to get on top.

"Continue the retreat!" Facehopper said. "I'll get him!"

Rade finally managed to mount the alien, pinning its slithering torso between both legs while pummeling the head with his fists. One of the watching beasts struck out at him, knocking him from his opponent.

"You don't want to play fair, then?" Rade said. "Fine."

He launched a smoke grenade and activated his jumpjets as confusion enveloped the alien ranks. Floating above them, Rade switched to frags and fired into the smoke, aiming at the spot where he had last seen the big hammerhead. A moment later body parts erupted into the air.

"Good bye," Rade said.

He spotted Facehopper below; the chief was halfway between the platoon and Rade's location.

"I'm up here, Facehopper!" Intending to clear some of the creatures from Facehopper, he tried to fire another frag but the launcher did nothing. A message flashed on his HUD.

Frag inventory zero.

Facehopper abruptly thrust into the air. He shook off the creatures that clung to him, then jetted again, joining Rade.

"Let's get back to the others."

The pair jetted past the smoke and landed beside the rest of the platoon. Rade found himself on the foremost edge of the circle, pushing toward the rock formations.

"Why don't we just jumpjet over all these bastards?" Manic asked.

"Can't," Facehopper returned. "Not enough fuel, for one. And secondly, didn't you see how many of them grabbed on to me? We'll waste even more fuel trying to get them off."

"Launch a bunch of smoke grenades like Rade did, then," Manic persisted.

"We still won't have enough fuel to clear them all," Facehopper said. "Not yet, anyway."

And so they continued on foot.

Half an hour passed like that, with Rade alternating between the inner and outer circles in the formation. It seemed an eternity.

And then finally, when he was on the foremost edge, the pressure before Rade abruptly ceded.

"We've broken through!" Chief Facehopper said. "Pick up the pace, people!"

Rade slowly increased his pace as the ranks on the leading edge thinned, and soon he and the others were able to retreat at a jog.

Up ahead, he could see the shoulders of the rock formations, about two hundred meters away. There, the sixteen combat robots had assumed a wedge shape, and were firing their plasma rifles into the incoming aliens, picking them off one by one, doing their best to keep the route clear before the Hoplites. HS3s swerved back and forth among them, unsure of what to do.

"Bender, get those robots climbing the rocks," Facehopper said. "The Centurions won't last a minute against these things in close combat!"

"Roger that," Bender said.

The robots retreated, running up the rock shoulder, but they continued to fire. When the Centurions reached a steep cliff face they began scaling the heights, using their individual jumpjets to lessen the required effort, and unleashing their AR-51's into the enemy below when they could.

The mech platoon surmounted the moderately sloped shoulder but soon found themselves backed against the cliff face.

"Cyclone, Mauler, Skullcracker, Grappler, Snakeoil, you're with me," Rade said. "The rest of you, continue up the face while we cover you. Use your jumpjets. When you get to about twenty meters high, grab onto the wall and issue suppressing fire so that we can follow you."

He knew the chief was okay with his orders, because otherwise Facehopper would have countered them.

While Rade and the others kept the swarm at bay, the other mechs fired their jumpjets in rapid succession, quickly attaining the prerequisite height. They latched onto the cliff face there and began firing down into the enemy.

"Rage, you're good to go!" Chief Facehopper said.

Rade swapped out a smoke grenade and launched it a few meters in front of him. "Let's go, people! Leapfrog time!"

He fired his jumpjets. Tahoe and the other four joined him in the air, and together they proceeded upward, floating alongside the wall. Rade retracted his shield in preparation for latching onto the rock, and he fired his jumpjets three more times in succession until he had leapfrogged the other ten mechs attached to the rock. When he was ten meters above them, he grabbed onto the rock with his thick fingers.

"Secure!" he announced.

The other five with him echoed the word. They formed a line of mechs thirty meters from the ground. Located above them by another thirty meters, the combat robots continued to climb.

"Uh, they're still coming," Bender said from below.

Rade glanced down. Underneath the remaining mechs, the creatures were using their claws to scale the heights. They moved fast, but their lack of jumpjets gave the Hoplites a distinct advantage.

"Keep climbing, people," Facehopper said. "Try to conserve your jumpjet fuel, if you can."

The Hoplites scaled the rock face. Whenever someone lost their grip on the wall, they utilized their jumpjets as a safety net, sending themselves upward in a long spurt.

Rade and the others paused occasionally to shoot down at the climbing aliens. He restricted his firing to cobras, as he wanted to conserve the last of his electromagnetic grenades. He found that if he shot his infrared laser at the rockface, he could sometimes cause a section to break away, bringing down two or three of the creatures at the same time. The falling hammerheads would trigger a cascade as they smashed into any aliens underneath them, creating a small avalanche of bodies.

"Eyes east!" Mauler shouted.

Fearing an attack, Rade glanced eastward, where a brightness drew his gaze. He saw what looked like a meteorite burning up in the atmosphere. He zoomed in at maximum level, and could make out the vague outline of what looked like a UC starship.

"That can't be one of our ships?" Bomb said.

"I think that's exactly what it is," Fret replied. "I'm picking up a faint distress signal from it. Definitely UC."

"Do we know who it is?" Rade asked.

"No," Fret said. "But its design is similar to the *Rhodes*."

"But if that's the *Rhodes*..." Grappler began.

No one finished his sentence. No one needed to. Because if the *Rhodes* was sinking, that meant their lieutenant commander was either dead or on his way down to the planet in a lifepod.

"Your orders, sir?" Chief Facehopper said over the line.

Commander Parnell was quiet for a time. "We continue our mission. That's all we can do. And we hope to hell the fleet survives, because if they go, we go. Climb, people! For all you're worth! Climb!"

Rade and the others continued to pause now and again to fire at the pursuers. Rade noticed that the clambering aliens appeared to be growing weary below, and some of them began to fall off the cliff without anyone even firing at them: either they had missed a hold, or their exhausted limbs had lost the strength to carry their weight. Without the luxury of jetpacks, there was nothing to protect them from plunging to their doom.

"I think they're giving up," Manic said.

Rade glanced farther down the cliff. A wave of vertigo came, but he ignored it. At the bottom, only a few were continuing up the wall; many of the aliens milled about uncertainly, obviously not wanting to commit to the climb. Some seemed to be retreating through the incoming swarm. He glanced at the plain beyond. The horde had finally reached its terminus, with the black masses gathered in a half circle around the cliff; a circle that only reached a quarter of the way across the plains behind them.

"Keep climbing, people," Facehopper said.

Rade continued to scale the rock. He lost his grip, and then activated his jumpjets to thrust five meters higher before attempting to latch onto the wall again. He couldn't find a hold—the rock kept breaking away. Suppressing a panic, he thrusted higher, and finally found purchase three meters up.

He glanced down toward the base. Again he felt the vertigo and suppressed it. He noticed that the aliens were now indeed retreating. The half circle was moving away from the cliff, and no others were committing to the climb. Those aliens that yet scaled the wall were slowly dropping away, either from weariness, or because they were shot down by the Hoplites.

"They're going back to the jungle," Rade said. He could feel the palpable relief in the air.

"Keep climbing," Facehopper replied.

"We really need to capture some of them for study at some point," Harlequin said. "NAVCENT will want specimens."

"Right now, all I'm concerned about is getting the lot of you back alive," Chief Facehopper said.

"I'll have to concur with that," Commander Parnell said. "The capture of an alien creature is right at the bottom of the objective ladder. Especially considering that the fate of the fleet is currently up in the air."

"The Centurions have found a cave," Bender announced a short while later. "About fifty meters above and to our right. I'm sending the coordinates."

"Have one of the HS3s continue to the top of the rock formation," Facehopper said. "I want eyes up there. Send the rest inside the cave to explore. Dispatch the Centurions meanwhile to secure the entrance. People, pilot your mechs toward that cave."

Rade and the others continued their climb. They were about five hundred meters up, by then. He had stopped looking down, as the vertigo was proving too unsettling.

"There goes our way home," Manic said over the comm.

"What do you mean?" Commander Parnell asked.

"Have a look at the plains," Manic replied.

Double-checking his grip on the rock face, Rade twisted his torso slightly and glanced over his shoulder. The swarm had swept up the shuttle from the middle of the plains, along with the mech booster payloads farther south, and they carried them off toward the jungle.

"Let's just hope they don't destroy the shuttle," Snakeoil said.

As long as the swarm kept the shuttle intact, Snakeoil and Fret would be able to piggyback off the comm node it contained, and thus communicate with any ships or repeaters in orbit and beyond. But if the hammerheads destroyed the shuttle, the comm node variants Snakeoil and Fret carried weren't powerful enough by themselves to reach a ship beyond the upper orbit. Unless of course the comm specialists knew the coordinates for a precision burst.

"Snakeoil, advise the fleet that we may lose the shuttle and its comm node," Facehopper said.

"I'm no longer getting a communications ping," Snakeoil said. "So I can't."

"Keep trying," the chief said.

"HS3s are reporting an extensive cave system," Bender said a short while later. "They've also found signs of human habitation. But no actual humans so far."

"Well then," Fret said. "Looks like we found out where the majority of the *John A. McDonald* survivors went after their lifepods crashed. Before the local inhabitants had them for dinner, anyway."

"Send in some of the Centurions to help secure the cave system," Facehopper said.

"Based on early echolocation readings, it's fairly big," Bender returned. "The robots will only map out a quarter of it by the time we arrive."

"Then secure the outer cave system," Facehopper transmitted.

The group reached the cave entrance and gathered. It was wide, able to fit seven Hoplites abreast.

As he stood there on the ledge, Rade noticed for the first time how beat up the other mechs were. Like his right arm, many of those limbs jerked badly when moved. Several of the Hoplites limped. The once burnished hulls were covered in dents and gashes, and smeared with alien blood.

"HS3s and Centurions have secured the outer cave system," Bender announced.

"Snakeoil, I want you to stay here and continue trying to contact the fleet while you stand watch," the chief said. "Mauler and Grappler, join him. You're going to act as our sentries. Bender, string out some of the HS3s between us and the entrance to act as repeaters so that we can stay in contact with them at all times. Send the rest deeper into the cave system to explore." After the ensuing chorus of 'aye sirs,' Facehopper finished with: "Headlamps on, people. We're going inside."

Rade gazed at the plain below one last time and saw that the last of the aliens were retreating into the jungle. He zoomed in on them and picked out one of the ugly creatures: like him, it was looking back. The creature abruptly turned around and dived into the jungle.

In the distance Rade discerned more meteorites in the sky. Fearing the worst, he zoomed in: he recognized the distinctive outlines of starships burning up.

"See something, Rage?" Tahoe asked.

Rade shook his head. He decided not to tell the others. He hoped at least some of the fleet would survive up there, because like Commander Parnell had said, without them there was no going home.

Heavy-hearted, Rade took his place near the center of the platoon and proceeded into the cave.

ten

The tunnel soon narrowed, and the mechs were forced to march in five rows of three abreast.

Though Rade advanced at a crouch, the upper portion of his mech still scraped the roof. The cone of his headlamp illuminated the weathered black rock beside him, along with the rank of Hoplites immediately in front. A strata of brown and red ran through the rock in some areas, providing some variety to the dark monotony.

Rade kept the forward camera feed of the mech on point piped into a corner of his HUD, which allowed him to see past the Hoplites blocking his vision; nonetheless, there wasn't much for him to witness up there, as the light cones of the lead mechs illuminated only more of the seemingly endless rock.

"At this rate, we're going to have to abandon our Hoplites," Manic said as the cave tightened once more.

"I'd rather not," TJ said. "If I have to crawl forward on the hands and knees of my Hoplite, I'll do so before I give up my mech."

"You and me both, brother," Bender agreed.

"Well, look on the bright side," Lui said. "At least we're not operating ATLAS units. We'd be on our hands and knees already if that were the case."

They arrived at a portion of the tunnel that looked like it had collapsed at one point, though someone—or something—had dug it out. Piles of smaller rocks littered the floor near the edges of the cave-in, though further in those piles rose to block the entire lower half of the tunnel, reaching to the waistlines of the mechs. A choke point.

"A partial collapse?" Bomb said.

"Seems too convenient," Manic said. "More likely the survivors dug out the cave so they could set up their base deeper inside."

"Doubt it," Fret said. "More like the survivors triggered the cave-in to keep the aliens out."

"And failed," Skullcracker said.

"We'll have to crawl through," Facehopper said. "Though according to the data returned by the Centurions, it gets nice and wide after this. So in theory, you can keep your mechs. But let's just hope that none of us gets stuck in there. Any volunteers to lead the way?"

"All right," Tahoe said, stepping forward. "Let's do this." He rotated cobras into either arm. "If I get stuck, I'm going to be melting myself some rocks."

Rade waited for his turn to come and then he advanced on hands and knees, eventually switching to a crawl. He shot his arms forward, pulling with them, while he pushed with his legs. The tunnel roof scraped against the topside of his mech, while the walls on either side pressed into his flanks. The rocks underneath him varied in size from that of sedimentary grains all the way up to human heads; the material flowed loosely, and at times he had difficulty finding purchase. At other times, the passage of the mechs before him caused the rocks to shift into the unpassable, and he had to dislodge several of them before continuing. He used his cobras to dissolve the more stubborn blockages.

He crawled onward like that for at least two minutes.

"Sheesh," Bomb said at some point. "Whoever dug this out sure was persistent."

"My claustrophobia is acting up," Manic said.

"It's acting up for all of us," Rade said. "Work through it."

"Yes, boss," Manic replied.

Rade definitely was feeling a bit claustrophobic himself, but he forced himself onward. He remembered a story Tahoe had told him once about alien insects following him and then crawling all over his body when he was in a similar situation, and Rade shuddered at the thought. It certainly felt like there was something following him, though he knew it was only a figment of his imagination.

He nervously glanced at his HUD. Skullcracker was just behind him. He felt better all ready. There was no one he would have rather had bringing up the rear. Except Tahoe, maybe. Too bad he was on point.

"I just lost reception with the comm node in the Dragonfly," Snakeoil said. According to the overhead map, he was still at his post near the cave entrance. "Looks like we won't be communicating with the fleet for a while."

"Assuming they've left orbit," Manic said.

"As I mentioned earlier, I stopped receiving replies to my pings a while ago," Snakeoil said. "So that's a good assumption."

"Oh, they've left I'm sure," Fret transmitted. "And they're probably never coming back."

"Fret, enough," the chief's scolding voice came over the comm.

Rade abruptly slipped through an opening, sliding down a sloping pile of rocks. He rolled away to let the next mech through, and was relieved when he could stand to his full height. He resided in a cavern of some sort. Two Centurions acting as sentries by the entrance greeted him.

Rade stepped forward to survey the area. Geodesic domes were scattered along the floor, though ragged holes had been poked into the fabric of all of them. He spotted punctured tanks and vats beside them—any gases or liquids they had contained had long since evaporated. In one of the domes, whose outer layer had been ripped away entirely, he saw shriveled, dead plants. Four other combat robots stood watch at different points throughout the cavern.

"So what are we looking at?" Commander Parnell transmitted.

One of the combat robots by the entrance answered him. A Praetor unit. "Hydroponic and berthing domes. Plus the oxygen extractors and water reclaimers to support them."

"The survivors managed to bring a few 3D printers down with them it looks like," Vicks commented from Rade's passenger seat.

"Have we found any bodies yet?" Parnell asked the robot.

"Negative, sir," the Praetor said. "Neither human, nor alien. Exploration of the inner portion of the cave system is ongoing, however. I have dedicated a squad of HS3s and Centurions to the task. Would you like me to recall them?"

"No," the commander said. "Keep them out there. I want the cave system mapped out in its entirety ASAP."

Rade checked his overhead map, and sure enough he saw the farthest tunnel segments continually expanding as the scout units proceeded deeper.

"And if we encounter hostiles?" the Praetor asked.

"If you encounter hostiles, withdraw immediately without engaging," Commander Parnell said. "That'll be your standing order from now on."

"Aye, sir," the Praetor replied.

Rade heard the clank of metal coming from his passenger area.

"Let me down, Mr. Galaal," Vicks said. "I want to collect some samples of alien blood from your mechs."

"If you wouldn't mind, call me Rage, ma'am," he told her. "It's my callsign."

"I prefer Mr. Galaal," she said.

Rade suppressed a sigh, and he knelt the mech so she could climb down.

When she was on the floor, Vicks retrieved some sort of swab from the kit she carried in her utility belt, and she swiped it over an area on his torso. "I should have done this earlier, before anyone navigated that cave-in."

"Why, you're not finding any blood?" he asked.

"Most of it has been scraped off, yes," she said.

Lieutenant Vicks moved from mech to mech, seeming like a small child beside the three-meter tall Hoplites. She finally found an ample quantity of blood on Skullcracker's mech.

"That's Skullcracker for you," Manic joked. "Always steeped in the blood of his enemies."

"I wouldn't have it any other way," Skullcracker said.

"Should I tell the tale of how I found you all those years ago?" Manic asked. "For the newcomers on the team? The story of your callsign?"

"Probably not," Skullcracker said.

"I'm going to tell them," Manic stated emphatically.

"Later, Manic," Facehopper said.

"Wait a second," Bomb said. "That blood she's collecting... shouldn't it have boiled away by now in this atmosphere?"

"Boiled away?" Vicks said. "The atmospheric pressure isn't that low, I'm afraid."

"But it's low enough," Bomb argued. "Human blood would evaporate in half the time here."

"You're wrong, actually," Vicks said. "The pressure is only a little lower than Earth's atmosphere. And besides, this isn't human blood."

"Chief," TJ said. "George is telling me it found some holographic drives in a cave chamber not far from this one. They're all smashed though, and George is convinced the data is unrecoverable. I'd like permission to check it out anyway."

"Who's George?" Commander Parnell asked.

"One of the Centurions," TJ said, his voice sounding a bit sheepish. "Unit G."

Manic turned his mech toward the commander and explained: "Our drone operators like to name them. Kinda like pets."

"I see..." Parnell's expression seemed somewhat amused behind his faceplate.

"Go ahead, TJ," Facehopper said. "But take Keelhaul with you."

"Aye, Chief."

Facehopper's mech turned toward Parnell. "Assuming that's okay with you, Commander?"

The commander inclined his head in consent.

"How much oxygen do your mechs have remaining?" Parnell asked when TJ and Keelhaul were gone.

"About five days worth," Facehopper answered.

"The lieutenant and I only carry two days worth," Parnell said.

Facehopper's Hoplite bobbed up and down, which Rade interpreted as a nod. "Our first priority should be to get these oxygen extractors back online so we can replenish our supplies. We could be down here for quite some time. Bender and Tahoe, you're the most qualified to work on those extractors. Get on them immediately. Harlequin, you help them—I'm sure your AI brain has a database containing thousands of extractor schematics."

"I have the same database Bender and Tahoe possess in their Implants," the Artificial said. "Nonetheless I will do my best to help them."

"The rest of you," Facehopper continued. "Split up and rummage through these domes. Let me know if you find anything the robos missed. A few battery packs for the suits of the commander and his chief scientist would be great. Otherwise we'll have to let the two of them take a turn in the Hoplites to recharge via our atomic reactors."

"My jumpsuit needs to recharge, too," Harlequin said.

Facehopper ignored the Artificial and turned toward Vicks, who sat crossed-legged in her environmental suit on the cavern floor, swiping her hands across a display screen only she could see. "Lieutenant, update us as soon as you've finished analyzing the blood. Then I want you to help Bender, Tahoe and Harlequin with the extractors."

"I can update you now," she said.

"All right..." the chief told her.

"This blood is certainly interesting," Vicks said. "The things that attacked us definitely aren't natural, or even native to the planet. I wouldn't even call them aliens. But rather, mutants."

"What are you saying?" Commander Parnell asked.

"They're bioengineered from Terran species," she replied.

"Terran?" Parnell said. "Are you sure?"

"Unfortunately, yes," she answered. "The DNA has several base pairs that match up to species from Earth, lumped together in long sequences by animal. Snake, alligator, shark, even human nucleotides are in the make-up. There are several insect genes, too, notably scorpion. Just a hodgepodge of characteristics borrowed from the genetic spectrum of Earth's phyla. I believe the base animal they started with was the chicken, however."

"The chicken?" Commander Parnell said, the disbelief evident in his voice. "We were attacked by big chickens."

Vicks looked up from where she sat. "The chicken is a descendant of the Tyrannosaurus Rex. It would make sense to use the DNA of the bird as a starting point, activating various genes to express characteristics of its ancestor. The clawed hands. The large tail. The extensive jaw. The massive size. Once they had reverted the animal, it was simply a matter of splicing in genes from other species to get the genetically engineered animal they desired, one that could breathe the harsh atmosphere of the planet. A weapon of war."

"Who is this 'they' you're talking about?" Parnell said. "The creators of this bio-weapon. You mean the aliens who attacked the *John A. McDonald?*"

"Possibly," the lieutenant replied. "Someone used the DNA of the human survivors, and that of their food sources, to bioengineer the creatures that attacked us. Either the aliens that attacked the *John A. McDonald* did it, or the scientists who survived the attack themselves."

"Why would the scientists create them?" Grappler asked. He was obviously listening in from his faraway sentry post at the cave entrance.

"Perhaps to protect themselves from the other native animals of the planet," Vicks explained. "Or from the aliens who attacked their ship in orbit. It's possible their plan backfired, however, and they lost control of their own creations. The creatures turned on them."

"Wait a second," Lui said. "I highly doubt the survivors had any bioengineering experts among them. And gene splicing equipment, plus the incubation chambers that go with them, are fairly specific. Very few starships have the necessary infrastructure aboard. It's not something you can simply jury-rig from a 3D printer and a geodesic dome. And you say DNA from the food sources was used? I don't think the survivors had any shark, snake, or alligator meat in their ration packs. Nor any scorpions. But they would have had chicken, I'll give you that."

"The survivors could have easily retrieved the base pair information from the database," Vicks said. "Though I'll agree, it was doubtful they had the necessary equipment to splice and incubate the bioengineered creatures."

"I'll tell you all what we're facing here," Lui said. "These hammerhead things weren't manufactured by the survivors of the *John A. McDonald.* Oh no. These kind of bio-weapons are the specialty of the Sino-Koreans."

Commander Parnell glanced at Lui's Hoplite. "You think the Sino-Koreans, or one of their factions, attacked the *John A. McDonald?*"

"That's exactly what I think," Lui said. "I'm willing to bet the other herds of animals we detected from orbit are also based on DNA from Earth phyla. And the plants? Probably genetically modified as well. That dodecahedron ship must be some new prototype of theirs. The secondary Slipstream in this system probably loops back to SK space. See, I'm willing to bet the SKs were using this planet as a breeding ground for organic weapons. At least until we showed up with our Builders and the *John A McDonald* to crash the party. Something they weren't too pleased about."

"It's an interesting theory," Parnell said. "And until we have any more evidence to the contrary, I'll go with it. Especially considering that our Raptors were attacked by rockets from that jungle. That's certainly tech the SKs would possess."

"Unless those mobile silos were captured from the wreckage of the *John A. McDonald* and used by an alien enemy," Manic said. "That's a possibility, too. I'm sure the Decatur class supercarrier carried a few types of artillery in its inventory, after all."

"I'm sticking with the SK theory for now," Parnell said.

"Do we know yet where the secondary Slipstream leads?" Rade asked.

"No," Parnell admitted. "The captain launched drones to measure the farther Slipstream, but they weren't due to arrive for a few more days yet."

"All right," Facehopper said. "Let's split up and see what we can find. Lieutenant Vicks, since you're done with your analysis, please join Bender and Tahoe."

"And Harlequin," the Artificial piped in.

Rade marched his Hoplite directly toward one of the domes near the center of the cavern. He avoided its airlock, which wouldn't fit his mech, and forced his way through a tear in the outer fabric instead. He found himself in what looked like a berthing area, replete with 3D-printed bunk beds and lockers. He began rifling through the latter, which was tricky, given his large fingers.

Manic's voice came over the comm.

"You thought you were going to get away from me telling your story, huh Skullcracker?" Manic said. "You thought I'd forget?"

Skullcracker didn't answer.

"Well," Manic continued. "Skullcracker was still a caterpillar, three months new to the team, when we were deployed to Mongolia. In our very first mission, he was separated from my fire team. The insurgents bagged him, temporarily disabling his Implant. It reactivated again a few days later, allowing us to track him down. I led a rescue party to retrieve him. We found him in a house inside a village under rebel control.

"When we broke into that house, I thought at first he had been skinned alive or something, because he was completely naked and covered in blood. 'Not mine,' he said. I checked my HUD and sure enough most of it wasn't his. And his vitals were fine, though he exhibited signs of physical and psychological torture. We sent combat robots to clear the rest of the the house, and we got some brutal footage back in return."

"From the combat robots shooting up the rebels?" Grappler asked.

"Not at all," Manic said. "The occupants were already dead. Let's just say none of the seven individuals scattered throughout the place were identifiable. He had cracked open all of their skulls with a blunt force weapon. I reviewed the video logs recorded by his Implant, and apparently Skullcracker had told them all before they began his interrogation: if they touched him, he was going to break their skulls. One by one. They laughed.

"When we brought him back to the forward operating base later that night, and he washed the blood off his face, we discovered he had tattooed a skull into his face during his captivity."

"Where did he get the ink?" Keelhaul asked. His voice warped slightly, because he was still in the adjacent chamber with TJ. "And the needle?"

"The ink was their blood," Manic said. "The needle was the syringe his captors used to interrogate him."

"That doesn't sound very... hygienic," Harlequin said.

Rade hadn't known the story, and it made him think of that incredibly detailed skull tattoo in a completely new light. He wasn't sure whether everything Manic said was true or not, but he had a feeling the MOTH hadn't embellished the story very much.

"You tattooed that yourself?" Grappler said over the comm, the incredulity evident in his voice. Or was that awe? "You must have been an artist in a past life."

"I was a welder apprentice," Skullcracker said.

"I didn't even know there *were* welder jobs anymore," Keelhaul said. "I thought the robos took them all."

"There is still some demand for manmade welded goods," Trace said. "Though it is small, admittedly."

"Okay people," Facehopper said. "I'm going to have to ask for quiet on the comms, please. I can't concentrate with you blokes incessantly chattering away like that, and I don't want to mute the line in case the scouts or another one of you has something to report."

On the one hand, Rade was relieved at the ensuing silence, but on the other he missed the camaraderie. It was a good relief of the tension knotted into his nerves from the fight. Even so, he knew there would be more than enough banter to come later. It was time to do his job.

Rade found nothing of interest in the lockers, other than a few personal belongings—lockets, hair clips, clothing. He departed the dome empty-handed to search another. As he left, he marked it purple on the overhead map so that no one would search the same place. Then he made his way toward the next closest dome.

He discovered no items of note there, nor in the three other domes he searched thereafter, one of which proved to be a waste reclamation unit. He left that latter with his mech coated knee deep in fecal matter.

When all the domes were marked purple on the map, Facehopper reconvened the platoon for a situation report. TJ and Keelhaul returned from the adjacent chamber, carrying the damaged holographic drives; Tahoe, Bender, Harlequin and Vicks were still working on repairing the oxygen extractors; Snakeoil, Mauler and Grappler reported in from the entrance—all was quiet, and the HS3 dispatched to the top of the rock formation detected no sign of hammerheads anywhere upon the surrounding terrain. The others meanwhile relayed what they found in the domes—a few broken 3D printers, bunks and lockers, personal items, ruined foodstuffs. Rade could have sworn he heard a few of the MOTHs sniggering at him over the comm when his turn to report came.

Facehopper ordered them to dismount their mechs, so that they could rest while they waited for the HS3s to complete the mapping of the cave system.

As Rade abandoned his Hoplite, Bender joked: "Hey, boss. What the hell did you step in? I can smell your mech through my jumpsuit!"

Rade didn't bother to look in his direction. "I stepped in your backyard, bro. Wish you'd told me beforehand you fertilize your shrubs with your own excrement."

Manic chimed in: "By shrubs, you mean his genitals right?"

"Funny," Bender said.

eleven

R ade and the others positioned their unoccupied Hoplites in a circle around the makeshift camp and activated "guard" mode. The mechs rotated their lasers into place; some of them remained near the edge of the camp, while others patrolled the cavern.

When outside of the mechs, the oxygen usage of the MOTH jumpsuits automatically switched to the local tanks. The individual canisters contained two days worth, just like the commander and the chief scientist, but if it came to it they could transfer oxygen from the mechs to their suits, restocking O2 levels.

Rade passed the time by moving between the men, trying to maintain morale. The chief did much the same. Commander Parnell meanwhile kept mostly to himself, though he hovered near Lieutenant Vicks and those working on the oxygen extractor. The commander probably felt out of his element surrounded by so many enlisted personnel, preferring the commissioned officers he was used to.

Rade noticed that Tahoe seemed to be joking a lot with Vicks, or at least that was the impression he had, because whenever he looked at the group by the oxygen extractor, she seemed to be always laughing at something or other he said. Rade wasn't sure what to think. Tahoe was a married man. He shouldn't be leading her on like that. Then again, men and women always wanted what they couldn't have.

As an LPO, Rade had no right to interfere with the private life of the MOTHs who served beneath him, unless those private lives interfered with their duty or violated navy regulations. If Tahoe wanted to lead her on, then so be it. Still, Rade wondered if he should take Tahoe aside for a short talk. Though the question was, should he approach the conversation from the point of view of the LPO, or the friend?

Maybe it's time to move the friendship to the back burner, Rade thought. *And the LPO to the forefront. At least for the short term. Because I'm not sure I can continue to be both.*

Rade decided he would let the behavior pass for the moment. Because honestly, Tahoe wasn't doing anything wrong.

After two hours Bender announced: "The HS3s and Centurions have nearly completed their survey of the cave system. The only thing of interest discovered so far is a cavern near the deepest sections. It looks like some of the survivors made a last stand there. Laser burns line the walls of the tunnel leading to the chamber. Inside, a long row of stalactites has collapsed. The HS3s found powder burns in the jagged edges left on the ceiling. It's likely the survivors laid a trap for the enemy there. A few Centurions are combing through the broken stalactites, but so far they've found no bodies, neither human, alien nor mutant. There isn't even any of that bioengineered blood we found coating our mechs. Whoever attacked sure did a good job of cleaning up."

"Let me know if they find anything," the chief said.

A few minutes later Bender spoke once more over the comm. "Well this is interesting. Very, very interesting."

"What is it?" Commander Parnell asked.

"Two Centurions just found an armory near the last-stand chamber. Surprisingly wasn't looted by the enemy. There are still several frags and electromagnetics in stock. They also found an Energy M7." The M7 was an MRAAWS—a Multi-Role Anti-armor Anti-tank Weapon System. Useful against tanks. And mechs.

Facehopper nodded behind his faceplate. "It looks like the survivors of the *John A. McDonald* definitely had time to plan their evacuation of the ship."

"There might be a few Dragonflies out there we overlooked," Parnell said.

"Maybe," Rade said. "But it's likely those hammerheads dragged them away into the jungle, like they did yours."

"Have the Centurions gather as many of the grenades as they can carry," Facehopper told Bender. "Tell them to bring us the goods. And get me that M7."

"That begs the question," Harlequin said. "Why didn't any of you bring an M7 in the first place?"

"Shut up, bitch," Bender told him.

"You were the only one of us who didn't have a mech," Rade said. "You could have chosen an M7 to haul around for yourself. Instead, you picked a plasma rifle."

Harlequin shrugged. "I suppose I believed your Hoplites would be good enough."

We all did, Rade thought.

An hour later a troop of combat robots returned, along with several HS3s. Several fresh grenades were attached to the harnesses of the former. One of the Centurions carried the M7 hoisted over one shoulder. They reported straight to Bender.

After a few minutes, Bender said: "The Centurions found something of interest while they combed through the smashed stalactites."

"What's that?" Commander Parnell said.

Bender handed over a large corrugated cylinder.

The commander held up the object to examine it. "Why didn't you report this earlier?"

"Would it have made a difference?" Bender said. "I wanted to have a peek at the item personally."

Commander Parnell continued to study it. "Looks like a mech servomotor of some sort."

"That's exactly what it is," Bender said.

"Is it possible the survivors had a mech with them?" Vicks asked.

Commander Parnell's eyes seemed to defocus behind his faceplate. "According to the manifest in my archives, the *John A. McDonald* launched with several ATLAS 5s in its inventory."

"This servomotor definitely ain't the kind found in an ATLAS 5," Bender said. "The design appears more Sino Korean than UC, actually."

"Lending credence to my theory that the SKs are behind this," Lui chimed in.

"What are you saying?" Fret asked. "The SKs attacked with bioengineered weapons, *and* mechs?"

"I don't know," Bender said. "But some sort of machine attacked them in that cavern. One, or many."

The platoon members were quiet for a moment.

"Misdirection," Skullcracker said suddenly.

"What's that?" Facehopper asked.

"Misdirection." Skullcracker stepped forward. "Could be that whoever did this wants us to *think* the SKs were behind it."

Facehopper thrummed a gloved hand on the opposite arm assembly.

"Snakeoil," Facehopper transmitted. "Have you received a response from the fleet yet?"

"No," Snakeoil said over the comm. "But the white flashes have stopped in the sky. I'm not sure if that's good or bad."

Rade waited for Fret to make his usual pronouncement of doom, but thankfully the pessimistic comm officer held his tongue.

Facehopper pursed his lips behind his faceplate. He glanced at the nearby Centurions with their grenade-laden harnesses. "Restock your Hoplites with grenades, people. Harlequin, the M7 is yours."

The MOTHs reloaded their mech launchers with frags and electromagnetics. Harlequin dutifully grabbed the M7, depositing it near his work area beside the oxygen extractor.

When that was done, Manic swiveled toward Facehopper and said: "So what now, Chief?"

Facehopper in turn glanced at Commander Parnell.

"We wait here until communication is reestablished with the *Rhodes*," Parnell said. "At least until the oxygen extractor is repaired. Seems the safest location, for the moment."

"That's what the survivors thought," Fret said. "Until they were wiped out."

"I say we relocate somewhere else entirely," Lui said. "Those hammerheads saw us go into the cave. They know we're hiding here. They'll relay our position to the SKs. We can expect an attack."

"You don't know they're capable of that level of intelligence," Tahoe argued.

"And we don't know they're not," Lui said. "But wouldn't you rather err on the side of caution? And even if they didn't have the intelligence to communicate our position, the SKs—or whoever attacked the *John A. McDonald*—were likely observing from the jungle the whole time. Someone launched those missiles, after all. We're going to have to investigate that at some point or other."

"Go into that jungle?" Bomb said. "Hell no! Not with those hammerheads waiting to ambush us. It's a death trap."

"We can send a few HS3s in at the very least," Lui said. "With orders to retreat at the first sign of trouble."

"How long until your men have the oxygen extractor and water reclaimer repaired?" Commander Parnell asked Facehopper.

"Bender?" the chief relayed.

"We're looking at, well, probably at least another three hours," Bender replied.

"And how easy will the two items be to carry out of here?" Parnell asked. "Considering that we'll have to climb down a rock face."

"Not easy," Bender said. "We'll probably have to expend the jump fuel of a few mechs. Might be better to stash the devices here, or in a side chamber, and come back as needed."

"If we leave, I don't think we're coming back." Parnell touched his faceplate as if he were about to rub his chin but the polycarbonate stopped him. "All right, Chief, I'll give your men two hours to repair those devices. Once operational, we'll replenish our oxygen and water reserves. After that, we relocate, bringing the devices with us. Do we know the day-night cycle of this planet?"

"We do," Vicks replied. "It'll be dark in about an hour."

Parnell nodded. "We can move out under the cover of darkness, then."

"It won't matter," Lui said. "If we're dealing with SKs, they can use thermals to spot us just as easily from afar."

"Any advanced race could," Tahoe said.

"But let's say we destroyed any SK presence when we took out those rocket launchers in the jungle..." Parnell said.

"Not likely," Manic piped in.

"But let's say we did," the commander pressed. "And that the hammerheads were the only enemies lying in wait. Wouldn't you agree that it would be safer to travel by night? Maybe they can't see in the dark."

"Lieutenant," Lui said. "When you analyzed the DNA, could you tell if any cat or tiger genes were spliced in? Maybe owl?"

"If you're asking me if the bioengineered weapons can see in the dark," Vicks replied. "I don't know. But I'd say it's a good possibility that whoever designed them would have planned for every contingency."

"We'll dispatch an HS3 across the plains when it grows dark," Parnell said. "Sending it into the jungle. We'll place another one in the center of the plain to act as a repeater. The rest of us, meanwhile, will clamber down and advance west, away from the jungle, utilizing jumpjet fuel as necessary to convey the extractor and reclaimer."

"Wait," Rade said. "What if the HS3 draws out the hammerheads as soon as it enters that jungle? We'll be stuck in the open on those plains again. We should send it now, and only when we determine that the jungle is clear, should we proceed."

"I agree," Facehopper said.

"Can we ever truly be sure something like a jungle is clear?" Mauler said. "There are a lot of places to hide in such a place. Ask our snipers."

"This is true," Trace agreed.

"We can't ever be completely sure," Facehopper admitted. "But at least we'll have some idea if they're waiting to spring an obvious trap."

Parnell frowned, his face momentarily darkening. But then his features smoothed. "You're my tacticians. I'll trust your collective judgment. Chief, send out an HS3 to scout that jungle now. And leave another in the middle of the plain to act as a repeater."

"Will do," the chief replied.

Bender dispatched the necessary HS3s and then returned to his work on the extractor with Tahoe, Harlequin and Vicks.

"The lead HS3 has entered the jungle," Bender announced several minutes later.

"Keep us posted," the commander said.

A minute later, Bender said: "It just reached the site where the two missiles launched. This is odd... there should have been some debris from the mobile silos, but all I'm finding is tracks leading away west. I was sure our Raptors got them."

"Maybe they did," Rade commented. "And the hammerheads dragged them away, along with the shuttle and boosters."

"Have the HS3 continue exploring," Commander Parnell ordered. "But I want it to return to the edge of the jungle by nightfall so that the rest of us can proceed west."

Half an hour later TJ spoke up. "I managed to recover a lone log entry from the damaged holographic drive. The last entry ever made." He sounded grim. "I'll play it for you all."

"Wait," Parnell said. "Send it to me only, for now."

TJ glanced at Facehopper, who nodded in assent from behind his faceplate.

"There you go," TJ said.

The commander was quiet for several moments. His face seemed to grow pale behind the photochromic polycarbonate of his helmet.

He abruptly sat down on the cave floor. Toppled, really. After several moments he waved a hand wearily. "Play it for everyone else."

The holographic image of a woman appeared on Rade's vision. She was relatively attractive, though at the moment appeared very haggard-looking: her cheeks sagged, accentuating her frown lines, and her eyes were dark hollows. She was dressed in command fatigues.

"This is Commander Julie Amati," the woman said. "Of the *John A. McDonald*. We thought we were safe after we sealed the cave. We stayed inside, laying low, planning how we would survive the next year or more until rescue. But unknown to us, they were digging the whole while. Slowly coming for us. We realized it too late. They destroyed everything we built here to sustain ourselves.

"We've retreated to the inner recesses of the cave system to make our last stand. I've dispersed the combat robots throughout the tunnels to buy us some time. We'll do our best to drive off the enemy, but I don't have high hopes: there are simply too many of them. Marik has come up with a last ditch plan to stop them, involving the stalactites. If it fails, this will be my last entry. Commander Amati out."

Her image faded.

The platoon remained very still, observing reverent silence for several moments. How could they do otherwise? They had just listened to a message recorded by a woman moments before she was about to die, wherein she proclaimed her intention to fight to the end. Any MOTH would have done the same.

"How do we know that was really Commander Amati?" Lui finally said. "Could be a computer-generated stand-in."

"That's her," Parnell confirmed. "I knew her from the academy. Did you see the way she rubbed her right eye when she mentioned making her last stand? She did that often in real life."

"Computer-generated stand-ins can be very convincing," Lui said. "Capable of matching the unconscious habits of a given subject down to the micro-tic level."

"Lui, mate," Facehopper said. "I think we'll assume she was real, for now."

"Just saying," Lui replied.

"Bender!" Snakeoil transmitted from his sentry position at the cave entrance. "I think I discovered the source of your mysterious servomotor."

"What are you talking about, bro?" Bender returned.

Snakeoil ignored the question, and instead said: "Chief, it was probably a bad idea to send that HS3 into the jungle."

"Why," Facehopper transmitted. "What's going on?"

"Attackers are streaming onto the plains," Snakeoil replied.

"More hammerheads?"

"No," Snakeoil said. "These are mechs."

twelve

Rade glanced at Facehopper.

"Say again?" the chief said. "Mechs?"

"Yes," Snakeoil returned. "Either mechs, or giant robots. Of a design I've never seen before. Their torsos are thick, built like tanks. Definitely could hold at least one occupant, if not more. Their legs are powerful, meant for running. And their upper bodies have four arms—two in front, and two in behind. They've got swivel mounts on their hands, for swapping out weapons. And they've got what look like shoulder-mounted rockets."

"How many of them?"

"I'm counting thirty."

Rade exchanged a look with Facehopper. "Twice as many as we have."

"Snakeoil, pipe me into your feed," Facehopper said.

The chief shared it with the platoon.

Rade saw the plains, dim in the twilight of the waning sun. He knew Snakeoil's display was brightening the light levels, as it was almost night. Rade focused on the dark masses that approached, zooming in on his local copy of the stream.

The mechs were precisely as Snakeoil described. Massive torsos connected to long, powerful legs. It appeared the upper bodies were rotated sideways so that all four arms were facing forward. Those arms were spread out so each weapon had an unobstructed line of sight. He observed what looked like a projectile launcher, an incendiary, and a missile launcher. And on the shoulders were mounted what looked like lasers, not the rockets Snakeoil had originally surmised. Their heads were small nubs with yellow "eyes" near the base. Based on the height measurements provided by the AI, the mechs were a little under twice as tall as the Hoplites.

The computed trajectories of the mechs matched up with the rock face directly below the cave.

"They look like insects standing on their hind legs or something," Bomb said. "Like roaches waving their arms when you've turned them upside down."

"Roaches," Manic said. "That's what I'm going to call 'em."

"Snakeoil, have you tried pinging them?" the chief asked.

"I have," Snakeoil replied. "On all frequency bands, encrypted and unencrypted. No response."

"Snakeoil," Rade said. "Do we still have contact with the foremost HS3?"

"Negative," Snakeoil replied. "But we do have contact with the repeater. I've already recalled it."

"Did we get any interesting video footage before the HS3 went down?" Rade asked.

"Not really. I'll send you the last ten seconds so you can judge for yourself."

Rade streamed the feed to the rest of the platoon as he watched it.

The HS3 hovered through the purple foliage. Because of the thick canopy overhead, and the twilight, the light levels were extremely low, and the footage was marred by the grainy streaks caused by the camera digitally increasing the brightness.

Rade saw a sudden flash of metal, then darkness.

"Smith," Rade said. "Replay that last second, eight times slower."

The footage replayed. That flash of metal turned out to be a large, metallic arm, striking down through the trees toward the HS3.

"That tells us everything we need to know," the chief said. "Everyone, to your Hoplites! We're going to assume strategic positions at the cave entrance."

"About that," Snakeoil said. "We've been surveying the rock face immediately surrounding the entrance. We got some hides for the rest of you. I'm sending the positions now. I'll leave it up to you, Chief, on how you want to distribute the platoon."

"Rage," Facehopper sent. "Allocate the positions. Commander Parnell and Lieutenant Vicks, we'll deposit you just inside the cave entrance. Try to stay back during the fighting. Harlequin, you'll fight from Bender's passenger seat. I'll expect you to put that M7 to good use. Snakeoil, Mauler and Grappler, target the incoming mechs with your cobras and fire when they are within range."

"They're already within range," Snakeoil said. "Targeting and firing."

Rage loaded into his Hoplite and hurried into the choke point of the tunnel exit with the others; they crawled their mechs through the partially collapsed section as fast as they were able.

We should have dug out this damn section.

Halfway through the choke point, Rade received the hides Snakeoil had picked out. He decided that only four of them were suitable for deployment. The remaining positions were too exposed.

"Snakeoil, how far is it to the top of the rock formations?" Rade asked.

"About another kilometer," Snakeoil replied. "We won't be able to position any mechs up there in time, though, if that's what you're thinking."

Rade finally emerged into the wider portion of the tunnel and picked up his pace.

"Cyclone, Keelhaul, Skullcracker, Bender," Rade said. "When you reach the cave entrance, I want you to deploy to the following hides." He marked off the locations on the topographical wireframe overlaying the upper right of his vision. "Cyclone and Keelhaul, take the two crevices near the entrance. Skullcracker, your place is behind this outcrop. Bender, you get the upper ledge here. Before going outside, stow a combat robot in your passenger seat."

"I have an Artificial taking up space in my passenger seat already," Bender said.

"That comment was meant more for Cyclone, Keelhaul and Skullcracker," Rade replied.

"Gotcha."

Rade assigned the remaining eleven mechs to the cave entrance—seven in kneeling positions, side by side with shields deployed, four standing behind them. He instructed two combat robots to remain with Vicks and Parnell, and had the remainder deploy into the available passenger seats of the mechs.

The tunnel shook.

"What was that?" Facehopper sent over the comm.

"We just took a missile hit," Mauler returned. "No casualties, but we lost half the ledge."

"Can we still squeeze seven mechs into the cave opening?" Rade asked over the comm.

"We can," Snakeoil replied. "But it's going to be a jagged line of mechs."

"That's fine."

The platoon of Hoplites reached the entrance. Mauler hadn't been kidding when he said they'd lost half the ledge: the entrance curved inward, forming a ragged, gaping hole that fell away onto the cliff face.

Tahoe, Keelhaul, Skullcracker, and Bender jetted out to assume their hides, while the remaining mechs took their places along the edge.

"Be ready to fire your cobras at any incoming missiles," Rade instructed those who had remained by the entrance. "But be prepared to retreat."

"One of us needs to stay behind at all times," Snakeoil said.

"What do you mean?"

"To launch a Trench Coat," Snakeoil said. "We have to do everything we can to destroy any incoming missiles. If we allow any more to strike, we risk collapsing the entire entrance."

"All right, we'll alternate when missiles come in," Rade said. "I'm sending the combat order now."

He randomized the list of mechs at the entrance and fed it to the platoon. He set the AIs to automatically alert the next person in the queue when a missile attack came.

"Those of you assigned to the front line when an attack comes," Rade said. "I want you to launch as many Trench Coats as necessary to stop the missiles, but then pull back."

"Only common sense, boss," Manic replied.

"And so it is," Rade said. "But you'd be surprised at how quickly common sense goes out the window in the midst of combat."

"As do most plans," Lui added.

Rade had assigned himself one of the standing positions in back, and he stared over the shields of those in front of him to survey the rapidly approaching enemy. They were about a kilometer from the base of the rock formation.

"Tell me you've downed some of them already, Snakeoil," Facehopper said.

"We got three of the roaches so far," Snakeoil said. "With the assistive AI of the Hoplites, we've been repeatedly targeting identical spots on the same mechs. Their armor seems thickest at the center of their torsos, and I'm guessing that's where their power sources or AI cores are housed. So we've been concentrating on the legs, bringing them down that way. Unfortunately, that doesn't disable them entirely, and the fallen are still able to fire nano-second pulse lasers in return. Our shields have been holding up so far, but they won't last forever."

The shields were mirror-like, designed to reflect as much laser light as possible. However, that wouldn't stop the more powerful lasers from penetrating.

Rade pulled up the stats of his platoon, and saw that Snakeoil had borne the brunt of the laser strikes so far: his shield had a huge groove carved into the middle where the enemy seemed to be concentrating fire.

"Snakeoil, you're relieved from the front line position," Rade said. "Fret, take his place. Everyone, link your cobra targeting system to my own. I want us firing at the same roach." He muted the outgoing comm and spoke to his AI: "Smith, target the legs of the leading mech. Aim for the knee joint. I want you to update the position in realtime so that we're constantly hitting the same spot. Let's see if we can blow its feet out from under it."

"Ready," Smith replied.

"Fire."

Rade watched as the mech collapsed. "Let's do the same thing with the next enemy." He targeted the knees of the adjacent roach and fired. In unison, all the infrared lasers in the group pulsed.

"Incoming missiles!" Mauler announced. "Thirty of them!"

"They're firing everything at once, are they?" Facehopper said. "Target them with your cobras! Take them down before they break into smaller warheads!"

"Don't think these ones can break into smaller warheads, Chief," Snakeoil said.

"Even so, I want them out of the sky!"

Rade unlinked the cobras so that the others could fire at will. The mechs did just that, and half of the missiles either exploded or dropped. Rade raised the laser of his other hand and fired again, as did other Hoplites, and those Centurions that had switched to laser rifles. Fourteen missiles were terminated in that next volley. The last two detonated moments before Rade was about to give the order to retreat deeper into the cave.

"Another wave!" Snakeoil said. "Thirty more!"

Again Rade and the others defended. The enemy wasn't giving the MOTHs enough time for their lasers to recharge, and Rade and the others were forced to fire at half strength. Six missiles closed.

"They're going to hit!" Rade said. "Into the tunnel people!"

Rade and the others retreated while Grappler, the first MOTH assigned to remain behind, activated his Trench Coat countermeasure twice. The missile defenses moved outward, thirty-four pieces of metal that used 360-degree homing radar to seek out incoming rockets. Grappler dove into the tunnel a moment later.

The cave entrance shook violently. At least one of the missiles got through, then.

"Grappler, you okay?" Rade asked. He instinctively glanced at Grappler's vitals. All green.

"Fine," Grappler responded. "I only took out three of the missiles, though."

"The entrance is definitely messed up," Tahoe said from his hidden perch outside.

When Rade and the others returned to the entrance, they discovered it had partially collapsed. Only three mechs could stand there abreast.

"They're using the missiles as a distraction!" Keelhaul said from his hide. "To close with us!"

Rade took a place behind Manic, Trace and Lui, who had already knelt at the opening and raised their shields. He saw that the first of the roaches were already arriving at the base of the rock formation below.

"On the bright side," Bender said. "I don't think they have any more missiles left."

Even though six mechs were able to occupy the opening by alternately kneeling and standing, the Hoplites couldn't all target those roaches that were scaling the rocks, not at the same time, because the angle was too steep. Only the three kneeling in the forefront could do that. Not unless he made them lower their shields a bit, potentially exposing Rade and the others who were standing.

"Manic, Trace, Lui, target the same enemies down there," Rade said. "Knock them off the rock one by one. The rest of us, meanwhile, will try to stop the remainder from approaching those rocks in the first place."

He kept expecting Facehopper to order him to the side so that the chief could take command, but the order never came. He was happy to let Rade work, apparently. Rade *had* gotten to the entrance first, after all.

Rade and the two others standing with him focused on one of the roaches that was still approaching from the plains, and managed to destroy its knee joint after four shots. But by then the rest of the enemy mechs had reached the rock formation.

"We got twenty-five climbers," Tahoe said.

Rade decided the risk of losing one arm was acceptable, so he ordered the mechs in the forefront to lower their shields slightly. He lifted his arm over them, crooked the elbow, and switched to the point of view of the laser's scope. He spotted the climbers immediately.

"Everyone who has a view of the cliff," Rade said. "I want you to target the rock face fifty meters above the lead mech. Let's see if we can cause an avalanche. Coordinate with your AIs to determine the best points of impact."

The AIs generated a firing matrix, and gave them precise targeting information. Rade and the others launched their lasers, employing frag grenades generously. Harlequin joined in, launching his M7 in turn.

Dust began to rise from the rock face. Rade heard a deep rumbling sound, and the cave floor shook underneath him.

"One avalanche coming right up," Tahoe said.

The tumbling rocks tore more matter in turn from the wall, until an all out avalanche made its way down the cliff. The incoming roaches were swept from the wall and vanished in a cloud of dust and rock. The seven near the bottom managed to break away from the rock face in time, and retreated before the onslaught.

"Concentrate on the seven survivors on the plain," Rade said. "Let's eliminate them. As usual, link your cobra targeting systems to my unit."

Rade picked off the survivors on the plains in that way, concentrating fire on their torsos one by one until all were immobile and smoking.

By then the dust had cleared below.

"No sign of any survivors," Keelhaul reported.

"TJ," Rade said. "Send a few HS3s down there just to be sure."

"You got it, *LPO*," TJ replied. The scorn when the drone operator said the word LPO was obvious. He never called Rade boss, and rarely referred to him by his callsign anymore.

Rade ignored the disrespect. He had already privately chewed out TJ a few times for displaying obvious contempt in front of the men. He had to choose his battles.

"External Hoplites, remain in your hides for the time being," Rade said.

While the HS3s proceeded down the cliff, Facehopper came forward in his mech.

"Good job, Rage," the chief said on a private line.

"It was nothing, Chief," Rade said. "Thanks for letting me lead the assault."

"And thank *you* for actually leading it," Facehopper responded. "It's not every chief who can rely on his LPO unfailingly in combat."

"That's because not every chief will give his LPO a chance to prove himself," Rade responded.

"Oh you've proven yourself many times over, Rage," Facehopper said. "It's why we made you LPO in the first place. And I know that you'll only continue to demonstrate courage under fire."

A few moments later TJ reported: "Nothing is moving down there, and the EM-band is clear. Looks like we got them all. The metal torsos of a few of them were split open during the avalanche. It seems there are no occupants in any of them. Only electronics. Combat robots, people. Big ones."

"You said electronics?" Lui asked. "So it's something you would expect to find in a SK-made robot?"

"Sure," TJ replied. "Or in a UC robot. But, while the individual electronic components are all readily identifiable, their arrangement is peculiar."

"Peculiar?" Commander Parnell said. "In what way?"

"Well," TJ continued. "It's almost like the kind of robot someone would make if they got their hands on the tech but didn't really understand it. Like they didn't have a manual on to how to put it together properly, nor the training. There are a bunch of extraneous components whose placement makes no sense. And the layout is super inefficient, requiring larger than normal heat sinks, among other problems."

"Thank you, TJ," Facehopper sent. "The mystery deepens, people."

"That mystery is going to have to be moved to the back burner real quick," Tahoe transmitted from his position outside. "Got more incoming. Apparently those roaches were only the first wave. And these newcomers, well, they're not like anything I've ever seen before."

thirteen

Rade immediately turned his attention to the jungle. The land was completely dark by then, and he observed the scene via the thermal band.

True enough, a black swarm had once again emerged from the foliage. He thought at first Tahoe was mistaken and that those were hammerheads, but when he zoomed in and digitally enhanced the image, he realized he was looking at mechanical legs, not biological. It seemed their hidden enemy had sent another variant of mech or robot at them: these were four-legged walkers that reminded him of scorpions because of the long tails that curved over their bodies.

"TJ, recall the HS3s," Facehopper said. "Secure them in the tunnel."

Rade had been about to issue that very same order but the chief had beat him to the punch.

"They didn't fully commit the first time," Bender said. "Those initial thirty robots were throwaways."

"They were testing us," Fret agreed. "Probing our defenses to prepare for the real attack."

"This isn't the behavior of SKs," Manic said.

"Probably not," Rade said. "Because in theory, the SKs would have known the full capabilities of our Hoplite units already, thanks to their moles in the manufacturing plants. If these were SKs, likely they would have committed everything they had from the get-go. Including their bioengineered weapons. They wouldn't attack piecemeal like this."

"Unless they had to relocate their robots from some other location," Lui argued.

As the HS3s returned from below, zipping past into the tunnel, Rade zoomed in closer on the enemy and activated tracking to study a single incoming unit. He didn't think those scorpions had missiles launchers. In fact, as far as he could tell, the new mechs only had laser units, judging from the small mounts at the tips of their tails.

"Are those lasers?" Rade asked no one in particular. "On the tails?"

"I'm definitely detecting laser fire!" Trace said. "It's weaker than the previous mechs had. Our shields are holding up nicely, at least at the current range. Even when they combine their beams. But when they close, we'll definitely have to fall back. There are too many of them."

"That's fine," Rade said. "The tunnel will serve as a choke point. Ever heard of the Battle of Thermopylae?"

"Um," Fret transmitted. "Didn't the three hundred Spartans and six thousand Greeks defending the pass of Thermopylae perish?"

"Bad example," Rade said. "Pretend I didn't say Thermopylae. You only heard choke point. Because inside this tunnel, we can fend off an army. We can fight here all night if we have to."

"The survivors of the *John A. McDonald* probably thought the same thing," Fret said. "And look where it got *them*."

"But you forget they didn't have Hoplites." Rade cleared his throat. "Front ranks, link your cobras to mine."

Rade aimed down at the plains, targeted a mech, and fired. The scorpion split in two. He switched to his left laser and fired another round.

"Front ranks, swap out!" Rade said.

He moved back, allowing the next group of Hoplites to surge to the front. They assumed the same pattern as the previous rank: three down on their knees with shields raised, three standing right behind them.

Rade continued cycling the platoon in that way, swapping out the front ranks so that they could fire at the enemy with cobras at full capacity every time.

"You know, when those scorpions get closer, we won't have to combine our beams," Manic said. "Nor wait until full charge."

"I know," Rade said. "Get ready to employ the avalanche strategy, people."

About five hundred meters from the base of the rock formation, and two hundred meters from the outer edges of the avalanche matter, the incoming scorpions began to move upward in spurts. He heard it then: the sound of a thousand jumpjets firing in random bursts. Because there were so many of them, that thrust-like noise was nearly continuous, and growing in volume. The resultant heat smears overwhelmed the thermal imagers at first, until the AI turned the sensitivity way down.

Now that they were airborne, each enemy unit had begun to move in a coordinated, seemingly random zig zag pattern on the way to its destination—the cave. They employed their lateral thrusters judiciously like that, making them extremely difficult to target.

Rade switched to the visual light spectrum, and realized he didn't need the thermal band anymore, not with the flames from all those jumpjets brightening the scene.

"So much for the avalanche strategy," Bender said. "Damn these bitches."

"External Hoplites," Rade sent. "Return from your hides! Get the hell in here!"

A few moments later:

"Coming through!" Bender transmitted.

The Hoplites at the front moved aside to allow Bender entry.

"I was getting roasted alive out there!" Bender said.

"The lasers are starting to cut real grooves into our shields," Lui said from the front line. "More and more of them are combining their firepower as they get closer."

"How long can you hold out?" Rade asked.

"I think this is the last time I'll be on the front lines," Lui said. "Those lasers will pierce right through my shield in about five seconds."

"Make way!" Keelhaul said, returning from his hide.

The mechs at the entrance made room for Keelhaul. Skullcracker followed just behind.

"Front rank, swap!" Rade said. He took a step back, and the next line of Hoplites moved forward to take his place and the positions of the others.

Rade waited impatiently as those at the front opened fire. All of the external Hoplites had returned, save Tahoe.

"Cyclone, where the hell are you?" Rade said. He glanced at the overhead map, and noticed that Tahoe's blue dot hadn't moved from his hide.

"Coming," Tahoe said. Finally his dot started moving. He had kept firing until the last possible moment, apparently.

"They're almost through my shield..." Mauler said.

"Clear the opening!" Rade said. "Everyone, get back and stay back! And Tahoe, get your ass in here on the double." In his haste, he realized he had accidentally used Tahoe's real name. Not that it mattered.

Rade held his position against the tunnel wall as the others squeezed past him and cleared the opening.

"It looks like we're going to have to put our choke point to use, blokes," Chief Facehopper said.

Rade glanced at his overhead map. Tahoe was still several meters from the opening. "Cyclone, where are you..."

"It's a shit-storm out here!" Tahoe said. "Fuck!"

Tahoe never swore. When he did, it meant he was really in trouble.

Suddenly worried that his friend had been injured, Rade pulled up Tahoe's status indicator. His Hoplite's shield contained multiple perforations, and he had laser damage all over the mech. His cockpit had been penetrated, too, but so far the jumpsuit he wore underneath remained unscathed, as far as Rade could tell.

Tahoe's mech abruptly diverted course, plunging downward rapidly. His mech passed by the opening five meters to the left, and continued down.

"Cyclone!" Rade said.

"They got my jumpjet feed!" Tahoe sent. "Can't... jet... up... going to eject... use the jumpjets of my suit."

"No!" Rade said, running forward. He held his shield out in front of him, toward the incoming enemies, and leaped over the ledge. As he plummeted, he continued: "You go out there in your unshielded jumpsuit, the enemy will burn multiple holes through you in seconds." Rade muted the comm and told his local AI: "Smith, fire corrective thrust. Line me up with Cyclone's mech. I want my right hand in position to grab him. And keep my shield arm directed toward the enemy at all times."

"Firing corrective thrust," Smith responded.

"What are you doing?" Tahoe sent. "Get back to the men."

"I'm coming for you, my friend," Rade replied.

The rock face moved past at a blur beside him under the dim light as Smith made the necessary trajectory changes. The Hoplite thrusted dorsally once, too, to prevent the mech from careening off the cliff face.

Rade checked the stats on his shield; though much of the incoming laser fire was reflected, the surface was still taking a battering. It didn't help that the mech's fall was predictable. As soon as he collected Tahoe, he planned to shake things up a bit, trajectory-wise.

Facehopper spoke to Rade over a private line. "Rage, we talked about this. You're an LPO now. You can't put yourself at risk like this."

"I'm sorry, chief," Rade replied. "But I couldn't ask anyone else to do this. Feel free to make TJ the LPO."

"I'm not making TJ the LPO," Facehopper said. "Because you're going to get through this. You and Cyclone both."

"Thank you, Chief."

"Don't thank me," the chief replied. "You thought I made you do a lot of push-ups before..."

"I've lined up with Cyclone," Smith said.

"Fire off a good solid burst, Smith," Rade said. "Help me grab him."

"You do realize we don't have enough fuel to carry both mechs back to the opening, right?" the AI asked.

"I didn't think we did," Rade said.

"But you jumped anyway..." Smith said.

"I did."

"Firing downward burst," Smith said.

Tahoe's Hoplite came up fast in the dim light. Smith took control of Rade's free arm and latched on to Tahoe's torso.

"Got you, Tahoe," Rade said. "Smith, fire lateral thrusters randomly. Make us a harder target for these bastards."

"Now what?" Tahoe said.

Because of the darkness, Rade couldn't see the ground at all. "Smith, how long before impact?" he asked.

"Imminent," the AI answered.

"Fire braking thrust!" Rade said. "And take cover!" He was anticipating being stunned the first few seconds after impact, and unable to perform the latter maneuver himself.

The Gs of braking thrust hit him hard and the mech slammed into the ground a moment later. As expected, he was completely incapacitated while the inner actuators of the cockpit moved his arms and legs—Smith was navigating the jagged terrain the rockslide had created and bringing him into cover. Hopefully.

When he finally regained his wits, he realized his Hoplite had maneuvered behind a rather large boulder. Tahoe's mech crouched beside him. They were completely shielded from the enemy. For the moment. Tahoe no longer had a combat robot attached to his passenger seat; he had lost it in the fall, apparently.

"Ernie, you all right back there?" Rade said. That was his nickname for Unit E.

"I've taken a hit in the side," the Centurion mounted in his passenger seat said. "There has been some damage to my power transference unit, but diagnostics report I am otherwise fully operational. I still retain my laser rifle."

"Good." Hardy fellow.

Above, the sky possessed the red glow one would associate with a firestorm, thanks to all those firing jumpjets. It was darker down where Rade was, even under the grainy enhanced brightness of the cameras, so he switched over to a combination of thermal and night vision.

"You guys all right, Rage?" Chief Facehopper said over the comm.

"Fine!" Rade sent. "We've taken cover behind a boulder. The enemy isn't paying us any attention at the moment. You worry about yourselves up there. Defend that tunnel!"

"Already two steps ahead of you," the chief responded. "Take care, mate. Things are going to be getting a bit hectic up here, so don't mind my lack of communications."

"Good luck, Chief," Rade transmitted.

"Luck has nothing to do with it," Facehopper replied. "As you're so fond of saying."

The landscape began to brighten around him and Rade realized some of the enemy were coming down on them.

"Looks like we got incoming," Rade said, forming a private line between himself, Tahoe, and Unit E. "Prepare to defend."

Rade covered the ninety degree approach vector from the top down to the right, while Tahoe targeted the opposite side.

Enemies began to drop into sight beyond the peripheries of the boulder.

Rade fired. The target's jumpjet's immediately cut out. At that close range, only a single pulse at full charge was needed to disable the enemy, apparently. He, Tahoe and Unit E kept firing sporadically like that, until a scorpion suddenly emerged from the right side of the boulder directly in front of him.

Rade couldn't react in time, and in moments he found himself grappling underneath the robot. It lifted its glowing tail to his torso.

Rade pushed upward and to the left with all his strength, and shifted his body to the right at the same time. He saw the momentary pulse on the infrared band as the robot fired its tail laser. A hole burned into the rock beside him.

Smoke abruptly erupted from its torso, and the robot collapsed on his mech. Rade tossed aside the deadweight, expecting to find Tahoe standing there beside him as his rescuer, but it was Unit E: the Centurion had tumbled free of his passenger seat during the tussle, apparently.

Tahoe loomed above the crimped remains of another robot that had attacked him in turn.

Rade was about to thank Unit E when two pincer-like forearms wrapped around the Centurion from behind and split it in half. A scorpion dashed forward, its laser pointed at Rade.

He dodged to the right, smashing his shield into the tail, deflecting the laser just in time. That move left him with a crescent-shaped notch in the top of his shield.

From the periphery of his vision, he saw that Tahoe was facing a similar attack on the other side of the boulder.

Another scorpion came in on Rade's side before he could offer any assistance.

Rade retracted his ballistic shield and grabbed the closest scorpion, which was still active, and he lifted it in front of himself. He advanced toward the newcomer; the first scorpion struggled in his grip, but Rade refused to let go. The second one abruptly fired, disabling the robot he held.

Rade tossed the wreckage at the second mech, then leaped onto them and fired his laser at point-blank range, disabling the second unit. He tore away a large piece from the mess of robot limbs and swung it like a club at the next scorpion that rounded the boulder on his side.

He deployed his shield once more and glanced at Tahoe. He seemed to have everything under control on his side. Rade spared a look for Unit E. It was definitely out of service. Permanently.

Goodbye, Ernie.

Movement drew his eye upward and he dodged to the side as another scorpion came crashing down. Rade swatted it with his makeshift club and broke away the laser on its tail. Another scorpion unexpectedly pounced on him from the side.

Rade struggled: the entire right half of his body, including his arm, was pinned by the scorpion. He retracted the shield on his left arm and pointed his laser at the robot's head. The precise moment before he squeezed the trigger, the robot dodged and the laser struck the boulder instead. It would be at least another ten seconds before he attained full charge.

The tail of the scorpion coiled back and lit up slightly; Rade realized it was about to fire. He reached up with his free arm, grabbed the tip of that tail, and pointed it toward another scorpion that just rounded the boulder. The incoming robot fell to the ground sparking.

Rade squeezed his fingers, bending his arm, and managed to wrench the laser section clean away from the tail. He tossed it aside and then plunged his fist squarely into the torso of the scorpion. At the same time he fired his laser at half charge. The combined blow caused his fist to tear right through the robot. Those mechanical limbs ceased all motion and he tossed the wreckage aside.

He loaded the grenade launcher into both hands and fired two frags into the four scorpions that rushed next around the boulder. Their robotic body parts erupted into the air.

Rade retreated until he stood right next to the boulder and then planted his backside up against Tahoe, and they fought back to back. Rade alternated between lasers, grenades, and fists, defending against the scorpions that attacked from the side and above. He lost a large chunk of his right leg, and the grenade launcher on his left arm was torn away. Tahoe was forced to eject his shield, which was so pocked that it had become useless. The robot body parts piled up around them, forming defensive cages they could fall back to.

As they fought, scorpions from the main assault randomly fell out of the sky, smashing into the rocks around them as the other platoon members shot them down far above. Their bodies only added to the debris.

Finally, after what seemed an eternity, the incoming ranks thinned until eventually the scorpions stopped coming entirely. Above, the sky no longer glowed with the red of jumpjets, and the stars gleamed.

Rade peered past the boulder. The rock-littered area beyond was clear, as was the sky. He saw only the bodies of the machines that had fallen out of the sky, some of them twitching. He aimed at those that were still moving and put them out of their misery in succession.

When that was done, he lay back against the boulder, panting. Tahoe joined him.

Rade checked the time on his Implant. Only forty minutes had passed since the start of the attack.

"Well done," Smith said.

"Thank you," Rade managed, out of breath.

"Remind me... why... I joined up," Tahoe said.

"Because you're sexually deprived at home?" Rade said.

"Oh yeah."

"Rage, sit-rep," Chief Facehopper's voice came over the comm.

"We're alive and well, Chief," Rade said. "The enemy robots simply stopped coming."

"Same thing happened up here. We successfully repelled them. It's clear all the way to the jungle. I'm sending down some HS3s to survey the wreckages, along with a couple of Centurions to finish off any survivors. Do you need assistance returning to the cave?"

"Negative," Rade said. "Got a hole in my mech's leg the size of a basketball, and Tahoe has lost his shield, but our Hoplites are otherwise none the worse for wear. We should be able to climb on our own."

"Please wait until my finishers have eliminated the survivors down there," the chief responded. "You don't want to take a shot in the back while you're in the middle of your climb, mate."

"No, I don't," Rade agreed.

"I don't mind waiting," Tahoe responded. "Not at all." His cockpit cracked open. "I can use the time to repair my jumpjet feed line. Still got half a tank of fuel left. I want those jets available when I climb—little insurance policy in case I lose my grip."

"How long will that take?" the chief asked.

"I should be done before your Centurion finishers give the all clear." Tahoe surveyed the wreckage of the countless scorpions scattered across the rocks. "Looks like that's going to be quite some time from now. There are a lot of robots down here..."

fourteen

Rade waited while Tahoe worked on fixing the jumpjet line of his mech. True to his word, he finished the job a full half hour before the Centurions gave the all clear.

After Facehopper okayed the ascent, the two of them spent the next ten minutes in a slow, controlled climb, trying to save as much jumpjet fuel as possible on the way up. It was entirely unlike the frantic, no-holds-barred retreat that had seen them scale the rock the first time around.

Rade listened to the conversations taking place over the comm as he climbed.

"You did well back there, Harlequin," Facehopper said.

"So have I earned my callsign?" Harlequin returned eagerly.

"Hell no," Bomb said. "I hate to contradict the chief, but you did jack back there."

"Chief?" Harlequin asked uncertainly.

"I'm sorry," the chief said. "Not to take away anything from what you did, but firing an M7 a few times doesn't earn one a callsign."

"See!" Bomb transmitted triumphantly.

"I did more than fire the M7," Harlequin said in a somewhat whiny voice. "I employed the weapon strategically. I kept the tangos from reaching the cave. And I even took out a few of them before they reached Rage and Cyclone below."

"I don't give two shits about what you think you did," Bomb said.

"What about just one?" Harlequin quipped.

Bomb didn't answer right away. Then: "What?"

"What about just one shit?" Harlequin said.

"Shut that mechanical mouth of yours before I staple it shut," Bomb replied.

When he had attained the entrance, Rade paused to survey the plains below using his combined thermal and night vision. Everything was completely quiet down there. His gaze ended on the jungle, silent beneath the stars. He stared at that mysterious, black mass that ate up so much of the landscape; that darker blotch amidst the gloom.

What unknown enemies do you conceal? he thought. *What secrets?*

Snakeoil was crouched beside him in the opening, apparently acting as a sentry. The rest of the group was arrayed in a line down the tunnel, resting against the walls in their Hoplites. The downed bodies of several scorpions were dispersed between them; the damaged machines spilled wires and circuits onto the cave floor.

"Looks like you guys had a bit of trouble up here," Rade said.

"Just a bit," Mauler replied.

"This is only about one hundredth of the robots we fought," Manic said. "The scorpions kept tossing out the bodies of their dead. Keeping a clear path to their targets. Us."

"You lucky bastards got to have all the fun," Tahoe said. Rade wasn't even sure if his friend was being sarcastic or not.

"Anything on the comms, Snakeoil?" Facehopper asked.

"Nothing," Snakeoil replied.

"Like I said before, the fleet has been destroyed," Fret transmitted. "When are you going to listen to me?"

"No, think about it," Lui said. "If there was an attack, it's highly likely a few of the enemy would have made their way toward the Gate. If the fleet in orbit survived, the remnants would be racing back to protect the Builder—we only left two destroyers guarding it. As you all know, without that ship, we're truly stranded here."

"The fleet abandoned us to protect the Builder, then?" Manic asked. "That's your theory."

"It's the best theory we have right now," Lui said. "I just wish we hadn't lost our comm node, because there's no way to confirm it."

"But I thought Snakeoil lost his comm ping before the shuttle was taken?" Manic said.

"That could mean anything," Snakeoil said. "Might have been a temporary glitch. Or the fleet could have been on the far side of the planet. If the repeaters in orbit were destroyed, which is likely, of course I would have momentarily lost signal."

Lui spoke up. "As I was saying, without the node, we have no way to confirm that either way."

Commander Parnell stepped forward, joining Rade at the ledge.

"Those hammerheads couldn't have taken my Dragonfly far," Commander Parnell said. He gazed toward the dark mass of the distant jungle. "If we can find it, there's a chance we can salvage the node."

"We could send another HS3 to scout the jungle," Manic suggested. Like Rade, he sounded eager to expose the secrets of the place, even if the unveiling was done remotely. "Might even find a few of our booster rockets."

"Is that such a good idea?" Snakeoil asked. "The last time we sent an HS3 inside, we triggered an attack."

"Probably a coincidence," Grappler said. "I'm willing to bet they meant to attack during the night all along."

"Up to you, Commander," Facehopper transmitted.

Parnell stared at the jungle for several moments longer, then went back inside the tunnel.

"Send another HS3 into that jungle," the commander said. "Let's find the wreckage of my Dragonfly."

Facehopper had Bender dispatch four HS3s onto the plain. Three of them were meant to act as repeaters, though that was probably overkill, considering the reception was very good on the plain. Then again, once the HS3s traveled into the jungle, the signal quality would definitely drop.

"We can reach a ship in low orbit with the comm nodes Fret and Snakeoil carry on their backs," Manic said. "And yet we can't keep in touch with HS3s twenty klicks away on the surface without repeaters. Never ceases to amaze me."

"Physics, bro," Fret retorted. "In the open air, there's nothing between us and a ship in orbit. If we know the location of that ship, it's a simple matter to send a concentrated beam. But once those HS3s pass into the jungle, all those trees are going to get in the way."

"Can't you use a shorter wavelength or something that can more readily penetrate those trees?" Manic asked. "Or boost the signal?"

"No," Fret said. "Unless you want me to fry you all with the equivalent of gamma rays."

"These mechs are rated for deep space use," Manic argued. "With shielding in place for gamma rays, energetic protons, and whatnot. They're like mini shuttles."

"To a degree," Lui responded. "But they're not meant to operate in outer space for very long. Let's just say, you wouldn't want to fly a Hoplite through the low orbit of a blue star. Mech's have nowhere near the rad shielding of a starship, or even a shuttle. As a mech specialist, I thought you would have known that."

"Oh, you so clever!" Manic said, mocking the Asian accent Lui didn't have. Lui occasionally invited the platoon to a certain dim sum place for lunch, and the waitresses usually said that line at least once, mostly when one of the MOTHs was trying to be smart.

"Cleverer than you," Lui said. "And that's all that counts."

The HS3s advanced across the plains below. The three repeaters halted halfway to the jungle while the lead HS3 continued; the dark eaves soon swallowed the scout.

Rade tapped into the video feed from the lead unit. He observed the foliage under the thermal band—there wasn't enough light beneath the thick canopy of leaves to use the night vision portion. He saw dark bands of foliage everywhere around him, and it was hard to pick anything out, visually. But after a moment the HS3's built-in LIDAR caused a three dimensional wireframe of the nearby topography to appear on Rade's HUD, and as it advanced, a small area slowly filled out on the overhead map.

"No sign of anything yet," Bender said.

"Keep advancing," the commander told him.

"This is going to take all night," Bender replied. "There's too much foliage. I'm going to have to double-back, and double-back again, criss-crossing the jungle to fill in the blanks. If you really want to properly search this mess, we're going to have to dispatch all the HS3s."

"Do so, then," the commander instructed. "But give the HS3s standing orders to return at the first sign of trouble. I don't want to lose any more of our scouts."

"Help me send them out, TJ," Bender said.

Soon twelve HS3s were rummaging through the perimeter of that jungle, while three remained on the plain. As the lead drones advanced, the repeaters moved up in turn, ensuring that the signal strength between the HS3s and the platoon remained at optimal levels. The map of the jungle grew outward, repealing its fog of war bit by bit.

"See that," Grappler said. "Nothing has attacked us so far. Told you the earlier attack was coincidence."

"Don't jinx us," Fret said.

The video feed from the scout Rade was observing pixelated and froze.

"Just lost the feed on HS3 J," Rade said.

"Damn it," Fret said. "You should have kept your mouth shut, Grappler."

Rade's display abruptly jumped and the video feed returned. The HS3 had moved forward several meters.

"Just a temporary glitch," TJ said. "The HS3 probably passed behind a particular thick grove of trees. Momentarily blocked the signal."

"You were saying, Fret?" Grappler asked.

The comm officer didn't answer.

The scouts continued forward. Six of them emerged into a partial clearing. Partial, because the canopy overhead was thick as ever, but some of the jungle had cleared underneath.

"Would you look at that..." Keelhaul said. "Are those buildings?"

"They're some kind of buildings, yes," Bender replied. "Ancient, judging from the trees overgrowing them."

"Nature always reclaims that which we take from her," Tahoe's soft, reverent voice intoned over the comm.

The LIDAR revealed spherical structures of different sizes, covered in what seemed alien moss and vines.

"It appears these spheres are composed of bricks taken from this very rock formation," Bender continued. "Eroded steps lead up to a few of them, and there are the remains of cobblestone paths on the jungle floor."

"We've found ourselves an alien village, boys!" Bomb said.

"Don't get too big of an erection," Bender added. "I did say *eroded*, and *remains*. Radiometric dating puts the structures at two million years old. Whoever built these is long gone."

"Have the other scouts converge on that location," Parnell said. "I want that ancient city mapped out."

More HS3s joined in. The structures continued for several hundreds of meters.

"Found one of the booster rockets," Bender said. "It's been punctured. No fuel."

The remaining booster rockets were discovered in turn. Each and every one had been pierced, the fuel drained or left to spill out onto the jungle floor.

"So much for any of us getting off this planet on their own," Fret said when the last was discovered.

About a kilometer in, the centermost HS3s passed a crater. There were broken pieces of stone along the edges: it looked as if something had reached down and literally ripped one of the structures away.

"Someone took a souvenir," Bomb said.

The HS3s continued forward for another kilometer. And then:

"Got something," TJ said. "In the northeast quadrant. Looks like what's left of the commander's Dragonfly."

Rade switched to the HS3 in that area and saw the debris. The Dragonfly lay in pieces, spread out across the ground, nearly unrecognizable. He saw the UC symbol stamped into the broken fuselage but recognized nothing else. It was like a crash site.

"Looks like the hammerheads decided to use our shuttle as toilet paper," Bomb said.

"Bet they don't take as big shits as you," Mauler taunted.

"What's that structure, in front of the fuselage?" Parnell asked.

Rade zoomed in to the leading portion of the fuselage. A long stone slab protruded from the ground there.

"Looks almost like an altar," Skullcracker said. "Maybe the hammerheads brought the shuttle here as part of some sort of offering or ritual sacrifice."

"What?" Manic retorted. "Ridiculous. They sacrificed our Dragonfly to their gods? I thought the hammerheads were bioengineered?"

"They are," Lui said. "That doesn't mean they don't have the sentience to develop their own culture and religion. We've seen it in bioengineered species before. The precedent was the Javier Ape Experiment. Before the scientists shut it down, the apes, genetically engineered to possess the equivalent of human intelligence, began to sacrifice their newborns annually to the unseen beings who provided food through the small slot in their enclosure. The apes did it in the hopes of promoting a 'bountiful harvest,' according to the translation of their pidgin English. Their actions were a bit startling, to say the least, especially considering they were receiving an ample amount of food already, and there was no need to make any sacrifices."

"So these hammerheads," Manic said. "They bring this shuttle back to their altar, and they tear it apart to pay homage to their robot masters?"

"Sounds about right," Lui said.

"Scour the wreckage," Facehopper said. "And the outlying area. Let's see if we can find that comm node."

Rade continued to observe the scene through the video feed of one of the HS3s. The scout moved along the east side of the fuselage, continuing onto the remains of the wing section. As it maneuvered across the far eastern edge of the wreckage, there, partially covered by a broken wing tip, was a cylindrical object half the size of a Hoplite.

"Is that what I think it is?" Facehopper said, apparently watching the same feed.

"The shuttle's comm node," Bender agreed.

"Attempt to interface the HS3 to it," Commander Parnell ordered.

Bender paused. "Nothing. It's offline. I've had the HS3 attempt a diagnostic, but without power the results are inconclusive. Could be that the node's local battery has drained, and we need merely connect it to a power source. Or it could be damaged beyond repair."

"Chief, can we send the combat robots in to retrieve it?" Parnell asked.

"Looks pinned by the wing tip," Grappler said.

"A few Centurions could easily move that, couldn't they?" Parnell said.

"But look at the way the wing is interconnected with the rest of the debris," Bender said. "We send Centurions down there, they're going to spend at least an hour cleaning the surrounding debris before they can move that node. We send some mechs, and they'll be in and out in five minutes."

"What if the Centurions fired a plasma rifle?" Parnell said.

"That's certainly an option," Bender agreed. "But there's a chance the powerful magnetic field induced by the rifle could irreperably damage the exposed node."

"Laser rifles?"

"I already factored that into my original estimate," Bender said. "Fifteen minutes or more to cut through the wing. Then they have to move the parts."

Facehopper's mech lifted a hand toward the upper part of its torso but then stopped and retracted the arm. He had probably been about to rub his forehead in thought, until he remembered that wasn't possible while aboard—the actuators composing the inner layer of the cockpit would have stopped the movement of his arm the instant the mechanical hand touched the thick torso.

"Wait a second," Lui said. "Has anyone bothered to consider that the comm node is a lure? Put there by our attackers?"

"Bender," Facehopper said. "Have the HS3s circle the city, and confirm that nothing is watching, waiting in ambush."

Several minutes later. "HS3s have reached the farther perimeter of the city, and report all clear."

"That doesn't mean its clear..." Lui said. "Not really."

"Well, we have to get that comm node," Parnell said. He glanced at Facehopper's Hoplite. "If it is a trap, and we send Centurions alone, we'll lose them, and probably the node, too. But if we dispatch Hoplites, at least we have a fighting chance. Send your best men. Make it work, Chief. In and out."

Facehopper remained quiet for a moment, likely mentally weighing his options. "In and out," he said finally. "Here's what we're going to do. I'm splitting the platoon into two squads. Squad A will be composed of myself, Bender, Harlequin, Grappler, Trace, Snakeoil, and Mauler. We're going to stay at Gray Gate"—that was the codename the chief had come up with for the cave—"and protect the water reclaimer and oxygen extractor while Bender and Harlequin continue the repairs. Rage, you'll lead Squad B down there: Cyclone, TJ, Lui, Manic, Skullcracker, Bomb, Fret and Keelhaul. Load Centurions into your passenger seats and go out there, retrieve that comm node, and get back here as fast as possible."

"Shouldn't I stay to repair the extractor with Bender?" Tahoe asked.

"No," Facehopper said. "I've been talking to Bender. In regards to the extractor, we've got too many carpenters in the belfry, so to speak. Bender tells me he'll work faster if he can concentrate on the system alone. Use your skills out there, Tahoe: assess the damage to the comm node. If it's readily repairable, something you can fix in a few minutes on the spot, then do so. That way Snakeoil can get a message out to the fleet while your squad hurries back."

"I should go with them," Vicks said. "As chief scientist, it's my duty to study the ruins of that city. If I can't help out with the oxygen extractor, and I'd rather do that than be useless."

"You can always work on the water reclaimer with Harlequin," Facehopper said.

"Excuse me," Harlequin said. "Like Bender, I'll work faster if I'm alone."

Vicks turned toward Parnell. "Commander, let me go. I might discover something that can help us understand who these attackers are, and what they want."

"All right," Commander Parnell said. "Go, then. But be careful."

"I'll see that no harm comes to her," Rade said, allowing her into his passenger section.

"You do that," Parnell replied.

"Be vigilant out there," Facehopper said. "Like Bender said, it could very easily be a trap."

"We're always vigilant, Chief," Rage replied. "We're MOTHs."

"And so you are. Squad A, distribute some of your grenades and fuel to B. Let's make sure B is ready for anything out there. And Harlequin, give your M7 to one of the Centurions going with B."

"Get ready, people," Rade said. "We deploy in ten!"

The members of Squad A moved their mechs off to one side and ejected from their cockpits to transfer the aforementioned gear. During the bustling, Rade spoke to Facehopper over a private line.

"Thank you for letting Cyclone come with me," Rade told him.

"Truthfully, I should probably split the two of you up, mate," Facehopper said. "Especially after what you pulled back there, leaping over the cliff to come to his rescue. You have to learn to let go. I don't want you to risk your life for him again. If you find yourself in such a situation, send someone else to get him next time.

Can I rely on you to make the right choice going forward? Or should I move Cyclone to Squad A?"

Rade swallowed uneasily, uncertain he would be able to let go if it came to it. But he said: "You can rely on me, Chief."

"Good," Facehopper continued. "Because I meant what I said about wanting him to use his skills out there. Besides, I know the two of you work better together, and I'm all about efficiency in my platoon." He reached out and patted Rade on the shoulder assembly with the open palm of his Hoplite. "Watch yourself out there."

fifteen

Rade divided his squad into two fire teams once they reached the jungle. He placed TJ in command of the first fire team, whose other members included Lui, Manic, Fret and Keelhaul. Rade resided amid the second fire team, in the middle position; Skullcracker took point on his team, followed by Tahoe, with Bomb on drag.

In each fire team, the individual mechs maintained a distance of two meters from one another, forming a zigzag line. He had placed the fire teams themselves in traveling overwatch formation, separated by ten meters, with Fire Team I in the lead. The foliage reduced the effectiveness of said formation, but because of the large size of the Hoplites, he could still occasionally see the members of TJ's fire team through the trees in front of him, under the thermal band. That was the only band they could really use, as it was otherwise pitch black under the canopy, with not even the starlight penetrating. Local-beam LIDAR helped clarify the topography, indicating trees and other shrubs to avoid.

In those times when the foliage became too thick to provide overwatch, Fire Team I remained visible on the overhead map, marked in blue dots. Rade's use of the formation was only partially for overwatch, however; mostly, he wanted to prevent the entire squad from being knocked out of action due to a missile or other mass casualty attack. Only untrained idiots advanced in a clump through an enemy jungle, where hidden mines, nets or other traps waited to be sprung.

Their advance was slow, and as quiet as they could manage in the large mechs they piloted through the heavy undergrowth.

An icon appeared in the lower right corner of his vision. It was Vicks, sending a message from his passenger seat. Apparently she wanted to talk to him on a private line.

He tapped her in. "What is it, Lieutenant?"

"I finished analyzing the plant samples I collected," she said, the excitement obvious in her voice. "These organisms seem to be native to the planet. They're not bioengineered, as far as I can tell. And get this. The nucleic acids at the core of their cell nuclei are different than our own. The biochemical composition of the bases are completely foreign to those of animals that evolved on earth. There are five combinations, not four, and one of them can match with three others. And the nucleic acids come in triple strands, not pairs. Cells divide into threes, not twos, with the strands splitting into three parts. That said, the chloroplasts still use ordinary molecules of chlorophyll for photosynthesis. Well actually, I suppose it's not *really* ordinary, as chlorophyll d dominates, which absorbs infrared light. That's somewhat odd, given the prevalence of visible light on the planet. I'm guessing the plant life native to this particular jungle developed in the oceans, and only recently migrated to the land masses, probably in the last one hundred million years or so. And—"

"I'm going to have to ask you to observe radio silence like the rest of us, ma'am," Rade finally interrupted. "If you wouldn't mind."

"Sorry," she said. "I plugged my comm port directly into your mech, so technically I didn't transmit anything externally."

"Even so, I need to concentrate now." He was about to close the connection.

"Wait," she said. "This means that the other animal herds we detected from orbit might be native to this planet, too. The hammerheads are the intruders, here. Just like the mechs."

"That doesn't change our situation." He tapped out.

Eventually the foliage gave way slightly to the partial clearing containing the ancient, overgrown ruins.

The squad continued forward in formation, passing between the spherical structures of stone. They paused beside each booster rocket they encountered: some of the tanks were merely pierced, others crumpled beyond repair. There was never any fuel left inside any of them, precisely as the HS3s had indicated.

A kilometer later the platoon arrived at the shuttle site. Rade passed one of the HS3s that secured the outer perimeter.

"Wreckage in view," Keelhaul reported, breaking radio silence for the first time since entering the jungle.

"Deploy in defensive pattern Triple Cigar, people," Rade said. "Centurions, you take the middle ring."

The eight Hoplites formed a circular perimeter around the shuttle. The Centurion passengers leaped down and scattered, forming a wider cigar shape. The HS3s had nothing to do—they were already in the necessary formation beyond them.

Rade glanced at his display, and confirmed that the three layers of dots representing his units were nested within one another. The mechs formed the inner layer, the combat robots the middle, and the HS3 scouts the outer perimeter.

"Secure the comm node, Keelhaul," Rade said.

He watched Keelhaul's blue dot move toward the flashing area on the overhead map. A moment later Keelhaul announced: "Secured!"

"Cyclone, do your stuff." Rade watched Tahoe's dot join Keelhaul at the flashing area, then returned his gaze to the pitch-black jungle beyond, which appeared gray on the thermal band.

"You wanted to study the ruins, Lieutenant?" Rade asked Vicks.

He moved toward one of the overgrown spherical structures that was enveloped by their defensive deployment, and knelt so the chief scientist could properly dismount.

"Thank you," she said.

"Unit F," Rade sent the closest combat robot. "Get over here and help me watch Lieutenant Vicks."

"Roger that," the Centurion returned.

In moments the combat robot joined them at the spherical structure.

Rade watched the gray representation of her environmental suit on the thermal band as it reached out and extracted a small piece from the object.

Meanwhile, Tahoe said: "This comm node isn't something I can easily repair. We're going have to bring it back."

"Let me have a look," TJ said. His dot started to break from the cigar formation.

"No," Rade said. "I trust Cyclone's judgement. We're packing that comm node up. Lui, join Keelhaul and Cyclone. Clear away the necessary debris pinning down the node, and load it up. Let me know when you're good to go."

A moment later Rade heard a loud ripping sound coming from the direction of the comm node, as transmitted by the directional speakers inside his cockpit. His gaze was momentarily drawn away from Vicks. He realized the noise was the shuttle's wing breaking in half as Keelhaul broke it away. He zoomed in and watched on the thermal band as Tahoe easily removed the wing tip after that and freed the comm node.

"The comm node is away," Tahoe said. "Securing it. Keelhaul?"

Keelhaul moved forward and placed the comm node in Tahoe's passenger seat, then secured it in place with carbon fiber cords taken from the utility compartment of his Hoplite.

"Just lost Unit F!" TJ said.

Rade spun toward Vicks. Where she had stood there were only shaking branches. The Centurion lay smashed in half on the ground.

He glanced at his overhead map. The blue dot representing her moved east, rapidly.

Rade broke into a run "Lieutenant Vicks, do you read, over?" Rade sent. "Ma'am?"

No answer.

"Vicks!" He glanced at his overhead map once more. "She's moving toward you, Unit G! Hoplites, on me!"

"Unit G just went offline," TJ said.

Rade tripped over an unseen root and his mech crashed ponderously into the undergrowth, tearing through leaves and branches. He scrambled to his feet and continued the pursuit.

"Have the HS3s nearest her in the outer perimeter converge on her position," Rade said. "I want to see what the hell has taken her."

On the map, he watched the two HS3 indicators ahead of him converge on her incoming dot. The HS3 indicators winked out.

"We just lost the HS3s," TJ said.

"Did you catch what took them out?" Rade said, doing his best to navigate the foliage under the thermal and LIDAR band.

"Only a blur of darkness," TJ said.

Rade continued his pursuit. He glanced at the display and saw that Skullcracker and Bomb were just behind him. But the lieutenant's dot was still pulling away from him.

"Centurions, join the fray!" Rade said. "TJ, get half of the HS3s to pursue as well!"

When Rade abandoned the ruins for the jungle proper, the foliage thickened. Branches and leaves constantly whipped and pulled at his mech. He nearly tripped thrice more, and he had to pause several times to regain his balance.

The Centurions made better progress because they were smaller, and nearly all of them passed him. The HS3s made the best progress of all, but even those couldn't outpace whatever had taken her. Obviously it had been designed to readily traverse that jungle.

"Rage, wait," Bomb said. "Rage. We can't outrun her captors. They could be leading us into a trap. Rage. We have to turn back. Rage!"

Finally Rade halted. "Damn it. Full stop, people. TJ, have four of the HS3s continue their pursuit. Best speed. They are to maintain full stealth mode, and avoid discovery. String out other HS3s as necessary to maintain signal strength. If we can't catch her, maybe we can at least find out where they're taking her."

According to her suit status report, her helmet camera remained active, so Rade attempted to tap in to her viewpoint. He saw only darkness. The overhead map wasn't updating around her, either, like it ordinarily would have when entering a previously unexplored area.

"Her camera and LIDAR seem to be down," Rade said. "Either that, or whoever took her has blocked them out."

"Black spray paint?" TJ asked.

"Maybe," Rade replied. The platoon members all carried aerosol cans of black paint in the utility belts of their jumpsuits. It was part of their kits. Sino-Koreans would likely possess similar gear. "Though I suspect it's something simpler, like a sack over the helmet."

"What about her comms?" Manic asked. "Why would we still get a tracking dot if her comm system was offline?"

"Her comm system obviously isn't offline," Lui stated.

"Then why doesn't she answer?"

"She has to be unconscious," TJ said.

"No one stays unconscious for more than ten seconds after a blow to the head," Lui said. "Unless some extreme head trauma has taken place."

Rade glanced at his HUD. "Her vital signs seem stable."

"There is another option," Skullcracker said. "A sedative."

"A sedative?" Manic said. "Wouldn't her suit depressurize if someone tried to inject her?"

"No, Skullcracker is right," Rade said. "If you penetrated an environmental suit with an old school syringe, and left the needle in, it would act as a sealant. That would explain her vitals."

"Unless her vitals were being faked somehow," Lui said.

"You don't trust anything, do you Lui?" Manic said.

"Rage, do you have the comm node?" Facehopper's voice came over the line, distorting very slightly.

Rade glanced at Tahoe's mech. "We do. Your orders, chief?"

"It's the commander's call here," Facehopper responded.

The commander didn't answer immediately. He had a fairly big decision to make: allow Rade and the others to continue their pursuit of Vicks, or order them to return the comm node immediately.

"I want that comm node back here, secure in the tunnel," Commander Parnell finally said. "Send back at least two of the Hoplites to escort it. The rest of you are to continue following the lieutenant, and report back if and when it becomes possible to stage a rescue."

"Will do," Rade said. That was an acceptable compromise.

"But if she doesn't stop her retreat within the next hour," Parnell continued. "I'm going to have to ask you to turn back. It's too dangerous out there."

"She'll probably move beyond comm range before then," TJ replied. "And we'll have nothing *to* track."

"All right," Parnell said. "Proceed with caution. I'll leave it up to you, Rage, whether you want to turn back before the hour is up."

"Understood, sir," Rade answered. He turned toward his Hoplites to relay the orders he had in mind, but Tahoe spoke first.

"Keelhaul," Tahoe said. He was using the Squad B comm channel, Rade noticed, which excluded the distant commander and Squad A. "Untie the comm node from my back."

Keelhaul obeyed.

"What are you doing, Cyclone?" Rade asked.

"I'm not leaving her," Tahoe said. "Send someone else to return the comm node."

"Cyclone..." Rade said.

"Send someone else!" His Hoplite spun toward Rade's. "If we lose her signal, we're going to have to track her using the old ways. I'm the best man for that and you know it."

Rade sighed mentally. Perhaps it had been a bad idea to let Tahoe come along with the squad after all, just not for the reasons the chief had originally thought.

He glanced at Keelhaul, who was still holding the comm node. Rade considered assigning him the task of returning that comm node, but he wanted experienced mech pilots in case events took a turn for the worse back there. So he chose the specialists.

"Bomb and Lui," Rade said. "Secure the comm node and carry it back to Gray Gate. Take four of the Centurions with you, and two HS3s to act as advance scouts."

"You got it, boss," Lui responded.

"Thank you," Tahoe transmitted.

Rade considered sending another mech with Bomb and Lui, but he would very likely need all the Hoplites he could muster if he wanted to continue pursuing Vicks into that uncharted jungle.

In moments Bomb and Lui were gone. Rade glanced at his overhead map and saw the lieutenant's dot continuing to move away eastward, pursued by the lagging HS3s, and the Centurions beyond them. Her dot flickered occasionally as the signal strength weakened.

"The rest of you," Rade said. "We have a hostage to rescue. Resume traveling overwatch. Fast jog."

sixteen

Rade and his reduced squad advanced at a slow jog through that thick, pitch-black jungle. He had given up the zig zag distribution, as well as the traveling overwatch formation; instead the squad moved forward in single file. At least that way, the route proved easier for those who resided in the latter portion of the line. Foliage still constantly whipped at their hulls no matter their position in the queue of course. There wasn't a moment when branches ceased to snag and sap them.

Even with the autopilot enabled, at first the Hoplites routinely tripped and fell—especially those in the front sections. But then Rade had TJ, who was on point, reduce his pace, and that helped them circumvent the more difficult topography. Even so their advance proved incredibly noisy, at least compared to their earlier, stealthier progression. Any creatures slumbering nearby in that alien jungle were likely wide awake by then, and watching from the shadows.

Rade half-expected an ambush to occur at any moment. If the hammerheads came, the squad would be hard pressed to fight its way out alive. Rade had a vague plan to take to the treetops in such a scenario, perhaps utilizing the jumpjets to break through the canopy, but he had doubts about the ability of the Hoplites to avoid being snagged by the upper branches. In fact, it was very likely the mechs wouldn't be able to break through at all, which was why he hadn't ordered the platoon to do that very thing in the pursuit of Vicks. There was another wrinkle, too: given the speed with which the unknown captors were moving away, even if he and the others managed to break through the overhead canopy, the Hoplites would run out of jumpjet fuel before they even got close.

A long thirty-five minutes later Bomb and Lui reported in. Their signal strength proved very low, and it took a few transmission attempts before Rade understood what they were trying to tell him: they had departed the jungle without incident.

Rade received a message from Facehopper shortly thereafter. "Rage... far enough. Only a little... no point... turn back when... lieutenant leaves signal range."

"Roger that," Rade sent. "We'll turn back as soon as Lieutenant Vicks moves beyond signal range."

The flickering indicators of Bomb and Lui blinked out on the plains a few moments later, halfway to the rock formation. The blue dots representing the rest of the platoon back at Gray Gate also vanished.

"On our own now, boys," TJ said.

"It feels so... isolating, somehow," Manic commented. "Stranded on an alien world, in a forest teeming with unseen enemies, cut off from the only brothers we have."

"We have each other," Rade said. "The only brothers we'll ever need."

Rade continued the advance for fifteen more minutes. On the overhead map, the lieutenant's indicator moved farther and farther away.

As her winking dot threatened to leave signal range, vanishing from the display more often than it remained, Tahoe stirred to life.

"Come on, pick up the pace people!" Tahoe said. "We're going to lose her!"

"It won't matter, Tahoe," Rade said.

"They'll have to stop eventually," Tahoe said. "They're taking her to some base. Isn't it obvious?"

"Not really," Manic said.

"We should turn back," TJ said. "It's obvious we're not going to catch her now."

Rade hesitated. He was intending to do that very thing, but if he gave the order at that precise moment, it would seem like he was listening to TJ. Rade cursed inwardly.

You're their leader. Make the choice. Forget about outward appearances and do the right thing.

"Full stop, people," Rade said. "TJ's right, there's nothing more we can do."

"But we can't just give her up," Tahoe said.

"Cyclone, I feel the sting more than any of us, believe me," Rade said. "She was my charge. But I can't justify continuing the pursuit. She's going to be out of range in seconds. There's no point in continuing."

"I can track her without a signal," Tahoe said. "I can read the trees. I learned how to track when I was a child growing up on the reserve."

"That'll take a long time," Rade said. "We're already cut off, too far away from our platoon. It's dark now, and while I'm sure we've awakened many jungle creatures with our passage, most of the remainder are sleeping. But what happens in the morning? Will we find ourselves stranded in the middle of the jungle, surrounded by a thousand fully awake hammerheads waiting to tear our mechs apart, hungry to get at the fresh tuna inside the tins of our mechs?"

"Did you just compare us to tuna?" Manic asked.

"Unfortunately, yes," Rade said. "I blame that one on Bender."

"But we don't know what they're going to do to her!" Tahoe insisted. "Torture her, if they're SKs. And if they're alien... dissect her. Alive."

"I'm sorry," Rade said. "The chief already gave me a direct order. We turn back when she leaves signal range."

"Do you remember when we were in boot camp?" Tahoe said, his voice becoming urgent. He reminded Rade of a drowning man grasping frantically for anything to hold on to. "We had a mantra then, one that we followed to the letter. No one gets left behind. That mantra defined us. Made us who we are today. We wouldn't have made it through MOTH training without it."

"Cyclone, we're turning back," Rade turned his mech around. "TJ, recall the HS3s and the Centurions."

"*You're* turning back," Tahoe said. "But I'm moving forward. *No one gets left behind.*"

"What's she to you, anyway?" TJ said. "I thought you were a happily married man."

"I am," Tahoe said. "She's a friend. And I don't leave friends behind."

"We don't have time for this childish behavior, *Cyclone*," Rade said, purposely emphasizing the callsign, wanting to remind Tahoe that he was speaking as his commanding officer at the moment, not his friend.

"Court martial me," Tahoe said, shoving past him to continue through the trees.

Rade leaped onto his Hoplite, pinning Tahoe against a tree. "Can't let you do it."

Tahoe swung his mech to the side with a sudden unexpected force and launched his arm outward. Rade hurtled backward into Manic's Hoplite, knocking it down.

"Hey!" Manic transmitted.

Rade got right back up and threw himself on Tahoe, who had turned his back on him to continue into the jungle. He attempted to subdue him by bringing the arms of the Hoplite behind its back, but Tahoe fired ventral thrust, rocketing the two of them upward.

Rade slammed into a thick overhead branch, arresting the jump, and the two of them tumbled back to the jungle floor, where they wrestled.

Tahoe thrust repeatedly at Rade's torso, aiming for the head section. His fist struck a glancing blow to one of the cameras embedded in Rade's torso; when that fist withdrew for the next strike, Rade swiveled, wanting to spare the camera. He received a nice dent in the side of his mech instead.

Another Hoplite intervened. "That's enough, boys," Keelhaul said, pulling Tahoe's mech off of him.

Tahoe spun and punched Keelhaul in the chest area, sending his mech sliding backward across the forest floor.

"It certainly is." Rade quickly pulled up the override controls on Tahoe's mech, and proceeded to lock him out.

Tahoe had forewarning, however. He must have sensed the giveaway stiffening of the limbs momentarily before all control was lost, because he managed to open his cockpit. He flew upward into the trees in his jumpsuit.

"Damn it." Rade jettisoned from his cockpit, too, loathe to send his mech up there. It would be too easy to hurt Tahoe with his Hoplite, not to mention an extravagant waste of mech fuel.

He spotted Tahoe's dark form on the LIDAR and thermal band, leaping from branch to branch, continuing toward Vicks. Rade tried to disable the jumpsuit, too, but Tahoe had some sort of failsafe in place.

With a sigh, Rade leaped into the air and thrust after him. Small branches broke away as he struck them, others whipped at the fabric of his suit so hard that he felt their impacts on his flesh underneath. His arm snagged on a branch, pulling him toward a tree. As he compensated with lateral thrust, he accidentally smashed into a bigger branch along the way, and it left a large circular crack in his faceplate.

"Shit."

He landed on a thick bough and raced forward, leaping toward Tahoe, who was in midair ahead of him. Rade hurtled into his friend and wrapped his arms around the waist area, and the pair landed on a wide branch just below.

"Obey my goddamn orders," Rade said, pinning him there. He reached around, gripped the feed to Tahoe's jumpjet, and ripped it away. "I've granted you lenience, more than any other man serving under me. Given you special treatment. Chauffeured you to and from the base in my personal vehicle. Allowed you to go home early every second Friday. Approved all your holidays no questions asked. Well, all of that's going to stop! No more special treatment. None! You're just another MOTH serving under me." He paused, panting. "Now. Are you going to stop struggling, dammit?"

He waited, but Tahoe said nothing. Rade couldn't see his face in the dim light of course; the LIDAR and thermal vision represented his faceplate as a smooth, black surface.

Rade interpreted Tahoe's lack of response as a yes and he sat up straighter. He was about to loosen his hold when all of a sudden Tahoe punched Rade underneath the helmet, hard, jerking his neck painfully backward.

Before Rade knew what happened, Tahoe managed to flip him over so that he was the one on top, with Rade pinned underneath.

Rade glanced to one side. He lay at the very edge of the thick branch, and there was only empty space beside him: if he fell, it would be a long way to the forest floor.

Rade struggled to get up. His arms were pinned to his sides.

Tahoe's gloved fists came in, repeatedly striking the faceplate. Rade's head ricocheted inside the helmet.

"I never wanted any of your damn special treatment!" Tahoe sounded like he was crying in his suit as he pounded away.

The crack in Rade's faceplate widened under the blows. He continued to struggle, but he couldn't get his arms free. He began to feel slightly nauseous, no doubt because of the way his head was bouncing around inside the helmet.

"You were my friend!" Tahoe continued. "My best friend. But then you became LPO. All of a sudden, it was like I didn't know you anymore. You became so goddamn full of yourself. Strutting around like some self-important prick. We stopped hanging together on weekends. We stopped working out together. And when you deigned to talk to me at all, it felt like you were implying I was lucky you made the time for a lowly petty officer like me at all. You never gave me special treatment. Not once. No more than anyone else anyway. You punished me, damn it. Starved me for hazing the Artificial, when the whole platoon was involved. You singled me out just to prove I wasn't your friend anymore. Well you know what, Rade Galaal? Fuck you!"

Tahoe abruptly stopped the assault. He sat up. The shoulder areas of his suit shook slightly, as if he wept.

Rade took a moment to recover from the blows.

"Is that how you felt?" Rade finally said. "I punished you, Tahoe, because I had to show the others I *could* punish a friend. Not because you weren't my friend anymore. And I put Bender at half rations, too, in case you forgot."

Tahoe didn't answer.

Finally Tahoe got up, freeing him. He took several wobbly steps backward.

"Are you going to have me court martialed?" Tahoe asked

"No," Rade said, standing himself. "In fact, I'm deleting the past few minutes from my Implant. Everyone else, do the same. This never happened, understood?"

"What never happened?" Manic said.

"Good," Rade said. "I'm glad we understand each other."

None of them were supposed to have the ability to alter their logs, but during downtime at the base TJ had found a bug that allowed him to escalate his privileges on his Implant, and he had shown them all how to do it.

"Now get back to your mech, Cyclone, so we can get the hell out of here." Rade unlocked Tahoe's mech.

Tahoe took a few uncertain steps backward, and then he summoned his Hoplite. The mech came to his side.

"Wait," Rade said. "Turn around."

Tahoe complied.

Rade reinserted the fuel feed into Tahoe's jetpack, and secured it with tape from his utility belt. "Good to go."

Tahoe leaped onto the arm of his mech without using his jetpack—likely he wanted to examine the feed on his own at some point to confirm the seal. Then he dove into the cockpit, which shut behind him.

Rade jetted toward his own mech. When the cockpit sealed behind him, he turned the Hoplite and prepared to begin the long return trek.

"She just stopped," TJ announced.

"What?" Rade glanced at his HUD hesitantly. The lieutenant's dot randomly flickered on and off, but as TJ had said, she had indeed stopped.

"She's still within signal range..." Tahoe said. The hope was obvious in his voice. As was the imploration.

Rade lingered only a moment longer. "We continue the pursuit. Stealth advance, people. TJ, resume point. Have the HS3s and Centurions enter stealth mode, too."

The mechs resumed their single file advance, but at a careful walk. They still made some noise, of course, but far less than previously.

"The HS3s have arrived at the perimeter of a camp of sorts beneath the trees," TJ said.

"Halt them there," Rade instructed. "But dispatch two of them outward along the perimeter. Let's see if the HS3s can map out the full extents of that camp. When the Centurions arrive, have the combat robots split up to assume hides along that perimeter. Full stealth mode."

"Aye, LPO," TJ said. There was no hint of TJ's earlier scorn. Maybe he was finally glad that Rade was the one in command and not him. Glad that Rade had to make the difficult decisions.

Rade switched to the video feed of one of the HS3s near the camp beneath the canopy. In the gloom, he discerned three geodesic domes placed amid the trees. Most of the undergrowth had been cleared around them. Near the larger dome, two of the 'roach' class mechs guarded a sealed airlock with their four-armed torsos. The lieutenant's signal was coming from inside. Smaller scorpion mechs patrolled the grounds between the remaining domes. He counted fifteen mechs in total.

"It must have been one of the scorpion mechs that took her," Manic said.

"Or a new type we haven't seen before," Skullcracker said. "Hidden somewhere out there."

"Either way," Rade said. "We have to act now. Like Cyclone said, we don't know what they're doing to her." He paused to consider his options. "All right. Here's what's going to happen. We're going to advance at our slowest possible speed, full stealth mode, and halt roughly eighty meters from the perimeter." Rade knew that was about as close as the Hoplites could get without alerting the inhabitants of the camp—even in full stealth mode, the ponderous machines made some noise. If there was less foliage, they might have been able to close to within twenty meters. But under the current circumstances, it was far too easy to snap a stray branch or crush a small shrub, and the resultant noise would readily reach the camp. He had based the eighty meter halting distance on the sound profile of the jungle as calculated by the HS3s. He just hoped the machines weren't wrong.

"Once we've taken up that position," Rade continued. "We're going to have one of the HS3s stage a diversion on the far eastern side. It's going to move into the camp, flash its lights and make a bunch of noise, then turn around and flee into the jungle. When the scorpions are drawn away, the rest of us will move in. We'll engage any of the remaining mechs, including the two roaches at the airlock, who will presumably remain behind regardless of any diversion. We'll draw them away, and while the rest of you keep them occupied, Cyclone and I will proceed to the geodesic dome alone. We'll dismount, leaving our Hoplites to guard the entrance, then we'll enter the airlock. We'll rescue Vicks, if she's still alive, and then get the hell out. With luck, we'll be able to leave the camp before the rest of the scorpions return, or before any other reinforcements arrive."

"You shouldn't be the one to go," TJ said. "Not as our LPO. And Cyclone is obviously too emotionally involved."

Rade could hear Facehopper's nagging voice in his head, reminding him of his duty.

He's right. Send someone else. You're LPO now. Start acting like one. Stay with your men. Lead them.

"She was my charge," Rade said, trying to ignore that voice. "I should be the one to get her. But maybe you're right about Cyclone."

"I don't care at this point," Tahoe said. "As long as *someone* gets her out."

"The longer we sit here and argue about it," Manic said. "The less our chances of rescuing her."

Rade delayed a moment longer.

You don't have to do everything yourself. Rely upon your men.

He made up his mind.

"All right," Rade said. "Skullcracker, you and Manic will enter the airlock and attempt the rescue while the rest of us provide a distraction."

"That's a Roger with a capital r," Skullcracker said.

Rade exhaled. It felt like a great burden had been lifted from his shoulders.

Rely upon your men.

"Let's move into position," he said.

seventeen

Tahoe and the others lurked in the undergrowth eighty meters from the periphery of the enemy camp. That was about as close as they could get without alerting the enemy to their presence, according to Rade.

White wireframes overlaid Tahoe's vision, outlining the trees and shrubs the HS3s had previously mapped in the darkness. And although the geodesic domes weren't discernible from his position, the video feeds and telemetry information provided by the scouts closer to the camp gave him everything he needed to spy on the enemy. Not that there was all that much going on in the camp at the moment anyway.

Tahoe thought of Rebecca Vicks. She had such a joyful, almost naive smile, yet it was entirely at odds with those eyes of hers, which had stared at him with such intensity. He could have sworn she was promising secret delights in the privacy of her bed while on the surface she discussed the vapid intricacies of extractor repair. She laughed at his jokes even when they weren't funny. She crossed her legs, asked him questions about his upbringing, and what it was like to train as a MOTH. She never asked him about his wife, never brought up a boyfriend or husband. It was obvious she had wanted him. It was a feeling Tahoe unfortunately hadn't experienced in a long time. She made him feel desirable again. It was a good feeling.

He tried to ignore her, at first. Tried not to flirt. But she had won him over with that vibrant spirit of hers, that *joie de vivre*. And soon he caught himself repeatedly trying to impress her. Repeatedly teasing her, flirting. Soon he wanted her just as badly, if not more than she pretended to want him. He felt like a teenager all over again.

And yet he knew theirs was a relationship that would never be.

It was a schoolboy's crush he had for her. A fleeting, unattainable lust. He was a married man. With two kids. He'd never betray Tepin. To do so would be to betray his children. Still, his lust for Rebecca boiled his blood. It was hard, being out on deployment, away from his wife for eight months. The virtual sex toys helped, but those couldn't replace a real flesh and blood woman. So when you were on deployment and a woman came on to you in any way, shape or form, it was very hard to resist. Especially given how terrible his home sex life had become.

Tahoe wanted to be the one to come to Rebecca's aid, a white knight riding forth on his trusty mech steed. Again, mostly because he wanted to impress her. That urge had driven him to fight Rade, his best friend. Looking back, he had been a fool to confront Rade like that in front of the men. He was very lucky that Rade had brushed the incident aside and agreed to delete it from the video logs. Still, he doubted their friendship would ever be the same.

When Rade had assigned Manic and Skullcracker the task of entering the airlock to rescue her, Tahoe had agreed, but at the time secretly decided he would disobey. But as he waited there in the jungle, crouching in the dark, the voice of reason at last returned. He realized it was probably better, even preferable, if someone else rescued her. He needed to distance himself from Rebecca as much as possible. For Tepin and the kids. Yes, let Skullcracker be her knight in shining Hoplite armor.

Besides, she was a strong woman. She probably didn't even need anyone to rescue her. She was likely already on the cusp of escaping on her own. In fact, Tahoe kept expecting her to come waltzing through the thick foliage, blaster in one hand, alien captive dragged along the forest floor in the other.

Then again, even a resourceful woman like her, faced with an alien foe, would find it difficult to escape captors such as these. Especially without a mech.

"The HS3 is in place," TJ said over the comm. "I'm just waiting for the support Centurions to assume their positions."

"Get ready, people," Rade transmitted.

Rade. Tahoe still found it hard to believe Rade was their LPO. Facehopper's promotion to chief had happened so fast; Chief Bourbonjack announced his retirement on the same day that Facehopper took over. Rade had already been in the process of studying for his LPO exam, and he took the test immediately. He was promoted to leading petty officer two days after Facehopper became chief.

Tahoe had been so proud of his friend. Many others in the platoon were happy for him, too. But not everyone was pleased. TJ had already taken the exam two years ago, and felt that *he* should have been the one who was promoted. He had talked shit behind Rade's back for the first two days until Tahoe and some of the others had confronted him about it.

"We can't function as a coherent team if you're going to constantly talk down our LPO behind his back like this," Tahoe had said. "If you keep this up, we're going to make your life so miserable, and I mean living-hell level miserable, that you're going to request a transfer to a different Team."

TJ never said a word behind Rade's back ever since. Even so, his disrespect was still obvious from the way he often scowled at Rade, sometimes in front of him, and the disgust that always entered his voice when he formed the word LPO. That disgust was present at the start of their current operation, Tahoe noticed, but had gone away as the mission progressed. TJ was finally learning to respect Rade as a leader.

Something that I would be wise to do, Tahoe thought, shaking his head once more as he thought of what he had done. *I always have to pick fights with those in charge. First Facehopper, now Rade. Guess I have a thing against people in authority.* He smiled wanly, remembering his upbringing. He always fought against the will of the elders growing up. But one of the hardest battles he had ever endured was leaving the reserve. Defying the elders in that final manner had been almost as hard as MOTH training. Almost.

"All combat robots are in place," TJ sent. "Ready to deploy the HS3 on your word."

"Deploy," Rade transmitted. "Here we go, people."

Tahoe cleared his mind and watched on the overhead map as the HS3 moved into the alien camp. He saw flashes of light through the foliage far ahead, and heard a wailing siren. The scout was doing its stuff.

The HS3 retreated into the jungle, still wailing and flashing its lights. The siren doppler shifted.

Nearly all of the red dots in the camp moved after it in pursuit.

Tahoe slowly rose to his full height, preparing to break into a controlled sprint. The HS3s had already mapped out the best path each of the Hoplites should take: his particular route overlaid his vision as a green trail through the wireframe representation of the surrounding topography.

"Hold," Rade sent. The plan was to give the HS3 a chance to draw the scorpions at least a klick away, because when the Hoplites attacked, any enemy tangos that remained behind would almost certainly recall the others.

Tahoe glanced at his overhead display. The scorpions pursued the scout extremely fast, slowly overtaking it, lending credence to the theory that one of the scorpions had kidnapped Rebecca. Tahoe ran a quick calculation and determined that the four-legged robots would outrun the HS3 in approximately ten minutes. The HS3 had instructions to shut off its lights and sirens and fly up into the canopy when the pursuers came too close. The scorpions would likely use their jumpjets to pursue, and if they actually succeeded in breaching the upper boughs, they would have a tough time finding that HS3, which would be in hiding by that point. When the enemy inevitably abandoned the pursuit, the HS3 was to attempt to coax them into chasing again.

Tahoe doubted many of the scorpions would continue the pursuit, given that Rade and the others were set to attack the main camp well before then.

"Hold," Raid transmitted.

Tahoe felt his stomach knot up. He hated waiting in the moments leading up to battle. The Teams, and the whole navy for that matter, were all about waiting, and he had developed an impeccable patience. Except when combat, that crucible of life and death, was imminent.

Come on. Come on.

"Hold..."

He wondered what the robots were doing to her in there. Maybe her body was already dissected. That was another reason he shouldn't be the one to attempt a rescue. He didn't need to see her like that.

"Transmitting attack pattern," Rade said.

Tahoe received two targets. He was part of the group that would take down the four-armed robots in front of the airlock, clearing the way for Skullcracker and Manic.

"Now!" Rade sent.

Tahoe sprinted through the undergrowth. "Hunts With Cougars, take over!"

"Aye, Cyclone," the mech's AI returned.

The Hoplite could navigate the thick foliage far better than he in that darkness, and it changed speeds between fast and slow depending on the obstacles. The advance was unfortunately noisy, but there was nothing to be done about that. By then, the Centurions in place around the perimeter would be opening fire, providing a further diversion. White flashes and thunderous booms from up ahead were testament to that.

The instant Tahoe emerged from the foliage and into the camp proper his missile alarm flashed.

"Missiles!" someone said over the comm.

Tahoe wrenched control of the Hoplite away from the AI, activated his Trench Coat, and dove to the side. The propellant-powered shards of metal expanded from his mech, and explosions detonated all around him. He was hurled against a nearby tree.

"I'm hit!" Keelhaul said.

Tahoe instinctively checked Keelhaul's vitals on his HUD. Keelhaul himself was fine, but his mech's left leg was completely blown off.

Tahoe glanced his way and on the thermal band he saw that Keelhaul had adopted a firing posture, and was unleashing frags and lasers from his position on the ground.

Good man.

Tahoe got up and dodged behind one of the smaller geodesic domes. TJ was there, peering past the far edge.

Tahoe joined him. Beyond awaited the main geodesic dome. The airlock was in plain site. There was no sign of the two roaches, nor any scorpions. He glanced at the overhead map and saw that most of the squad had gathered behind the farther dome, where many of the remaining enemy seemed to be taking cover. The scorpions that had been drawn away by the HS3 were already racing back toward the camp, tracked by the scout that had drawn them away in the first place.

"Skullcracker, Manic," Tahoe sent. "The airlock is free!"

"We're kind of pinned right now," Manic replied.

"TJ and I have a clear line to the airlock," Tahoe sent. "Do we have permission to proceed, boss?"

"Do it," Rade returned. He of all people would know that plans had to be fluid amidst the unpredictable ebbs and flows of live combat.

Tahoe exchanged a look with TJ's Hoplite. "Let's get her while we have a chance. Cover me."

Tahoe left his position and raced across the jungle toward the larger dome. He sensed movement beside him. Too late he realized it was one of the roaches, stepping out from behind a thick bole. Its missile launchers were rotated into both hands, and its shoulder-mounted lasers were pointed directly at Tahoe. Those glowing eyes glinted malevolently.

Two frags exploded in rapid succession on the enemy's hull, and the roach stepped backward. A hole appeared in one of its eyes as a laser bored through. Another frag detonated, and that head blew clean away. The roach toppled.

"You're welcome," TJ sent.

Tahoe reached the man-sized airlock. "Hunts With Cougars, protect!"

Tahoe opened the cockpit and leaped out as the mech assumed a guard posture. He dove for cover inside the protruding outer rim of the airlock. He retrieved the laser blaster from his belt, the only weapon he could fit in the mech's cockpit. He had stowed a rifle in the storage compartment of the Hoplite's back leg, but at the ranges he expected to deal with over the next few moments, a blaster was all he needed.

Through the sights he scanned the nearby foliage as TJ's Hoplite left cover. It seemed clear.

TJ reached the airlock and ejected. His mech immediately assumed a guard stance beside Hunts With Cougars.

TJ went straight for the airlock's control panel.

"We're never going to get this open," TJ said. "There's no way to interface with it. Looks like we're going to have to blast our way inside."

"What if she's not wearing an environmental suit in there?" Tahoe asked fearfully.

"Then she's probably already dead," TJ replied grimly.

TJ pointed his blaster at the hatch. Before he could fire it opened of its own accord. He exchanged a glance with Tahoe, then moved inside. Tahoe followed.

The airlock sealed behind them and the air vented.

There was dim light provided by some sort of HLEDs above, so Tahoe switched back to the visual spectrum.

White gas misted into the airlock from below. The fog became translucent as it dissipated.

"The atmosphere just became Earth-like," TJ said.

The inner hatch opened, revealing a brightly lit chamber.

Tahoe and TJ advanced at the same time. Tahoe went high, TJ low.

Tahoe scanned the compartment. It seemed to be a sick bay or other medical type facility, what with the hospital-like beds, intravenous machines, and other surgical instruments.

He spotted Rebecca lying unconscious on one of the beds. She was dressed only in her cooling and ventilation undergarments. There were clamps around her arms and legs, and a vise pinning her forehead. The long, telescoping fingers of a surgical robot had driven multiple needles into her shaven head, forming a claw-like pattern. Her chest still rose and fell, so that was a relief.

Tahoe suppressed the urge to run to her. Someone—or *something*—else was in that compartment. The hatch wouldn't have opened by itself, after all. Unless some kind of AI was running the place.

"I'll take the nine o'clock." Tahoe moved into the compartment on the left side, while TJ advanced on the right. The two of them proceeded to sweep the place.

Tahoe found more of those surgical robots beside other beds. They had the same basic design as UC Weavers, and yet they were different in subtle ways. Instead of a sphere, their heads were dodecahedral, for example, as were the cylinders that composed their torsos. The biggest difference was their exterior: instead of silver, they were made of a black metal polished to a mirror-like sheen. It reminded Tahoe of the Hoplites when he had first seen them in the hanger bay of the *Rhodes*, before their camouflage patterns had activated.

Tahoe found a man crouching behind one of the tables. He was dressed in UC-style fatigues—the bars on his sleeves told Tahoe he was a commander. Or had been, at one point. Assuming he hadn't stolen the clothing. His cheeks sagged, as if he had spent too long in the slightly stronger gravity of the planet. He had an olive complexion, and wore a pencil-thin mustache. His lips possessed nearly the same thinness, as did his eyebrows. And those icy blue eyes themselves, well, they seemed dead. An Artificial? But even the eyes of Artificials teemed with life. Not like these joyless, emotionless orbs. If it was an Artificial, it was malfunctioning.

"Found someone," Tahoe said over the comm. Then he switched to the external speakers. "Stand up," he ordered.

The man complied.

"So you speak English," Tahoe said.

He gave Tahoe a slimy smile. "Yes."

"You're from the *John A. McDonald?*" Tahoe asked.

"Right again."

"What happened to your ship?" Tahoe said.

"Destroyed. We escaped to the surface in lifepods."

"We know *that*," Tahoe said. "But what happened?"

"We were attacked by... something."

Tahoe sighed. "Turn around," he ordered.

When the man obeyed, Tahoe shoved him toward Rebecca. "Go to her." When the two reached her, Tahoe told him: "Remove those needles and unbind her."

Behind him, TJ finished his sweep of the room. "Clear on my side."

The man walked behind the robot and accessed some external interface. The needles of the strange Weaver retracted, and then the fingers telescoped inside one another, withdrawing. Small droplets of blood marked where the needles had penetrated.

On the bed, Rebecca continued breathing, but her eyes didn't open.

"What were you doing to her?" Tahoe said.

"Me?" the man said. He removed the vise from her forehead, and then the binds from her hands. "Nothing. It was *them*."

"Who?" Tahoe tried again.

"*Them.*"

Tahoe waited until the man released the clamps from her feet, and then he pressed the tip of his blaster into the man's temple. "You gotta tell me a bit more than that. Who are they?"

"I don't know," the man said. "They're aliens. And yet they are also human. And machine."

TJ approached the bed. "What's wrong with her?"

"He won't say." Tahoe turned to address the man. "Wake her up."

The man shook his head. "I can't. She will awaken when they deem fit."

The dome abruptly punctured in two places as a laser shot from outside tore through the fabric. The atmosphere began to rapidly leak out. Due to the existing pressure outside, the decompression wasn't explosive, but more like a large weather balloon deflating. Judging from the way the fabric was descending, the dome wasn't actually geodesic at all—it had no support frame.

"Cyclone, we really have to go," Rade transmitted.

Tahoe checked his map and saw that most of the scorpions had returned from their diversion into the jungle. He heard the M7 going off outside, thanks to the combat robot that wielded it, along with frags and electromagnetics.

Tahoe hastily surveyed the compartment, searching for something he had spotted earlier. There. An environmental suit in a nearby open locker. Likely Rebecca's.

"Watch him," Tahoe told TJ. He made his way to the closet and grabbed the suit, scooping up the helmet. He returned and began dressing Rebecca.

"Wait, that's mine!" the man said urgently.

"Where's her suit then?" Tahoe said. He felt no compunction at all.

"They took it," the man replied.

"The elusory *they* again." Tahoe finished pulling on her leg and waist assemblies, then shrugged on the torso and connected the arm assemblies. The suit was a bit loose for her, but it would do. He attached the helmet. The interface was standard UC, and he was able to remotely pressurize it.

"That's the only suit." The man glanced at the ever-deflating fabric of the dome. "What am I supposed to do?"

Tahoe didn't have any respect for traitors to humanity. "Guess you better hurry and patch the holes."

He carried Rebecca to the airlock. TJ followed him, keeping his blaster pointed at the man.

"You can't abandon me like this," the man said. "I won't open the outer hatch for you."

The inner hatch was still open, so Tahoe entered the airlock with TJ. He held Rebecca close.

"You won't open the hatch?" Tahoe said. "Then we'll shoot our way out."

He pointed his blaster at the outer hatch.

Unsurprisingly, the inner hatch immediately sealed and the air vented.

Tahoe glanced at his map and saw that his mech and TJ's had been driven from the airlock.

"Hunts With Cougars, I need a pick up," Tahoe transmitted.

The outer hatch opened.

The battle was ongoing outside.

Tahoe switched back to the thermal band and lowered Rebecca so he could assume a support position near the outer rim of the airlock. He fired off some shots as a scorpion raced past.

The scorpion spun toward him, and curled its tail backward to fire.

The enemy robot was abruptly bashed aside. Tahoe's Hoplite dashed onto the scene, along with TJ's.

"About time," Tahoe sent it.

"Sorry," the AI returned.

While TJ's mech provided cover, Hunts With Cougars knelt and opened its cockpit. Tahoe used his jetpack to bring Rebecca quickly to the passenger seat, where he secured her.

"You're going to be all right, Lieutenant," Tahoe transmitted.

She didn't answer.

He leaped into the cockpit and the inner actuators surrounded him as the chamber sealed.

He provided covering fire for TJ while the MOTH loaded into his own mech, then the two of them piloted their Hoplites behind the adjacent dome.

"Got her!" Tahoe transmitted.

"Coming to you," Rade sent. "And then we're getting the hell out of here."

The final two scorpions went down and the rest of the squad caught up with Tahoe and TJ. Only five combat robots remained, and the same number of HS3s. The Hoplites had varying degrees of damage, though it was mostly dents and the occasional scorch mark. Most seemed fully functional, except for Keelhaul, who hopped on one foot.

Manic apparently realized that Tahoe was gazing at Keelhaul, because he spoke up.

"He's gone and changed mech class on us," Manic said. "Keelhaul's dropped the lite, and now pilots a Hop. The first and only transforming mech class."

"Let's go people, before any reinforcements come!" Rade transmitted. "HS3s, Centurions, lead the way." He glanced at Tahoe's passenger section. "How is she?"

"Still unconscious," Tahoe said. "I had her suit inject a waking agent, but she hasn't responded. I don't know what they did to her. I found a crew member from the *John A. McDonald* in there, I think. He was helping the aliens subdue her. But he wouldn't tell me what happened."

"Where is he now?" Rade asked.

Tahoe nodded toward the deflated dome. "Dead."

"All right, let's go!" Rade said. "Marching formation, best speed! We've stayed long enough."

eighteen

Rade was relieved his squad had rescued Vicks without any losses. Though he had come fairly close to losing some men back there. That unexpected missile attack right at the start had nearly cost Keelhaul more than a damaged Hoplite, for example. And there were some other close calls after that, and some bad luck: they had lost the powerful M7 along with the Centurion carrying it, both destroyed in a single blast. But all of his MOTH brothers had pulled through, and that was all that mattered.

No longer caring about the noise they produced, the Hoplites moved at their fastest possible speed westward through the jungle, taking the same route their passage had carved through the foliage earlier. Their two-ton machines had formed a decent trail the first time through, making the return trip far easier. Only Keelhaul had some difficulties, as he had to "hop" his mech forward on one leg. Even with the onboard AI to assist him, he toppled every few minutes. But thus far he had refused any offers of assistance.

Rade had ordered the remaining HS3s and Centurions to encompass the group in a wide cigar shape to act as peripheral scouts and hopefully forewarn them of any ambushers. Unfortunately, there weren't enough of the robots to cover every attack vector.

About ten minutes into the march, TJ spoke up. "Aft HS3s are detecting pursuers."

Rade glanced at his overhead map. Red dots had begun to appear.

"Scorpion units," TJ continued. "I'm counting fifteen so far. But more are appearing by the second."

"We can't outrun them," Fret said.

"No, we can't," Rade agreed. "Into the trees, people. We hide. Low power mode. Radio silence, and LIDAR off."

"Our heat signatures will still be visible in the dark," Manic said.

"Then choose your hides very carefully," Rade responded. "Pick spots that aren't visible from the ground. TJ, have the Centurions and HS3s move into the trees as well."

Rade approached a tree that was about twice as broad as his Hoplite and hurried to the western side, away from the incoming enemy. He climbed until he stood on an upper bough four meters from the jungle floor. The branch was about the same thickness as his mech. Perfect. He huddled close to the wide tree trunk and waited.

He heard a few more cracking branches as other members of the squad moved into position. Keelhaul was the last; he seemed to be having trouble.

"Need some help, Keelhaul?" Rade asked.

"Nope, I got this," Keelhaul replied.

"He's going to hop his way up," Manic said over the comm. He snickered.

"Radio silence, Manic," Rade said with as stern a tone as he could manage.

Finally Keelhaul took his place on the upper branches of a nearby tree.

Quietude descended.

A distant rustling reached Rade's hearing courtesy of his helmet speakers. It quickly grew in volume as nearby branches broke away and foliage was trampled underfoot. The scorpions were moving fast.

Rade instinctively held his breath when he spotted the thermal outline of the first scorpion crawling past below. The movements were decidedly insect-like, and he found himself amazed at the ease with which those four legs navigated the uneven jungle floor. He could understand why the robots moved so fast in that terrain.

More robots followed in waves, and he was suddenly glad he had elected to hide rather than stand and fight. There had to be hundreds down there. Called in from the barracks of some other nearby camp, no doubt. Who could say how many more bases those robots had scattered throughout the jungle? He was only glad there hadn't been so many guarding Vicks. Either the enemy was overconfident, or these robots had already been on their way to the camp before the squad attacked. Rade suspected the former.

When the last of the scorpions passed, Rade exhaled in silent relief. He waited another fifteen minutes, then broke radio silence. Before he spoke, he set his transmitter to the lowest possible setting.

"All right people," Rade said. "We're going to stay here another forty-five minutes before we move out."

"Waiting to see if they'll come back?" Manic asked.

"Or if more arrive," Rade answered. He paused. "I don't think we need radio silence. But reduce the power of your transmitters to the lowest levels."

The group remained quiet for the next several minutes, despite that Rade had lifted the radio silence order.

He checked the lieutenant's vitals after authorizing himself with her new suit. She seemed fine, though she remained in a coma.

He tapped in Tahoe for a private conversation. "How are you holding up?"

"Fine," Tahoe said. "Thank you for not ordering us to abandon her back there."

"I had to continue," Rade said. "When it became obvious she'd stopped, and remained in signal range."

"I could have tracked her even if we lost her signal," Tahoe said.

"I know you could have."

"I'm sorry for what I did," Tahoe said. "Throwing around an expensive mech like that, pitting it against the Hoplite of my best friend. That was entirely unlike me. I don't know what came over me."

"Don't sweat it," Rade transmitted. "We're cut off from the rest of our platoon. Surrounded by enemies in an alien jungle. We're stressed out, to say the least. It's no surprise emotions are running high."

"Even so, I shouldn't have fought you," Tahoe replied. "*You* of all people. My LPO. And my friend. Not for a woman. Especially not for someone like Lieutenant Vicks. She's not my wife." He paused. "I said some things back there. Things I shouldn't have. I didn't mean it."

"I said a few things I regret, too," Rade told his friend. "Let's just pretend the whole thing never happened, all right? Our logs are already purged. Let's purge our memories, too."

"Easier said than done," Tahoe sent. "I'll do my best to get over my guilt. Just tell me you forgive me."

"Of course I forgive you." Rade paused. "Do you really think I've grown more distant now that I'm your LPO?"

"I told you, I didn't mean what I said," Tahoe answered.

"I know you didn't," Rade said. "But sometimes, the things we say in anger are closer to the truth than we care to admit. It's not going to hurt me, Tahoe. I'm a man. I can take it. Just tell me."

It sounded like Tahoe sighed over the line. "All right," Tahoe said. "The truth is, you have grown distant. To a degree. But that's not necessarily a bad thing. You have to lead us, now. You can't get too close to any one of us, lest it cloud your judgment at some critical juncture."

"I disagree," Rade said. "I think my friendship with you and the others makes my judgment clearer. I don't want to endanger my brothers, and my decisions reflect that, hopefully. Why do you think I was pressing so hard to abandon Vicks in the first place? Not because I *wanted* her to suffer at the hands of her captors, but because it was becoming too dangerous for us to continue the pursuit."

"What are you going to do," Tahoe said. "When someday you're forced to sacrifice some of us, so that the rest may live?"

"I hope that day never comes," Rade said grimly.

"Didn't your LPO exam pose a similar question?" Tahoe asked.

"It did," Rade replied. "And I gave the answer that was expected: of course I'll sacrifice the few to save the many. Yet that was just a test. Something administered through virtual reality. It wasn't real. And that's the crux of it: I don't know if I could bear to do that very thing in the field, if the time came. I don't think I could leave one of us behind. Some lieutenant who I barely know is one thing, but a brother I've fought and bled beside? Tahoe, it would destroy me."

"Then maybe you're not fit to be LPO," Tahoe said rather harshly.

Rade didn't answer. What did Tahoe expect him to say?

"You have to be strong, Rade," Tahoe said. "In the coming days. Promise me you'll do that."

Rade sighed. "I'll be strong." But those were just words, something intangible, unreal, like the exam. Tahoe couldn't understand the burden of command. None of them could. TJ yearned for it, and probably hated Rade because of his position, but if only he knew the truth, he wouldn't be so full of resentment. In that moment Rade found himself wishing more than ever that he was merely a grunt, and that TJ was in charge.

His eyes were drawn once again to the lieutenant's vitals on his HUD.

"You know, I still feel like it's my fault she was kidnapped in the first place," Rade said. "I looked away for only a moment, and then she was gone. I should have never let her down from the passenger seat. But she wanted to study the ruins. And I let her."

"That was the whole reason we took her along," Tahoe said. "So she could study this alien world. If she was kidnapped, the fault was hers alone."

Their conversation died at that.

A few minutes later Fret at last broke the general silence and spoke up over the comm: "So Keelhaul, is this everything you expected when you joined up?"

Keelhaul chuckled softly. "This, and then some."

"Why did you join up?" Manic said. "And don't tell me you're one of those who volunteered."

"No, I'm an immigrant," Keelhaul said. "Forced enlistment, like most of you. I'm Czech."

"Ah, time to enlist in the UC Navy," Manic said, mimicking his accent. "Czech that off from my bucket list."

"You've been with us six months," Tahoe said. "And it took you all this time to reveal your nationality? Where have you been?"

"Normally something like that would have been revealed during hazing," Manic said. "But he got to skip that, seeing as he came from Team Eight."

"He never really hangs around with us after hours, either," Fret said. "Kind of a loner. What's the matter, we're too good for you, Keelhaul?"

"Not at all," Keelhaul said. "It's just, well, I never really felt like I fit in with you guys. I hadn't had a chance to prove myself in combat, and I knew if I went out with you I'd be a fifth wheel. And I prefer working out to drinking anyway."

"Goodie two shoes," Manic said.

"I want to hear more about his background," Rade said, mostly for the benefit of the others, as he knew all about Keelhaul already—one of the privileges of his rank.

"I didn't join the MOTHs right away when I signed up," Keelhaul continued. "After graduation, I was handpicked by the Special Collection Service. I worked to hunt down terrorists who sought to infiltrate our country by joining the military as immigrants. I also hunted down Sino-Korean moles. I got so good at it that I developed a special algorithm that automated most of it, helping detect ninety percent of terrorists and moles at the application stage. Anyway, by that point, there were no more major challenges to solve in my position, and I got bored. So I signed up for the Teams and the rest is history."

"Why'd you transfer from Team Eight?" Skullcracker asked somewhat disinterestedly. "Your chief didn't like you?"

"No, I actually put in for the transfer myself," Keelhaul said. "I don't know if you realize it, but Team Seven is renowned throughout the Teams. Every MOTH wants to join. The waiting list is huge, mostly because you guys get the best missions."

"We get the best missions because we're the best," Skullcracker said.

"Exactly," Keelhaul said. "Everyone knows about your exploits. What you did in the last alien war, well, it's the stuff of legends."

"Waiting list is huge, you say?" Manic asked. "Then how did you get on Team Seven? You sucked off Lieutenant Commander Braggs?"

"Basically," Keelhaul said. "Though I'd like to think it was for my qualifications. During my Mongolia deployment, I racked up the most sniping kills of anyone in the military. *Ever.*"

"I didn't know Braggs was gay," Fret said. He added as an apparent afterthought: "Not that there's anything wrong with that."

"Hey, if you're the one being sucked, you're not gay," TJ said.

"You talking from experience, TJ?" Tahoe piped in.

"Nope," TJ said, and left it at that.

"So that means Keelhaul is gay, if he sucked Braggs," Fret said.

"Yup," TJ said.

"Don't worry, Keelhaul," Manic said in obvious mock sympathy. "We accept you."

"So what if I'm gay?" Keelhaul replied. "I still eat pussy."

"Wait, what?" Fret said. "How can you eat pussy if you're gay?"

"'Cuz it tastes good?" Keelhaul answered. "Oh and, I've got something I've been wanting to tell you all. Ever since I joined Team Seven, I've been in love with Manic. I've never met a man with such a big pussy. May I eat it, Manic?"

Manic remained silent. Rade was biting back his laughter, and judging from the barely suppressed snickers he heard over the line, he wasn't the only one.

Manic apparently decided to roll with it. "I love you, too, Keelhaul. When this is through, let's get hitched. On our honeymoon, I'll let you eat my shaved pussy for hours. I'll let you munch and munch until the pubes grow into stubble and start to get lodged between your teeth."

"A man's got to floss," Keelhaul said. "Might as well use pussy stubble."

"Sometimes I wonder if I'm fighting with warriors," Tahoe said. "Or a Team of juveniles. Eating the stubble of each other's pussies. Sheesh. Man up, people."

"You first, Tahoe," Keelhaul taunted.

The time passed uneventfully. The forty-five minute mark came and went. The scorpions didn't return, nor did more arrive.

"They likely made their way to Gray Gate," Tahoe said. "Facehopper is probably staving off the attack even now."

"Facehopper and the others are dug in fairly well," Rade said. "I don't think they'll have any problem repelling them."

"Neither do I," Tahoe agreed.

Rade wrapped his metal arms around the bole and began the climb down. "Let's move out, people!"

nineteen

Rade elected to take a different path through the jungle as they continued the return. It would make sense for the enemy to leave sentries hidden along the previous route, so he chose a course that diverged to the southwest before heading due west once more.

He had TJ redeploy the HS3s and Centurions into a cigar shape around them, and then ordered the Hoplite squad to advance in single file. The going proved difficult once more, since the mechs were breaking a fresh track through the jungle.

"I'm receiving comm pings," Fret said. "We're at the extreme range of communication with Squad A."

"Chief," Rade tried. "You there? Chief?"

"I... you," the chief's warping voice returned. "Sit-rep if... please."

"We've successfully retrieved Lieutenant Vicks and we're on our way to Gray Gate," Rade sent. "No casualties sustained."

"Say again?" the chief transmitted.

Rade repeated himself.

"Excellent news," Chief Facehopper returned. "I... forward to... full debriefing... return. We... an assault here ourselves... resilient little blokes. No casualties... either."

Rade continued the march. The blue dots of Squad A had returned to his overhead map. According to HUD, Gray Gate was twenty klicks away. That meant there was only sixteen more klicks of jungle left.

When the squad had plodded forward another five klicks, Facehopper's voice came once more over the line. The signal reception was better, but while no words were dropped, severe warping still affected most syllables.

"Be advised, Rage," Facehopper sent. "You have an hour before sunrise."

"Say again?" Rade replied. "An hour before sunrise?"

"That is correct," the chief transmitted.

"We're not going to make it out of this jungle before morning," Fret said, the dread obvious in his tone.

"Why does that matter?" Manic asked.

"Didn't someone theorize the hammerheads only attack during the day?" Fret replied.

"So?" Keelhaul said. "We'll kick their asses."

"Kind of hard for you to do that, Hop," Manic joked. "With your one foot and all. You'll fall down."

"Let's pick up the pace, people," Rade said. He didn't entirely share Keelhaul's enthusiasm, nor Manic's nervous merriment.

Unfortunately, when they tried to move faster, that only caused the autopilots on the mechs to trip up, and the squad members found themselves falling more often than not. Keelhaul most of all. Rade finally ordered him to accept assistance from Manic, but that didn't prevent the others from tripping. Rade was forced to return to their previous speed.

"We're not going to make it out in time," Fret said.

The jungle brightened around them as the advance continued. Rade switched to the visual spectrum when the sunlight began to lance down through small gaps in the canopy. It was good to see color again, even if the tones were a little disturbing. White trunks. Purple leaves and ferns. The occasional orange shrub. Well, that was what triple strands of DNA would do for you.

"Who was it that said we wouldn't last until morning?" Tahoe said.

"No one," Manic replied. "All in your imagination, Cyclone."

"Let's maintain radio silence, people," Rade transmitted.

They marched onward for several moments.

And then...

"Wait, stop," Fret said. "Do you hear that?"

Rade halted. "Hear what?"

"That rumbling," Fret said.

Rade listened. He thought he could hear a distant rumbling sound.

"I am detecting a slight seismic disturbance emanating from the jungle floor," Smith intoned. "It is growing in intensity."

The AI was right, because Rade soon felt it as the inner actuators of the cockpit transmitted the vibrations from the Hoplite's legs to his own.

"Aft HS3s are reporting incoming hammerheads," TJ announced.

Rade glanced at the overhead map. Red dots were appearing en masse behind them as fast as the rearmost scouts could pick them up.

"Into the trees, people!" Rade said. "You know the routine. TJ, get the combat robots and HS3s up there!"

Rade chose a suitable hide for himself in the upper boughs of the canopy; he sat against the thick trunk, facing away from the incoming hammerheads. He would be exposed to any creatures that passed his spot and decided to look up and back, but with the camouflage the mech applied to the external hull, blending him in with the bark, he doubted that would be a problem.

Unless of course they could see the thermal spectrum.

As usual, Keelhaul was last to find a spot, and finally out of frustration he used his jumpjets to expedite the process.

The rumbling continued to increase after they had all taken their places, until it became an all-out thunder. Rade watched from his hide as the squealing hordes of hammerheads raced through the foliage below. There were literally hundreds of them, if not thousands.

A louder roar came then, piercing the background noise. One of the hammerheads had halted. A large thing whose bony, spiked crest was at least twice the size of the others. It was looking up into the trees directly at Rade.

Nearby hammerheads began to slow down, and eventually stopped. They followed the gaze of the big one.

It roared again, baring its teeth in a snarl. It shoved its way forward through the ranks, spreading its arms, and advanced with a posture that could best be described as stalking. Others cleared from its path, moving aside to let the beast approach the base of Rade's tree.

It began climbing.

Guess they can see thermals after all.

Others swarmed the trunk and scaled the bole after the big one.

"Shit." Rade leaned over the side and aimed at the large one. Before he could fire, it crawled around to the other side of the bole.

He launched two frags toward the base of the tree anyway, blowing the other incoming hammerheads apart.

Rade stood up, turning his cobras toward the far side of the trunk. But before he knew what was happening, a clawed hand grabbed the ankle of his Hoplite and pulled him off balance.

He fell from the branch.

He plunged the long distance to the forest floor with the hammerhead hanging onto him. He struck multiple branches on the way down, and bounced off the sturdier boughs. Meanwhile Rade kicked at the beast, trying to get it off him. The hammerhead's spiked tail shot upward and impaled his torso. The tip passed into the cockpit, and he could feel the fabric of his jumpsuit compressing in front of his chest.

"That was a close one," Rade said.

"Yes," Smith said. "A few more millimeters, and your jumpsuit would have been breached."

He landed amidst the swarm, and other hammerheads were instantly upon him. They grabbed at his arms and legs, and stretched them outward to their fullest extents. Sharp probosces and claws dented his hull from all sides.

The sharp tail withdrew from his torso, and then the large hammerhead was on top of him. It continued the assault, biting at the edges of the hole it had made.

Rade fired his cobra at the hammerhead that was stretching out his right arm, and the creature collapsed. He used the now free hand to pummel the large hammerhead on top of him. He broke away half its proboscis with a solid connect. The squealing creature retreated, only to be replaced by another, if smaller, hammerhead.

He wanted to use the cobra in his left arm, but he couldn't rotate the grenade launcher there off the mount, as one of the beasts still had that arm pinned. And he didn't dare launch a grenade at such close range. He started to turn his torso, intending to bash the thing away with his free arm...

When another hammerhead grabbed his right arm and pinned it down.

He couldn't break free.

Plumes of smoke abruptly rose from the bodies of the creatures restraining him.

The other Hoplites were joining the fray, firing their lasers from their hides. His body was no longer restrained by the muscle of living organisms, but the deadweight of corpses. He broke free of them and scrambled to his feet.

Frags and electromagnetics detonated nearby, taking out droves of the creatures and driving the rest away from Rade, granting him a much-needed respite.

"Rage, what's going on over there?" Facehopper sent.

"We're under attack, Chief," Rade returned.

Nearby hammerheads squealed. They were gazing up into the canopy. Then they began climbing the trees the other Hoplites used as hides.

Rade fired indiscriminately as his lasers recharged, trying to help his companions, but he was soon overrun, and he fought with his back to a thick tree. He bashed mostly, and fired his cobras whenever they reached half charge, wanting to preserve his grenades as much as possible.

Other Hoplites were dragged from their perches around him as the hammerheads took to the trees. Rade continued to fight, directing some of his cobras toward any of his team members that seemed like they were in trouble. The hordes of hammerheads came in relentlessly.

Soon there were two distinct groups of Hoplites fighting with their backs to two separate trees.

Rade, Tahoe, and Skullcracker formed the first group.

Manic, Keelhaul, Fret, and TJ composed the second.

"Do you want the Centurions to fire from their hiding places in the trees?" TJ asked at some point.

"No," Rade said. "They'll just be spotted, and we'll lose them."

The hammerheads continued to come in relentless waves, lining up for their turn to battle the Hoplites, and to die. A wall of dead formed around both groups, but the creatures in behind merely tossed the bodies aside, clearing the way for the next wave as they themselves were either shot or pounded down.

"Both of my lasers just overheated," Tahoe said. "Looks like I'll be bashing for a while."

Rade's cobras shut off as well, and he deployed the shield in his left arm while utilizing his right arm as a club.

"Incendiaries would have probably proven useful right about now," Manic said. "Remind me to talk to the genius who thought that provisioning mechs without flame throwers was a good idea."

Rade knew they couldn't keep up that defense for much longer. Eventually the mechs would begin to fail due to sheer wear and tear, and because of damage inflicted by the enemy. Or one of the Hoplites would commit a fatal mistake.

He had lived through no-win situations before, but never anything quite like this. There was literally no way out.

I've lost my squad.

He bashed aside another hammerhead.

No. There's always a way out.

Beside him, Tahoe fired his jumpjets and swung both arms upward to intercept a hammerhead that leaped down at him from the trees. Tahoe's mech struck with such force that he instantly decapitated the thing.

Momentarily transfixed, Rade watched the lopped off head fly upwards: it passed through the javelins of light that pierced the canopy. He followed those pillars of sunlight to their sources in the upper boughs, and he had a sudden idea.

twenty

R ade aimed a frag toward the canopy and fired, blowing away half of the branches that blocked the way. He launched another, clearing the way entirely so that a wide swathe of sunlight streamed down from above.

"On me, people!" He activated his jumpjets and aimed for the opening. Without branches to snag him, he rose uncontested, and in moments he was through.

The ocean of purple trees stretched before him, their upper boughs seeming an infinite sea.

He thrusted again, keeping himself airborne while advancing away from the opening.

Behind him other mechs emerged in turn. Tahoe, Skullcracker. Keelhaul, Fret. Manic, TJ.

"Let's see if we can put some distance between ourselves and these hammerheads," Rade said, thrusting forward while maintaining his height.

Before he had gone five meters, two hammerheads burst through the purple canopy below and dragged him under. He fell, bouncing hard on the thick branches along the way, until he landed with a resounding thud. The vibration traveled up into his cockpit, momentarily stunning him, the momentary taste of freedom but a memory.

The hammerhead swarm was on him an instant later. Rade got up before they could pin him, and began bashing away.

Bogged down by the creatures, other mechs plunged through the trees in a similar manner.

"So much for that great idea," TJ muttered over the comm.

Rade joined up with the others, and soon the Hoplites were right back where they had started, fighting with their backs to the white trunks. Except they battled in three groups instead of two.

Rade fought on, feeling doomed. Exhaustion was setting in, but he refused to allow his autopilot to take over. Not yet.

"I'm down!" Keelhaul said.

On the overhead map, Keelhaul's dot quickly moved eastward. Rade zoomed in and spotted him. He was carried by four hammerheads. Rade shot one of them with his laser, but had to bring his focus back to the combat at hand when another hammerhead loudly struck his hull.

He defeated his latest foe, and when he returned his attention to Keelhaul, the MOTH was gone, swallowed by the jungle. His blue dot continued to move away on the map.

"I'm going to eject!" Keelhaul said.

"No wait!" Rade said. He worried that the hammerheads would tear him apart if he did that.

"Scratch that," Keelhaul said over the comm. "I can't. Nothing is responding. They've killed my AI!"

"We're coming for you," Rade said. "Come on people, we move east. After Keelhaul!"

The three individual groups of Hoplites advanced from the trees that covered their aft quarters, and instead formed a single unit, fighting back to back. They made their way eastward through the swarm, but progress was extremely slow. Keelhaul continued to slip away from them.

"Too many of them!" Tahoe said. "We won't reach him in time, not like this!"

Keelhaul's voice came over the comm. "Forget about me. Save yourselves."

"That's not an option," Rade said. To the others: "We have to find a way to spook them."

"Grenades?" Skullcracker suggested.

"They don't seem afraid of grenades," Rade responded as he fought. "We'll blow up a few of them, sure, but more will simply rush forward to take their places. In the end, it'll be a waste. We need something more shock and awe."

Rade remembered Manic's earlier comment regarding incendiaries, and found himself wishing he indeed had a flame thrower.

"I've got nothing," Fret sent.

"Me neither," Manic added.

They both sounded exhausted.

Rade battled for all he was worth. He dodged a spiked tail, caught the beast by the torso, and swung it around to bash the next foe. He fired his laser at point blank range, tearing through the torsos of two closely spaced hammerheads.

A distant part of his mind reviewed the failed jumpjet plan. He felt that there was something obvious he was missing, something that would have made the plan succeed. Maybe if he had ordered the Hoplites to jump higher... no, that would have merely made them exhaust their fuel faster.

Fuel...

And then he had it.

"Got an idea," Rade said over the comm as he dodged a proboscis.

"Not another one," TJ retorted.

"This one is going to work," Rade said as he bashed another hammerhead aside. "You say this atmosphere is five percent oxygen, Cyclone?"

"I did say that, at one point," Tahoe returned.

"I'm transmitting a pair of waypoints," Rade said. "Different for each of you. When you reach the first waypoint, open up your fuel lines. Let that fuel spray out as you proceed to the final waypoint. Pour it onto the jungle floor as you cut a swathe through the aliens. And when your tanks empty, turn around and ignite that fuel by whatever means necessary. Frag. Cobra. Whatever it takes."

"Should we siphon the fuel from our jumpsuit jetpacks into the mech tanks as well?" Tahoe asked.

"No," Rade said. "I want to save that for emergencies." He completed transmitting the coordinates to the respective mechs. "Maneuver to the starting position, people! And wait for my order!"

Rade hefted his shield like a battering ram as he drove a wedge through the enemy ranks and moved toward the waypoint he had selected for himself.

"I'm in place!" Tahoe transmitted.

The others spoke up in turn, until everyone reported in from their designated waypoints.

"Can't... hold them... much longer..." Manic sent.

"Open up your lines and move to your final waypoints!" Rade said. To his AI: "Smith, crack the pressure release valve on your jetpack. Time to unleash the bug spray!"

Rade fought his way forward, periodically firing his jumpjets when the swarm became too thick. He kept low to the ground when he jetted, and narrowly avoided the thick branches overhead. He landed quickly each time, not wanting to expend too much of the leaking fuel.

Three-fourths of the way to his target, a low fuel warning flashed on his HUD. He ignored it, fighting onward. In seconds a new indicator appeared.

Smith read it aloud: "Fuel levels zero."

Rade drilled a hole into a hammerhead with his laser, and shoved the next one aside with his shield. He moved two paces forward, turned around and then launched his last frag. Hammerhead body parts erupted into the air, and the long line of jet fuel he had carved through their ranks ignited like a rapid fuse. The foliage proved relatively flammable, and in moments those flames reached to the height of his mech, forming a wall that spread upward and outward. He was forced to retreat.

More fires ignited as the other Hoplites exhausted their fuel supplies, and long walls of flames formed in the midst of the horde. One of the HS3s hiding in the treetops updated the overhead map, and Rade saw that a nearly complete pentagram had been burned over an area of three hundred meters square, the five interlinking walls of flame hemming in hundreds of the creatures, and repelling hundreds more. Some of them attempted to dash through the flames and caught fire themselves. Other hammerheads were already alight thanks to fuel that had fallen on them. They flailed about, squealing in pain. Because they were in such close proximity, it was relatively easy for them to rub the flames onto other hammerheads unfortunate enough to be nearby. The effect caused a panicked stampede.

"They really don't like fire," Tahoe said.

"No, they don't," Rade said. "Use the confusion, people! We take flight! To Keelhaul! TJ, send the HS3s forward, and have the Centurions join us from their hiding places in the trees."

Rade scooped up the severed, burning torso of one of the hammerheads and used it to scare away any beast that crossed his path. His mech was impervious to the fire, of course, though Rade could still feel the heat generated inside the mech. Despite the cooling system and vented undergarments he wore, the environment inside the cockpit had reached body temperature, and his jumpsuit struggled to wick the perspiration away.

The other Hoplites regrouped with him, as did the combat robots, and together they continued eastward after Keelhaul. Conveniently, the horde of hammerheads had trampled much of the verdure in their mad flight. When Rade and the others had first entered the jungle the day before, none of the foliage had been flattened like that. It was another testament to the stark fear the fire had instilled in the beasts.

"Sit-rep!" Facehopper's voice came over the comm. The chief had likely observed the scene already via their video feeds, and was only asking out of respect.

"We're going back for Keelhaul," Rade said.

"Let me send more mechs to help you," Facehopper said.

"They'll have a hard time getting to us," Rade said. "The forest floor is still teeming with hammerheads behind us. And then there's the conflagration, raging out of control. By the time reinforcements arrive, Keelhaul will be well out of signal range. Sorry, chief."

Behind them, the conflagration generated its own wind system, which propelled the hungry flames outward through the jungle at an even greater pace. The hammerheads were in full flight by then, and those that were trapped within the fiery walls died a horrible death. Their agonized squeals drifted across the jungle, and Rade pitied the creatures in that moment.

"How's the lieutenant?" Rade asked Tahoe, checking her vitals at the same time. He was trying to distract himself.

"Still in a coma," Tahoe replied. "Though alive."

"Glad you still have her," Rade said.

"So am I," Tahoe said.

Rade knew how easy it would have been for her to succumb to a stray blow during the attack. Even though she was secured in the rear passenger seat, that didn't mean the hammerheads couldn't get at her, especially since she was unconscious and defenseless back there.

"We never win," Fret complained. "First they kidnap our scientist. We get her back, then they kidnap Keelhaul. The universe is against us."

Rade glanced at Keelhaul's tracking dot. Though the MOTH wasn't moving away as fast as when the scorpions had taken Vicks, Rade and the others were still gradually falling behind, despite their best speed through the trampled jungle.

"Hang in there, Keelhaul," Rade sent. "We're coming for you."

"They're moving too fast," Keelhaul said. "You won't catch up. Like I told you before, just leave me."

"No," Rade said.

Facehopper tapped in again, but on a private line. "Do what you have to do out there, Rage. But don't lose any more men to save him, you hear me?"

"I won't," Rade responded. But even he couldn't keep the doubt from his voice.

twenty-one

Rade and the others encountered no further resistance as they hurried eastward through the jungle. However, soon the undergrowth thickened once again, as the hammerheads had scattered in random directions, and the jungle was no longer trampled underfoot in that area. He spotted the occasional signs that a Hoplite had been dragged that way—broken branches, a crushed shrub—but otherwise most of the foliage remained meticulously intact and the squad was forced to slow.

An hour passed. Rade occasionally communicated words of hope to Keelhaul, telling him to "hang in there." Fret lost contact with the chief at the half hour mark.

Alone once more, Rade thought.

Unlike the scorpions that had taken Vicks, the hammerheads hadn't done anything to prevent Keelhaul's mapping software from updating, so on his HUD Rade was able to see the unmapped darkness of the jungle slowly fill out around the hostage, leaving a trail of terrain traced in his wake. The creatures were taking him on a slightly different path than the lieutenant's kidnappers had, though the general direction was still the same.

Rade was also able to tap into Keelhaul's camera, and he saw that four of the hammerheads ported the Hoplite upon their spiky carapaces, alternately carrying the mech via the protective plate of bony horns on their shoulder regions, or using their taloned gripping arms. He considered permanently positioning that video feed into the upper right of his vision, but the quality was fairly bad; he decided it was better to conserve bandwidth for communications anyway and shut it down.

"Something's different," Keelhaul said ten minutes later. "The terrain's changing."

"Changing, how so?" Rade asked.

"It looks like there was another fire here," Keelhaul said. "I thought at first the hammerheads had looped back, but then I double-checked the map. We definitely haven't retread. And this fire has already burned itself. It seems fresh, though. Maybe a day old? Which would explain why we didn't spot it from orbit. I can still see the smoke rising from some of the cinders the trees have become. The flames must have been really bad. I mean, the jungle here has been burnt to the ground. Wait a second..."

"What is it?" Rade pressed.

"There's something here," Keelhaul said. "Something big."

"What do you mean?" Rade sent. "Another creature?"

"No," Keelhaul said. "Not a creature. I think it's a ship. That has to be what razed the jungle. And when its thrusters activate again, everything within the immediate vicinity is going to fry. Like you guys when you get here."

Rade glanced at the HUD. The partial outline of a large object was displayed, courtesy of the mapping software in Keelhaul's mech. Rade piped Keelhaul's low-quality visual feed into the upper right of his HUD and studied it firsthand. The video feed halted and pixelated constantly, but Rade was able to discern the towering object well enough. It was composed of three black, pentagonal planes—Rade remembered the dodecahedral shape of the enemy vessel Lieutenant Commander Braggs had presented during briefing, and he thought it was certainly possible he was looking at three of the twelve faces from that very same starship.

Keelhaul's captors conveyed him toward the hull, and through the feed Rade saw regular patterns embossed on the surface. No, not embossed—he realized the hull was actually composed of small pentagonal tiles. The hammerheads halted about two meters from it.

"What's your status, Keelhaul?" Rade sent.

"We're just sitting here," Keelhaul replied. "Waiting for them to let us in?"

"All speed, people." Rade tried to increase his pace and promptly tripped. He scrambled upright and continued on autopilot.

"I don't know what they're doing," Keelhaul said. "But this waiting is torture. I wish they'd just kill me and get it over with."

"No one's going to kill you," Rade transmitted.

The advance felt agonizingly slow. Ten minutes passed.

"Almost there, Keelhaul," Rade sent.

He had kept Keelhaul's camera feed active in the upper right of his vision, but it abruptly turned black.

"Keelhaul," Rade said. "You turned off your camera." No answer. "Keelhaul, update me."

"You know, when I was a kid," Keelhaul said. "My parents owned an old-style galleon, the *Cestovatelský*. That's Czech for *Explorer*. They gave tours to well-heeled foreigners from the UC."

"Keelhaul, turn on your camera..." Rade said.

"My sister and I often worked aboard," Keelhaul continued. "My sister— she was such a beautiful thing. A little angel, with the looks and voice to match. At school, she stole the hearts of all her male classmates. And when she sang at the youth choir, she brought tears to every eye. Anyway, one time when we had a break from our chores, and all the deckhands were occupied below, we found ourselves gazing out from the bow as the ship moved rapidly over the waves. I was always a troublemaker, so I bet her she couldn't climb to the top of the forward mast before me.

"I never expected her to follow, but she did, scaling the ratlines on the shrouds like a little monkey. When I got halfway, I stopped, because I didn't want her to hurt herself. But she kept climbing the rigging. I swore to myself, and continued. As she neared the top, the mast broke free of its restraints. It was a windy day, and it flung forward, over the bow. She hung there, floating out in empty space, and I struggled to reach her. Strove for all I was worth. But she lost her grip and plunged into the ocean. The fast moving ship plowed right over her.

"When she came out the other side, what was left wasn't so beautiful anymore. Nor alive. It had been a long time since my parents had brought the *Cestovatelský* to dry dock for a proper cleaning, and the underside of the hull was laden with barnacles. The medic assured me she felt no pain. That she had been knocked unconscious by the very first barnacle. That she couldn't have felt those sharp shells ripping off chunks of her face and body. I'm not so sure.

"It's my fault she fell. She would have never gone up there if I hadn't dared her. I've always felt it should have been me, and not her who plunged overboard. I promised I would spend the rest of my life making reparations. It was why I chose the toughest rating school when I joined the navy. I wanted them to punish me—I couldn't get enough. It's also why, when I transferred to Team Seven, I changed my callsign. I told you it was Keelhaul. It's what I should have been called in the first place. So that every time someone said my name, I would be reminded of what I'd done: I was a man who'd keelhauled his very own sister."

"Listen to me," Rade said, reluctant to use the callsign now that he knew what it meant. Rade had thought it strange that the former Team Eight member had chosen a new name for himself, but when transferring Teams it wasn't unheard of. Still, he wasn't entirely sure whether Keelhaul was telling the truth, or perverting a name that was meant to honor the memory of his sister in some way. "It's understandable to feel emotional, given the circumstances. But you have to turn on your camera. Or at the very least, tell me what's going on down there."

"Forget me," Keelhaul replied. "Let them have me. I spent all these years trying to prove to myself that I was worthy of the name brother. I'm not. I don't want any of you to risk your lives for a worthless piece of shit like me."

"You're just as much of a brother as any of us," Rade said. "We're not going to abandon you. You're not worthless. I know what you're trying to do. You don't want us to risk our lives for you, so you'll tell us anything to make us turn back. But the fact is, we're not going to. MOTHs never give up. 'Surrender' isn't part of our vocabulary. And you're not going to give up either."

Keelhaul didn't answer. Rade began to wonder if the MOTH had deactivated his comm, too. And then:

"A ramp of some kind finally opened up," Keelhaul transmitted. "A couple of scorpions are coming out."

In front of Rade the jungle abruptly opened into the scorched region Keelhaul had described. The foliage layer was completely burned away, with some charred remnants still smoking. Because of the outward pattern of the damage, Rade thought it was definitely possible some sort of braking thrust had caused it.

The towering black object loomed against the sky at the center of the devastation. Rade spotted Keelhaul's mech at the base, near an open ramp. While the hammerheads held him down, two scorpion robots fired the lasers at the tips of their stingers in rapid succession, tearing open the Hoplite's cockpit. The scorpions dragged Keelhaul's squirming jumpsuit from the mech.

"They got me!" Keelhaul sent.

There was no need for Rade to link the cobra targeting systems at that short range.

"Select targets and open fire, people," Rade sent the squad.

The scorpion holding Keelhaul got lucky, in that it maneuvered behind a hammerhead just as Rade gave the order. All of the bioengineered creatures went down in the resulting assault, as did the second scorpion, but the remaining robot scurried up the thick ramp, which shut behind it as the squad fired again. The Hoplite cobras only cut small grooves in the hull. The laser rifles the Centurions fired fared no better.

"Keelhaul, do you read?" Rade said.

"The scorpion passed me off to something smaller." Keelhaul's voice warped heavily as it transmitted through the hull. "Another robot. It's got me in a vise... I can't escape. It's carrying me through dark passageways. Tight in here. You'll never fit a Hoplite. The scorpion is waiting for you by the entrance behind me. I saw other, larger passageways there. I think it might be calling in reinforcements."

Rade tried the helmet camera feed of Keelhaul's jumpsuit. That worked. At least he hadn't deactivated remote access to it yet, as he had done the Hoplite. Rade saw the tight, dark passageway around Keelhaul through the poor quality feed. It looked like a spiral, and as he watched, Rade felt like he was traveling through a corkscrew. He reduced the feed to ten percent size and placed it in the upper right of his HUD. While the bandwidth requirements could potentially interfere with any communications Keelhaul sent, Rade figured it was better to have eyes inside.

"Forward, people!" Rade sprinted toward the hull.

He tripped on a half buried log. He didn't realize it at the time, but the act saved his life.

He saw a flash above him an instant before he crashed into the charred ground.

"The object is firing some kind of point defense!" TJ said. "Take cover!"

Momentum carried Rade forward a few meters, and when he stopped he heard a sizzling sound behind him; it came from the deep tunnel that had been carved into the scorched earth where he had stood only moments before. If he had been hit, there likely would have been nothing left of himself or his mech but smoking slag.

Rade heard several loud bangs around him and thick gray fumes began to disperse throughout the area. He realized the others were launching smoke grenades.

Veiled by the smoke, Rade quickly got up and moved to a new position. He rotated the launcher into his left hand and released some of the same grenades. "Fill the space between here and that ramp with smoke! And use some flashbangs, too!"

He had Smith coordinate with the AIs of the Hoplites, and the mechs fired the grenades as the party moved forward. While the smoke would screen them from visual targeting systems, and the heat from the flashbangs would provide decoys on the thermal band, he knew the mechs were still vulnerable to other techniques such as radar, echolocation, and predictive algorithms, which is why he gave the order to proceed in a zig zag pattern.

He thought he heard the sizzling sound of impacts around him; either the enemy was firing randomly, or they indeed had a partially working targeting alternative.

The noises stopped when the party neared the hull. He hoped that meant the squad had passed out of the firing angle of the point defenses.

Rade moved toward the area where the ramp had sealed as the smoke cleared behind him. Though he couldn't actually see the outline of the ramp embedded in that hull, his Implant had recorded the precise location.

"Use your cobras like laser cutters, people," Rade said. "Line them up, and place them in a row. TJ, bring the Centurions in to participate. Have the AIs coordinate between us all. And I want those HS3s watching our backs!"

Though they all joined in, the going was slow. The biggest problem was the recharge period of the weapons, something that a commercial grade laser cutter wouldn't have suffered.

Rade abruptly remembered the conversation he had had with Tahoe earlier.

"I don't think I could ever leave anybody behind," he had said.

"Then maybe you're not fit to be LPO," Tahoe had answered.

Rade glanced at the Hoplites beside him, at these men who would follow him to the gates of hell if he commanded it.

What am I doing?

"Once we've cut through," Rade said as the AIs worked. "Some of you are going to have to stay behind. Maybe all of you. I can't ask any of you to go inside with me."

"You don't get to be the lone wolf on this one, Rage," Manic responded. "I'm in."

"Me too," Fret added.

"Wooyah," Skullcracker sent.

"We're all going, boss," TJ said.

Rade glanced at TJ's mech.

Boss.

"When we leave our mechs behind," Rade said. "We'll only have two days of oxygen left. You board this thing with me, and we become trapped, there won't be any going home."

"Then we won't get trapped," Tahoe said.

Rade turned to his friend. "You of all people are not going."

"I'm with you," Tahoe said. He sounded hurt.

"What about Vicks?" Rade told him. "You heard what Keelhaul said. There isn't room for a mech in there. Not in the passageways he's been taken down, anyway. You can't drag the lieutenant around inside there while she's unconscious. And you certainly can't leave her here unattended."

"We can have one of the mechs take her back via autopilot," Tahoe said.

"Do you really think that's a good idea?" Rade said.

Tahoe paused. Then: "No. But maybe, maybe I can bring my mech inside. Keelhaul spotted other, large passageways near the entrance. I can take one of them, cause a diversion or something."

"With her strapped to your passenger seat?" Rade said. "And her life at risk the whole time?"

Tahoe didn't answer.

"No," Rade continued. "It's too risky. Besides, I want those of us who go inside to stick together. It's an alien ship. We go straight to Keelhaul. And straight out again. No splitting up."

"I—" Tahoe hesitated. Finally: "You're right. Someone has to bring the lieutenant back, personally. I'll transfer her to whoever—"

"It's going to be you, Cyclone," Rade interrupted.

He knew his friend was torn. As much as Tahoe wanted to go with Rade, he probably wanted to protect Vicks at least as much. Removing the choice would make things easier for his friend, hopefully.

Tahoe exhaled audibly over the comm. Finally he said: "I'll bring her back."

"Fret," Rade said. "You're going with him."

Fret spoke up immediately. "But—"

"No buts," Rade said. "I won't have anyone navigating that jungle alone. Buddy system all the way, people."

"Our abandoned mechs will have to go with him," Fret argued. "So he won't be alone."

"No, I want him to have a trained human pilot at his side," Rade said.

"Manic is an official mech pilot," Fret said. "It should be him."

"I'm sorry, Fret," Rade responded. "I've made my choice. After we're done cutting through, you two take Vicks back to the chief, along with our mechs, and tell him what happened. Tell him we tried to save Keelhaul. Tell him... tell him we were MOTHs."

Smoke began pouring from the underside of the starship in profusion. It emerged from the entire length of the lower rim. The hull began to vibrate.

"Looks like they're priming their engines," TJ said.

"You're assuming this alien vessel is anything like our own," Tahoe said. "They could actually be taking off *right now.*"

"If we don't get inside before they launch..." Manic trailed off.

He didn't need to finish. Everyone knew the thruster outflow would melt them to the ground. Not even Hoplites could withstand heat like that for long. The squad would be incinerated.

"Smith," Rade told his Hoplite. "Can the AIs cut through any faster?"

"We're working as fast as we possibly can," Smith replied.

"Assuming we actually reach Keelhaul," TJ said. "How do we know he's going to have a working jumpsuit by then? We got lucky when there was a spare suit for Vicks. We can't rely on luck again."

"That's a good point," Rade said. "We'll just have to take one of the spares with us." The parts for at least two complete jumpsuits would be spread across the storage compartments of their mechs. "Smith, determine our inventories, and assign the pieces necessary to form a complete suit to myself, Skullcracker, TJ, and Manic."

"Transmitting assignments now," Smith replied.

"Anyone bring a plasma rifle?" Rade idly asked.

"I did." Tahoe responded.

"You could have told us before!" Fret said.

Rade agreed, but he held his tongue.

"Forgot." Tahoe dismounted from his mech.

"If it's anyone's fault, it's mine," Rade said. "I should have brought it up earlier."

Tahoe opened the storage compartment in his mech's leg and produced the aforementioned plasma rifle.

"Tell your AIs to hold their fire, please," Tahoe said.

He stepped between the Hoplites and Centurions and unleashed his weapon into the hull from nearly point blank range. A rent appeared.

"That's better," Rade said. "Keep it up, Cyclone."

Tahoe waited the necessary recharge interval and fired again. After about a minute of that, he had tunneled a hole five meters deep through the hull to the inner compartment. The rent was large enough to fit their jumpsuits, if the squad members crawled.

TJ's Hoplite glanced toward the underside of the hull. "Looks like they were priming after all," he said. "Considering they haven't launched yet."

Tahoe stepped aside, returning to his mech. He stowed the weapon and dusted off his gloves in self-satisfaction. "One hull penetrated."

Rade's arm abruptly began to melt. "Infrared laser!" he shouted, taking cover. He had Smith compute the source of the laser from the damage profile. "The fire is coming from inside that breached compartment. At the two o'clock position. Anyone have any frags left?"

"Frag out," Skullcracker replied, launching a grenade.

Manic echoed the call.

The two bombs hurtled inside. An instant later the hull shook even more vigorously, and then black smoke drifted from the opening.

"TJ, send two HS3s in," Rade transmitted.

The small spherical drones dove inside.

"HS3s report all clear," TJ reported a moment later.

"Assign the remaining HS3s to Cyclone," Rade said. "We'll keep the two already inside for ourselves." He glanced at the combat robots. "Centurions, go!"

The five combat robots crawled inside.

"Clear!" the Praetor unit leading them transmitted a moment later. "Three scorpions have been taken out by the grenades."

The smoke was pouring even more vigorously from the underside of the craft by then, and the hull vibrations were ever increasing.

"Abandon your mechs, people," Rade said. "And then grab the assigned jumpsuit components from your storage compartments!"

Rade knelt his Hoplite and opened the cockpit. "Take care of Cyclone for me, Smith."

"I will," Smith replied. "Tahoe is in good hands." Rade noticed it used Tahoe's real name. The AI apparently wanted to convey it knew how important Tahoe was to him.

Rade leaped down and quickly opened the storage compartment in the mech's leg; he grabbed the spare jumpsuit torso assembly and strapped it to his harness above the jetpack. He considered taking the laser rifle that was stowed in the compartment as well, but he knew the blaster at his belt would be far more usable at the close ranges he would be fighting.

"Incoming!" the Praetor unit transmitted from inside.

Rade paused.

"Taken care of," the unit returned a moment later.

Rade shut the storage cavity and prepared to move in.

"I'll take that," Skullcracker grabbed the plasma rifle from the open storage compartment of Tahoe's mech and slung it over one shoulder.

Rade realized the others had secured their necessary components, so he gave the order to proceed.

"Manic, TJ, lead the way." Rade turned toward Tahoe's Hoplite. "Tahoe, you and Fret better go!"

"Good luck, Rade," Tahoe transmitted as the abandoned Hoplites joined him.

"You too, my friend." Rade turned his back on them, drew his blaster, and then crawled into the breach after Skullcracker.

twenty-two

Rade wormed his way forward. The fit was tight in the five-meter long tunnel—his jetpack and the spare torso assembly strapped to it continually scraped the ceiling. He struggled to find purchase at times, with some sections smoother than others due to the irregularity of the plasma blasts that had drilled the bore, but shortly he was through.

He found himself in a mid-sized compartment. It seemed to be a staging area of sorts for infantry-type units. The bulkheads were black, and formed of the same pentagonal tiles as the hull outside. Broad passageways led away to the left and right. The only light came from the helmet lamps of his companions and the heads of the combat robots.

On the deck just in front of Rade were the wreckages of three scorpions. Inside a passageway directly to the right, another scorpion lay in ruins, courtesy of the Centurions. Directly ahead resided the smaller passage through which Keelhaul had been conveyed, according to the data Rade's Implant had received. There was no sign of any airlocks or hatches.

"TJ, send the HS3s down Keelhaul's route," Rade said over the comm.

"Sending HS3s," TJ replied.

The two small, spherical scouts swerved into the central passageway and quickly vanished from view.

Rade took a step forward, but then paused. "Do we know if the gravity we're feeling is artificial?"

"Not yet," TJ answered. "Once we take off, we'll know right away."

Rade nodded. "We'll assume it's artificial, for the moment." Rade glanced at the five combat robots. "Units B and C, you're on point," he said, taking direct control of the Centurions. If TJ objected, the drone operator hid it well behind his faceplate. "Follow the HS3s."

"Let's hope the inertial compensators of this scrapheap extend to breached areas," Manic said. "Otherwise, we're shortly going to be making pancakes. With our bodies."

"The only pancakes you'll be making are the toilet kind, bro," TJ said.

"That doesn't even make sense," Manic replied.

"I think he means your excrement," Keelhaul sent.

"Good to know you're still listening, Keelhaul," Rade said.

"Trust me, listening to you guys is all I have now," Keelhaul replied.

Rade sensed a momentary surge of Gs and he involuntarily flexed his thigh muscles to stabilize himself. The feeling quickly subsided.

"We're going up!" Skullcracker said.

Rade glanced over his shoulder. Through the hull tunnel he saw the landscape quickly receding outside.

"So it's a ship after all," Manic said.

"Gravity is remaining constant," TJ said. "And I'm not detecting any further G forces."

Rade nodded slowly. "Manic, TJ, you're up. Praetor, follow them."

Rade waited until the three of them had entered the central passageway, then he turned toward the last members of his team.

"Skullcracker, watch our six. Units D and E, take drag." That was a different E than the one Rade had lost earlier—TJ had done some relabeling.

Skullcracker grinned widely behind his faceplate. Because of the tattoo, Rade felt like he was looking at a grinning skull. "Let's go crack some heads."

Rade moved into the tight passage, crouching slightly to fit. The cone of light from his helmet cut a swath through the murk. The spare torso assembly tied to his harness scraped the low overhead occasionally. Skullcracker followed just behind, and the two remaining Centurions assumed the drag position. Those latter three essentially walked backward, keeping their eyes ever on the rear.

"The atmosphere has completely voided," TJ said. "Looks like we've moved into high orbit already."

"Fast little fellers," Manic said.

As he made his way forward through the black passage, Rade found himself missing his mech. He felt so much smaller without it. So much more exposed and vulnerable.

Suck it up.

He glanced at the video feed from Keelhaul's helmet. It looked like the MOTH had stopped moving, and resided in a slightly larger chamber.

"How are you holding up, Keelhaul?" Rade said.

"They've taken me inside an airlock," Keelhaul responded. "The atmosphere is venting out. My suit says it's being replaced with breathable air."

The video feed momentarily pixelated and froze: Rade thought the signal was lost. But then it returned, displaying a larger compartment.

"I'm inside some sort of operating theater," Keelhaul continued. "They're clamping me to a table. Some kind of alien Weaver is approaching. I think those are lasers on its telescoping limbs. It looks like it's going to cut me out of my suit. If that happens, I guess this will be our final communication. Thanks for coming back for me, boss. It's more than I expected, or deserve. If you turn back now, I'll understand."

"Keep fighting, Keelhaul," Rade said. "To the end."

The helmet camera feed went black. Rade tried to reconnect. The request was refused. They'd removed Keelhaul's helmet, then, which would have caused it to power down immediately.

The Implant in Keelhaul's head was capable of transmitting voice and visual data, too, but the range was severely limited, coming in at fifty meters at best—when there were no obstructions. The devices relied on an adhoc mesh network of Implants and other aReals worn by human beings in the immediate vicinity to act as repeaters. There were none of those aboard the alien vessel of course. At least, nothing human technology could interface with.

It didn't matter. Rade knew precisely where Keelhaul was being held, thanks to the mapping data already transmitted.

"HS3s have reached a hatch," TJ sent.

The rest of the boarding party gathered in single file before the hatch. "Skullcracker, pass your rifle forward please."

Skullcracker slid Rade the plasma weapon. "I want that back after."

Rade passed the weapon to TJ, who handed it onward. The combat robot on point accepted the rifle.

"Let's move back, people," Rade said. "In case we have a welcoming committee waiting for us on the other side."

Rade and the others retreated some ways down the tunnel, and dropped to the deck. The two HS3s landed.

"Proceed," Rade said.

The Centurion fired off three quick, well-placed shots, pausing in between to let the weapon recharge, and burned a man-sized hole clean through the hatch.

"Clear!" The Centurion said.

Staying where he was on the deck, Rade zoomed in on the opening. Inside, another hatch blocked access almost immediately beyond.

"Looks like we have our first airlock, gentleman," Manic said. "And here I thought it was a breach seal."

"Your orders, LPO?" the Centurion asked.

"Blast it down," Rade sent.

The combat robot, Unit B, fired. The first shot burned a hole the size of a human head through the inner hatch. The atmosphere beyond vented explosively—the Centurion was taken slightly off balance by the force of it, and had to grab onto the nearby bulkhead so that it wasn't knocked off its feet. Rade felt the pull of the passing air, too, but it was easier to resist, given that he was already flat on the deck.

The metal around the opening buckled slightly as the flow persisted, and Rade realized that something hard had struck the hatch on the other side.

In front of him, TJ held up one hand.

"What are you... doing, TJ?" Rade said.

"Analyzing."

"Analyzing," Rade deadpanned.

"Yes," TJ replied. "The composition of the inner atmosphere is similar to that of a Jovian. Mostly molecular hydrogen and helium, trace amounts of methane, ammonia, hydrogen sulfide, water. And the pressure is high."

"Just be glad that the artificial gravity doesn't match a Jovian," Manic said.

The drag on his jumpsuit began to subside and Rade heard a thud coming from the direction of the sealed hatch—the unseen object that had been pinned on the other side by the decompression had probably plunged to the deck.

"The atmosphere has completely vented," Unit B announced. It peered through the scope of its rifle and aimed into the hole. "Clear, so far."

"Then enlarge that hole," Rade said.

The Centurion fired two more shots, widening the gap to fit the jumpsuits of the party members. The robot leaped backward suddenly and pointed its rifle at the deck area immediately beyond the rent.

"What is it?" Manic asked.

"I found out what hit the hatch on the other side," Unit B replied.

Rade switched to the Centurion's point of view and found himself staring at a large, crab-like robot of some kind. The automaton was upside-down, its carapace touching the deck; its claw-like appendages clasped repeatedly at the empty air.

Rade suppressed a sudden chill. "I hate crustaceans."

"Why hasn't it righted itself?" Manic asked.

Rade studied the robot. Only half of the appendages appeared to be working. "Obviously, hitting the hatch has damaged it."

"This could be the robot that carried Keelhaul," TJ said.

"Could be," Rade agreed. "It certainly is big enough. Looks like it could easily reach my waist, when righted." He watched those appendages writhe for a few more moments, and then said: "Unit B, terminate the tango."

The Centurion pointed the rifle and fired. The robot melted into the deck.

"HS3s, resume scout position," Rade ordered. He and the others stood, then proceeded forward once more.

Beyond the airlock, the small passage quickly narrowed further. It looked like a spiral, and Rade had the eerie sensation he was traveling through a corkscrew; it was the same feeling he'd had earlier while viewing Keelhaul's feed remotely.

"Is it just me, or is this tunnel actually revolving around us?" Manic asked.

"According to my local AI," TJ said. "The bulkheads are stationary, but they're twisting slightly as we travel downward. And get this: the gravity field is bending to compensate. Craziest thing I've ever seen."

Rade's stomach knotted as the advance dragged out. It was a combination of the swirling nature of the place, and the tightness of those bulkheads. MOTHs were trained to feel no fear in confined spaces—they wouldn't be able to operate mechs otherwise. And while mechs could induce claustrophobia, at least with a mech he knew he could crack open the cockpit and emerge at any time. But in that twisting passageway, he had no such recourse. There would be no breaking out.

He supposed that was the source of his unease: the lack of control, the feeling that his life resided in the hands of the unseen alien masters who commanded the ship.

He halted, closed his eyes and took a deep breath.

I'm in control.

"You all right, Rage?" Skullcracker asked.

"Fine." Rade opened his eyes and pressed on. He concentrated on the overhead map, and gazed at the dots in front of him that represented the HS3s and other members of the party.

If they can do it, I can.

The bulkheads continued to tighten, until they had to stoop far forward. Eventually the passage became so cramped that they proceeded on hands and knees, or rather gloves and knee assemblies. It was nearly as bad as the five meter tunnel Tahoe had originally bored into the hull for them, except it went on for much longer than five meters.

"How the hell did that robot carry Keelhaul through *this?*" Manic asked.

"Ain't that tight," Skullcracker said. "Man up."

Thankfully, the route widened shortly thereafter, and Rade was able to stand on two feet once more. The passageway continued to spiral downward however so that he could never see very far in either direction. He lost track of his spatial orientation within the ship entirely, and without the three-dimensional overhead map, he would have had no idea where he was.

Occasionally other side passages branched off from the main but they, too, spiraled out of view—sometimes up, sometimes down—hiding what lay beyond. Rade always sent the HS3s a short distance into each of them to make sure nothing waited in ambush just beyond sight.

"Does anyone else feel like a lamb being led to the slaughter?" Manic said.

"Manic, please," Rade said.

"No, I like it when he spouts stupidities like that," TJ said. "Makes me feel good, knowing I'm not a pussy. Right, Skullcracker?"

The latter didn't answer.

"*Stupido*," Manic said, mocking TJ's Italian accent.

"The HS3s have reached another hatch," TJ said.

Rade checked his overhead map. Apparently, a wide compartment awaited on the other side. It narrowed into a smaller passageway after about ten meters, and fifty meters beyond that lay Keelhaul.

"Blow it open," Rade instructed Unit B, which was still on point. "But wait until we're in position."

Rade and the others, including the HS3s, retreated until the hatch was almost lost by the curve of the passageway, and then they dropped to the deck.

Unit B fired.

Once more the atmosphere vented explosively, and the robot on point had to brace its body against the nearby bulkhead to prevent itself from falling over.

As it waited for that atmosphere to vent, a circular hole abruptly appeared in the robot's midsection. That hole instantly widened, partially consuming the battery compartment. Unit B lost its balance, and the venting atmosphere carried it backward, slamming it to the deck. Its body slid silently across the metal.

The atmospheric leakage abruptly ceased and the damaged robot stopped moving. It tossed the plasma rifle across the passageway, toward the party. Unit C caught it from its position on the deck.

"Run," Unit B transmitted before its headlamp lost power.

twenty-three

The hatch slid aside and a scorpion robot waltzed into the passageway. Its legs and tail were all scrunched up to fit the narrow confines; its stinger was pointed right at Unit C.

"Fire!" Rade sent.

The group unleashed their weapons, and the scorpion crumpled, riddled by laser blasts. Another scorpion crawled into the passage behind it.

"Take it out!" Rade said.

Most of the group had fired their lasers already, and were waiting for the recharge. Unit C, however, had yet to unleash its plasma rifle, and it did so at that moment.

The stinger of the next scorpion melted away entirely. The tango continued to slither forward until it abutted against the first, disabled scorpion. It wasn't able to crawl past the blockage, so it began to push instead.

Rade and the others fired their recharged lasers, disabling the thing. It toppled forward, landing on the first, blocking the path.

He had only just exhaled in relief when the pair of robots began sliding forward once again, obviously pushed by another, as yet unseen, scorpion behind them. The uppermost body slid backward as something grasped it: whatever gripped the robot obviously intended to move it out of the way.

"Retreat, people!" Rade said.

Staying low, the party quickly backed up until the blockage was completely lost to the bend of the deck. There Rade stood to his full height and fell back to an area where a side passage branched off.

"We can take them," Skullcracker said.

Rade pulled up the footage recorded by one of the HS3s near the front when Unit B went down. He paused it after the Centurion fell, and then zoomed in on the head-sized gap burned into the hatch. Only darkness awaited within the wider compartment beyond. He enhanced the area, changing the focus and exposure levels—the lightfield camera in the HS3 recorded beams of light from all directions, allowing him to make these and other fine-tuning adjustments after the fact. Once he was satisfied, he maintained the zoom and let the video play on slow speed. Using the pattern recognition and extrapolation provided by the processor embedded in his jumpsuit, he quickly realized he was looking at several scorpion robots, tightly packed and milling about in that compartment.

"No," Rade said. "There are too many of them. Have a look." He transmitted the resultant video to his teammates.

"We can take them," Skullcracker insisted.

"Maybe," Rade finally conceded. "But it won't be easy. And it will take a while. Remember, time's ticking away. Every moment we delay is another moment Keelhaul suffers at the hands of our captors. Whoever they are. We'll find another route."

"The rest of the ship is unmapped," Skullcracker said. "We might spend just as much time wandering around, as we would fighting here. And we might find ourselves faced with another enemy bottleneck. Against worse opponents."

"Which is why we're staying right here, and dispatching the HS3s," Rade said. "TJ, send the first down this side passage. Have the second continue back the way we came, to the next available side passage. Activate the predictive algorithms—I want them choosing those branches that will take them closer to Keelhaul."

"You got it," TJ replied.

The party waited, guarding the forward quarter.

The map slowly filled out beyond the side passage the first scout had taken. The HS3 retraced its steps a few times after encountering dead ends in the form of other hatches, and eventually the scout began to close with Keelhaul's last known position.

"That looks promising..." Rade said.

"I just lost the second HS3 behind us," TJ announced. "It was ambushed by a scorpion robot."

"So they're already starting to outflank us," Rade said.

A scorpion came into view from the forward quarter. Apparently it had managed to break apart the previous two that blocked the passageway.

Rade and the others opened fire immediately, taking it down.

It crashed to the deck, revealing another scorpion approaching right after, stinger poised and ready.

"Drop!" Rade said.

The Praetor unit was struck before it could obey, and it collapsed to the deck with a finger-sized hole drilled through its head. A runnel was also carved into the pentagonal tiles of the bulkhead behind it.

Rade and the others returned fire, eliminating the next enemy. It collapsed onto the first, blocking the passage.

In seconds, that inanimate blockage began to slide forward as the unseen robots behind it pressed onward.

"Looks like we have an unobstructed route to Keelhaul!" TJ said.

Rade glanced at his map. Sure enough, the first HS3 had reached a hatch that appeared to be just outside the compartment where Keelhaul was held.

"Down the side passage, people!" Rade said. "Unit C, lead the way!"

The party assumed their previous combat order, minus the Praetor and Unit B, and proceeded onward.

The spiraling passage curved downward and outward. They took a left branch, and another.

According to the display, Keelhaul was thirty meters ahead.

"I thought the range of Implants was fifty meters?" Manic said. "Shouldn't we be getting pings from Keelhaul by now?"

"Not if his Implant is damaged," TJ said.

"Why would it be damaged?" Manic said.

"When we found Vicks," TJ explained. "She had steel probes sticking out all over her head. If the bastards are doing the same to Keelhaul, who knows what havoc that shit is wreaking on his Implant?"

"Could be something as simple as bulkhead interference instead," Rade said.

"What if they moved him after we lost connection?" Skullcracker said.

"Man, if they moved him," TJ said. "And all of this is for nothing, then I'm going to shoot Manic in the testicles."

"You can certainly try," Manic responded, sounding completely unfazed, and almost challenging.

They reached the hatch. Not unexpectedly, there seemed no way to open it.

"So what now?" Manic asked. "We blow it, and risk venting any breathable environment the captors have prepared for Keelhaul?"

Rade ran his gloved fingers along the outline. "There has to be a way to open it."

He stepped back and aimed his blaster at the hatch.

"What are you doing?" Manic asked nervously.

"Just using the sights to see if I can spot anything." The built-in scope acted as a stabilized zoom—it was much easier to aim than the zoom built into his helmet.

Without warning the hatch opened.

"What did you do?" Manic asked.

"Nothing," Rade said. He lowered the blaster. "Apparently, they don't want me to fire."

"I thought you had no intention of firing?" Manic said.

"I didn't," Rade replied. "But they wouldn't know that."

There was another hatch just inside. An airlock. Only two could fit the chamber at a time.

"Skullcracker," Rade said. "With me."

Skullcracker retrieved the plasma rifle from Unit C.

"You shouldn't be the one to go," TJ said. "You're our LPO."

"At this point it doesn't matter," Rade said. "There's only you and Manic left. If Skullcracker and I fall in there, you get to be LPO of a whole team of one, plus some combat robots."

"Wonderful," TJ said. "But I wasn't suggesting that Manic and I go. What I meant is, you should send two Centurions."

"And what if the hatch never opens again?" Rade said. "What if the combat robots have only one chance to free Keelhaul, and they fail? No, I want human beings to handle this. Load your spare jumpsuit parts into the airlock, people. And Skullcracker, with me."

Rade waited as the others piled the spare assemblies into the airlock, then he stepped inside with Skullcracker. Not unexpectedly, the outer hatch sealed behind them.

Rade felt his heart pounding in his neck, the collar of his jumpsuit feeling too tight all of a sudden.

Atmosphere began to vent into the airlock, judging from the white mist that was coughed up from the bottom of the two bulkheads on either side.

Rade checked the breathability with his suit samplers.

Atmosphere breathable.

He was tempted to remove his helmet if only to spare his oxygen stores, but decided it was best to leave it on, considering he had no idea what awaited on the other side.

The inner hatch opened. There was no decompression. The atmospheres were equal.

Rade and Skullcracker stepped inside.

twenty-four

R ade went high, Skullcracker low.

Holding the blaster with two gloves, Rade ran the sights across the compartment. It was indeed some sort of operating theater, as Keelhaul had said. He saw several beds placed side by side, with some in the middle separating the compartment into two aisles.

There were strange animals Rade had never seen before clamped to those beds. One looked like a giraffe grafted onto the body of a giant spider. Another seemed like a gorilla except with multiple tentacles in place of arms and legs. They were all unconscious. Weaver-like robots resided near most of them, and had telescoped large needles into the shaven heads of the animals.

Rade glanced uncertainly at the lower part of his HUD: the atmosphere was still rated as breathable.

The chest regions of those animals were rising and falling, partaking of that processed air; that told him the beings were definitely bioengineered from Earth stock. Once again, he found himself wondering who the aggressors were. Aliens, SKs, or what?

Keeping his weapon extended in front of him, Rade crouched, and slid the spare jumpsuit parts into the room from the bottom of the airlock—just in case the inner hatch were to close behind him.

"Search protocol," Rade transmitted when he was done.

Staying low, he proceeded forward through the compartment, branching out into the left aisle, while Skullcracker took the right.

He paused occasionally to search underneath groups of the beds, which were more gurneys than anything else, but spotted nothing. Eventually he reached the far side of the chamber, where Keelhaul was clamped into one of the beds.

"Clear," Rade said.

"Clear," Skullcracker echoed.

He stood up, some of the tenseness ebbing from his body. Only some.

"A monitoring AI must have let us in," Rade said.

"Why would it help us?" Skullcracker said.

Rade nodded toward the beds. "It saw my blaster, remember? Doesn't want to lose its precious specimens. Especially the new shining jewel of its collection." His eyes drifted to Keelhaul. Long needles were drilled into the unconscious MOTH's shaven crown, courtesy of one of those Weaver-type robots perched at the head of the bed.

When Rade pointed his blaster at the Weaver, those needles retracted, and the robot moved backward.

"Interesting," Rade said. He promptly fired his blaster, melting away half those telescoping arms and the component that held them.

"Careful," Skullcracker said. "You might make the AI mad."

"I hope so." Rade studied Keelhaul. Blood trickled from the areas where those needles had pricked his shaven head. Rade wondered how far the probes had penetrated. Was he too late?

He carefully used the blaster to cut away the clamps restraining Keelhaul's arms and legs. Skullcracker chipped in, speeding up the process. Before they got the last one free, Keelhaul opened his eyes.

Rade retreated a step, ready to point his blaster at the man. "Keelhaul?"

Skullcracker had backed away, and while his rifle was lowered, he too seemed poised to leap into action.

Keelhaul looked around, seemingly confused as to where he was. When he saw Skullcracker, his eyes lingered first on the weapon, then moved to his face. He seemed about to speak, but then his gaze moved on, eventually finding Rade.

He smiled then, broadly, and burst into tears. "You came for me. You came back. I thought you'd abandoned me. I thought you'd given up." He tried to hide his face, obviously ashamed that he was crying.

As Rade watched that big man who had served under him bawl his eyes out, he couldn't help but feel empathy. He held his blaster away from Keelhaul as he reached forward to touch his bare shoulder with one glove.

"It's okay, Keelhaul," Rade said. "Everything's going to be all right now. You're going home."

"They took my suit," Keelhaul said, finally getting the tears under control. "And my cool vents." The cooling and ventilation undergarments.

"We have one here for you. Minus the undergarments. Near the hatch."

"Oh." His red eyes gazed toward the hatch, and he brightened when he saw the jumpsuit pieces scattered there.

"We're getting you out of here." Rade cut away the last restraint with his blaster, then lowered the torso assembly of the spare jumpsuit—he had kept the piece secured to the rear of his harness the whole time—and tossed it to Keelhaul.

"Put this on," Rade commanded. "As I said, no cooling undergarment. You're going to sweat a bit."

He shrugged on the torso assembly and grimaced. "Does chaff quite a bit without the undergarment."

"You're a MOTH," Rade said. "You can take it."

Keelhaul finished donning the torso, only to have Skullcracker throw him the leg assembly.

Keelhaul paused as he pulled it on from the bed. "Did you hear that?"

Rade frowned. "What?"

Keelhaul tilted his head. "Tones. And now colors. It's them."

"Who?" Rade said.

"The aliens." He paused again. "At least, I think it's them... I have no idea what they're saying. Their language seems to be a mixture of flashing colors and pulsing tones. The kind of data you'd expect from a machine."

Rade exchanged an uncertain glance with Skullcracker.

"Looks like Keelhaul is going to need a wee bit of treatment when we get back," TJ transmitted from outside.

When the MOTH finished putting on the leg assembly, Rade offered him a gloved hand. "Can you walk?"

Keelhaul grasped the hand uncertainly and rose to his feet. He took a few tentative steps, then released Rade.

"Is that you doing the walking, or the jumpsuit?" Rade asked. The suit would only be half-powered by that point, but it would be enough to aid his brother in arms.

"All me," Keelhaul said.

Rade glanced at the O2 levels on his HUD. "By the way, I don't suppose you know where we can get some fresh oxygen?"

Keelhaul shook his head. "While these aliens might be trying to communicate with me, they certainly haven't revealed all of their secrets. Would you?"

"I hadn't actually meant to imply that," Rade responded. "But no. I wouldn't expect them to."

The spare jumpsuit had a half tank of oxygen, so Rade figured he could siphon some from Keelhaul if it came to it. Though that would only extend their collective oxygen levels by a few hours.

When Keelhaul attached the last component of the jumpsuit, the helmet, Rade checked that the suit was functioning properly.

"The fit is a bit off," Keelhaul said. "Especially without the undergarment. But it'll do." His eyes dropped to Rade's jetpack. "Don't suppose I get one of those?"

"Sorry, bro," Rade replied. He moved toward the airlock. "Skullcracker, blast the outer door." Since only two of them could fit at a time through the airlock, he didn't want to risk leaving one of them trapped in there. The bioengineered animals strapped into the beds would die when the atmosphere released, but they were abominations anyway.

"Clear the outside, people," Rade warned TJ and Manic. "We're coming through."

Skullcracker fired the plasma rifle. The air rapidly vented; beds shifted, and some of the smaller instruments tore past. Rade was nearly struck by a flying scalpel. Perhaps that hadn't been the best idea after all...

"Wooyah!" Skullcracker shouted.

The venting quickly ceased; unconscious specimens on the table spasmed for a few moments, then ceased all movement. A few body parts occasionally twitched in the cold of the void. Rade wondered how long it would take for them to freeze solid. He had heard that the SKs sometimes bioengineered antifreeze into the blood of their creations...

Skullcracker blew another hole through the hatch, bringing Rade's attention back to the airlock. In a few moments, he fired again, and they were through.

"So what's the plan now?" Manic asked.

"We go back the way we came," Skullcracker replied. "And jump out."

"Brilliant plan," Manic said. "Boss, what's the real plan?"

Rade didn't answer.

"Don't tell me that's the real plan?" Manic transmitted. He waited for someone to contradict him. No one did. "It *is* the plan, isn't it?" Again, no answer. "You know that route will be crawling with scorpions, right?"

"Send the HS3 forward, TJ," Rade said. "We move, people. Keelhaul, you're in front of me, after TJ."

They had retraced their previous route for only a minute when TJ announced: "Just lost the HS3. The return passage is blocked by at least two scorpions."

"We'll just have to shoot our way past them," Rade said.

Keelhaul halted beside a side corridor.

Rade paused beside him and stared into the darkness. His helmet light didn't penetrate very far, as the curvature of that passageway was even more extreme than usual.

"Keelhaul," Rade said. "We have to go."

Keelhaul hesitated a moment longer. "They're calling to me."

"Ignore them," Rade said. "You go down that passageway, you never return. Make your choice."

Keelhaul stiffened, and then continued along the original route.

"Incoming!" Unit C said from its point position. The Centurion toppled.

Rade glanced forward. The first scorpion had arrived. "Fire!"

The scorpion toppled under the party's laser bombardment. When the next appeared, Skullcracker aimed past the Centurions and melted away its upper body with his plasma rifle. It fell forward, completely filling the gap between the first robot and the overhead.

Once more the remains of the machines slid forward as other scorpions shoved from behind.

"Looks like we're going to have to cut our way through them to get back," Rade said.

"On drag!" Unit E said.

Rade spun as Units D and E fired. The pair took down a scorpion that had crept up on them from behind. Rade aimed his blaster at the space between its upper body and the overhead, and sighted the scorpion behind it. He squeezed the trigger; the robot went down, but when it fell, it hit the deck rather than the disabled scorpion in front of it, so that there remained a visible gap above the two machines.

Another scorpion lurked behind those two, its stinger glowing.

Rade instinctively dropped to the deck.

Behind him, TJ fired.

That scorpion toppled as well, also plunging straight to the deck, so that the gap remained. The curvature of the passageway was only slight here, so that the next scorpion behind that one had a clear line of sight above the wreckages of the fallen.

That glowing stinger brightened, and Unit D fell with a hole burned through its chest.

twenty-five

Guess we're taking your side passage after all, Keelhaul!" Rade said.

I just hope we're not being herded.

He aimed past Skullcracker and Unit E—both of them had dived to the deck, like Rade—and when he had the robot's stinger in his sights, he fired, disabling the weapon. "Skullcracker, on point!"

Skullcracker, who was the closest to the side passage, dove inside. The rest of the party followed at a crouch, essentially reversing their previous combat order so that Manic was at the rear. Unit E assumed drag.

It was impossible to see what lay ahead, due to the extreme curvature of the new passageway. Despite the deeply corkscrewing deck, the group remained steadily glued to the surface because of the compensating gravity vector.

The party approached a branch.

"Which way?" Skullcracker said.

Rade glanced at the overhead map. Right brought them closer to the core. Left took them outward again.

"Left," Rade said.

Skullcracker obeyed. Rade followed close behind him.

"Boss," Manic sent.

Rade paused. Glancing back, he saw that Keelhaul had halted beside the rightmost branch.

"I said _left_, Keelhaul," Rade said.

Keelhaul hesitated a moment longer, then turned left.

"How do we know this is the right way?" Manic sent.

"Because they're calling Keelhaul down the other passage," Rade replied.

The curvature evened out, and after two more left-turning branches they eventually doubled-back to the previously mapped route. They had skirted the whole scorpion-infested area.

"Lucky break," TJ said.

They continued along the upward-curving corkscrew, passing a hatch they'd breached before.

The deck suddenly rumbled, and the party began floating upward. Rade felt like he was going to throw up.

"What the—" Manic began.

"Looks like they lost their artificial gravity," TJ said.

"Or they turned it off on purpose," Skullcracker said.

"Keep going, people," Rade said, swallowing back the nausea. "Push off the bulkheads. You know the drill."

Before anyone could actually move, without warning gravity kicked in once more and the lot of them crashed to the deck.

"Well that was... strange." Rade pushed himself up. "Let's move."

The passageway tightened and soon they were crawling forward on gloves and knee assemblies. The path widened shortly, and they advanced at a crouch, reaching the final breached airlock.

"Almost out, people," Rade said.

They advanced through the rectangular passageway, and arrived at the edge of the staging area where the party had first boarded. Skullcracker paused at the opening.

Rade came up behind him. Their headlamps illuminated only a sliver of the mid-sized compartment beyond.

"Unit E, come forward," Rade said.

Rade and the others flattened themselves against the bulkhead to let the Centurion pass.

"Clear the chamber with Skullcracker," Rade said when the robot was in place.

Skullcracker glanced at the unit. "Ready?"

"I am," the Centurion replied.

The pair entered. The Centurion went high, Skullcracker low.

"Clear," Skullcracker said.

Rade entered the compartment, stepping over the wreckages of the original three scorpions. The larger passages that branched out on either side were empty, save for the one where another scorpion resided in a broken pile.

The far bulkhead still had Tahoe's five-meter long tunnel boring through to the stars. Floating there amid those myriad points of lights resided the planet they had left behind. It was currently the size of a thumbnail.

"There's our freedom, people," Rade said.

"I can't believe you guys came all this way to get me," Keelhaul transmitted. "You risked everything." He sounded like he was going to choke up again.

"Yeah, too bad we're never going to get back there," Manic said, his gaze on the distant planet.

"I'm hoping we won't have to," Rade said.

"What's that supposed to mean?" Manic asked. "You expect fleet to find us out there?"

"They'll find us," Rade said.

"If Fret were here, he'd tell you the fleet was long gone," Manic said. "Or destroyed."

"And he'd be wrong," Rade said.

"Wait," TJ said. "What are we going to do about the point defenses?"

"Maybe we'll be too small of a target for the defenses to detect?" Keelhaul said.

"No, TJ is right," Rade replied. "They detected us well enough on the planet's surface. They'll detect us in space, too."

"Too bad we don't have any smoke grenades," Manic said wistfully. "Or mechs."

"So what's the plan?" Skullcracker asked. "We thrust in random directions until we clear the ship?"

Rade shook his head. "No. We have to eliminate as many of those point defenses as we can before jetting from the ship."

Manic frowned behind his faceplate. "So what you're saying is, we're going to spacewalk across the hull."

"We are," Rade said.

"I'm only surprised our enemies didn't send any tangos to intercept us here," TJ said. "Scratch that!" He spun to the left and fired into one of the passageways, where a scorpion had appeared.

"Out people!" Rade said. "Unit E, cover us!"

Another scorpion appeared in that broad passageway, and Rade unleashed his blaster at it and then dove into the tunnel. He crawled the five meters to the opening, firing his jetpack in controlled, judicious bursts to aid him, and then pulled his upper body through into empty space. As usual, the sudden absence of gravity was disconcerting, but he ignored the nausea and braced his gloves against the rim of the opening to lift his legs through.

He set down his boots on the outer hull and activated the supermagnets in the heel. He felt the suction as his feet affixed to the black pentagonal tiles. Up until that point, he had been unsure as to the composition of those tiles—they might have been entirely ceramic or something, rendering the magnets useless.

Rade waited for everyone else to emerge. Keelhaul. TJ. Manic. Skullcracker.

"Where's Unit E?" Rade said. The blue dot of the Centurion was still active on the overhead map.

Abruptly the robot's head poked through the opening.

"Good to see you made it, Unit E," Rade said. "You've certainly lasted longer than the previous Unit E I had."

"Thank you, LPO," the robot replied, taking its place on the hull.

"Einstein," TJ said. "It's callsign is Einstein."

"Einstein," Rade said, smiling. "Well, you'd definitely have to be some kind of genius to survive what we just went through. Or a complete idiot, depending on your point of view." He studied the external hull blueprints provided by his HUD. "According to my Implant, the nearest point defense turret is here." He transmitted the location, and a blue square appeared in the distance, overlaying his vision. That was where his Implant had recorded the source of the point defense attack they had received on the surface. "Lead the way, Skullcracker. Let's go disable ourselves a turret."

Rade followed Skullcracker across the black surface. His boots varied the intensity of the magnets based on the angle and pressure applied by each foot, ensuring that he stayed glued to the hull while simulating a one-G environment for the user. It felt like slogging through mud.

As he spacewalked toward the target along that hull, he suddenly understood why the gravity had cut out earlier.

Streaks of light passed by overhead, slamming into the surface up ahead: Hellfire missiles, or their equivalents. Small craft also zoomed by.

The alien vessel was under attack. He could swear those were Avenger class fighters up there, flying past on strafing runs.

"Uh, I think we won't have to worry about those point defenses targeting us after all," Manic said. "Looks like they got their hands full already! And to be honest, the safest location right now is probably up there, out in space."

"UC Task Group 68.2," Rade transmitted on an open channel. "This is Rade Galaal, LPO of Alpha Platoon, MOTH Team Seven, assigned to the *U.S.S. Rhodes*. Requesting pick-up. Do you read, over?"

No response came.

"You think the comm nodes in those fighters received the signal?" TJ asked.

"I don't know," Rade said. "They should have."

"Maybe they did, but they think it's a trick," Manic commented.

"Might not even be the UC," Skullcracker said.

"I am detecting electromagnetic interference emanating from the hull," Einstein intoned. "I believe it is severely reducing the range of our signals."

"Wonderful," Manic transmitted.

A bright flash erupted from the hull just ahead as another fighter zoomed by overhead. The impact location corresponded with the blue square that marked the point defense turret. Rade zoomed in on the area: only a blast crater remained.

"Our friends just took out the closest turret for us," Rade said as more flashes went off in the distance around him—some on the hull, some in deep space as fighters were shot down. "I'm going to have to agree with Manic. It's safer, for the moment, to get the hell off this thing. The enemy has their hands full. Supermagnets off, people. Rendezvous at these coordinates."

He transmitted a location five kilometers from the hull, then wrapped his arms around Keelhaul. He deactivated his magnets and waited for Keelhaul to do the same, then released a quick burst from his jetpack. He discharged another burst that would take him to the rendezvous location, then fired lateral thrust, revolving his body. When he faced the enemy ship, he fired a countering burst, stabilizing his rotation: he wanted to watch the dodecahedral ship recede. Flashes continued as fighters flew past in more strafing runs.

He tried to make several more communication attempts with those fighters. No reply came. He couldn't see the supercarrier that had launched the craft, but that didn't mean a thing—any one of the stars around him could be a ship, thanks to the distances at which most space battles were fought. His overhead map didn't help... not even any of the fighters were displayed on it. He was starting to wonder if they were actually UC.

Have we wandered into some alien war?

The dark vessel quickly diminished in size; soon, the only way Rade could tell it was still there was because of the stars the vessel blocked. That and the flashes of light from the fighter attack. When the dodecahedron shrunk to the size of the planet behind him, Rade lost sight of the vessel entirely.

He reached the rendezvous point and fired stabilizing thrust. The others were already there waiting for him, floating within three meters of each other.

"Welcome to the party," Manic transmitted. "It was getting kind of lonely out here. Actually, it's still lonely as hell. Floating in the void, it's not like hanging out around a campfire if you know what I mean."

"So, what now?" TJ transmitted over the comm.

"Have any of you been able to raise the fleet?" Rade asked.

"Negative," TJ replied. "But according to Einstein, that ship is still sending out some sort of interference. But it's quickly weakening, the farther away we move."

"Would the fleet see us on the thermal band?" Keelhaul asked.

"No," TJ said. "The weak thermal signature of our suits blends with the background radiation after only a few klicks."

"Our PASS mechanisms are the strongest assets we have right now," Skullcracker said.

"That's a very good point," Rade replied. The small Personal Alert Safety System was attached to each of their utility belts, and could transmit a distress call up to ranges of several hundred kilometers. "If we join our power sources to one of the devices, we can boost the range."

And we might actually have a chance, then.

"Who's the lucky recipient?" Manic asked. "Because if we give up our batteries like you ask, the rest of us will be running on backup power. We'll have what, an hour left?"

"Take your pick," Rade said. "A small chance of rescue, but only an hour until your suit shuts down. Or two days floating in the void, waiting for your oxygen to run out, with no chance of rescue at all... "

"I'll take the small chance." Manic reached into his chest assembly and produced the battery. He gently flicked it toward Rade. "Here you go."

Manic's aim was off, and Rade had to fire a short lateral burst to catch it. He stuffed it into his utility belt. He handed Keelhaul over to Manic for safekeeping, then collected the batteries from everyone else, including Unit E. Then he jury-rigged the power sources to his PASS.

"Good to go," Rade said. "Let's hope this works. Now all we can do is wait. And hope. If no one answers in an hour, I'll return your batteries."

"For what?" Skullcracker said. "So we can merely extend the inevitable?"

Rade didn't answer.

The slow minutes passed. Rade stared at the infinite points of light around him. Phosphenes in his vision added to the starry panorama, and he found himself reliving memories from bootcamp, and then his rating school. He thought of Shaw, and wondered if he would ever see her again.

"In space, no one can hear you pee," Manic said, interrupting the quietude.

"You're taking a piss right now, aren't you?" TJ said.

"Maybe."

Rade glanced at Manic and saw the yellow crystals germinating outward from his leg.

TJ thrusted past and gave the eerily beautiful structure a kick; the crystals scattered in all directions. "Piss starburst!"

"The human fascination with bodily excreta never ceases to amaze me," Einstein said.

"You're just jealous that you can't piss, Einstein," Manic said.

It was good to see that they were in somewhat good spirits, at least. But that could be expected. These were *his* MOTHs, after all. Men who were used to staring death in the face.

Rade was never more proud of them than in that moment.

Forty-five minutes passed. Power levels were low. The others were careful not to make too many unnecessary movements, lest they drain the backups even faster. Once those levels reached zero, oxygen would cease to pump throughout their suits.

"I'm going to return your batteries," Rade said.

"Not yet," TJ said. "Give it a bit longer."

At the ten minute mark, Rade tried to give them back again. Still his brothers refused.

With five minutes to go, an Avenger pulled alongside.

A voice echoed in his helmet. "Greetings, leading petty officer Rade Galaal. This is Lieutenant Barnes. Nice day for a spacewalk."

"It is indeed," Rade said.

He did his best to suppress the tears of joy that came then, but he failed miserably.

His brothers weren't going to die.

He stared at the stars around him. They had never seemed more beautiful.

twenty-six

As soon as the *Rhodes* finished major combat operations in orbit, the captain of the vessel dispatched a Dragonfly to retrieve the commander from the planet 11-Aquarii III. New booster payloads were dropped for the stranded members of Alpha Platoon, facilitating the return of their Hoplites into orbit.

Every member of the landing party, including the chief and the commander, spent several hours under decontamination watch before being moved to the isolation ward for further observation. Those who had boarded the alien vessel were held separately from the others: Rade, TJ, Manic and Skullcracker shared the same glass-walled berth.

Keelhaul domiciled alone in a glass chamber across from them. He was kept isolated because the scientists had discovered some sort of nano machines reproducing inside his Implant; they had removed the device, but wanted to make sure none of the machines had spread to any other part of his brain.

No updates had been given regarding Lieutenant Vicks: she was held in a completely different part of the ship. But given the nano machines they'd found infecting Keelhaul, Rade feared the worst.

During their remote debriefing, Lieutenant Commander Braggs had explained what happened to the fleet. Coinciding with the attack experienced by the landing party, four of the dodecahedral vessels launched from the surface, where they had been masquerading as mountains. In the initial engagement, the enemy managed to drive away the fleet, causing severe losses among the UC task unit while suffering no casualties themselves.

The fleet returned a few days later, employing a strategy developed from detailed review of the first encounter. As an unexpected bonus, the UC only had to face three of the ships, as one of the enemy had returned to the surface—the same ship Rade and his team had boarded. By the time the final ship reached orbit, the other three were disabled, and the remaining enemy found itself facing the combined firepower of the task unit.

Shortly after Rade and the others were rescued, all four vessels self-destructed. Planet-side sweeps performed by drones reported no further sign of the enemy: the robots and biologically engineered lifeforms had gone into permanent hiding. Meanwhile, those UC personnel who had escaped the sinking of their ships by jettisoning in lifepods were rescued.

"So the four ships self-destructed," Rade had said. "Leaving us empty-handed."

"Yes, but we weren't left with nothing," Braggs had answered. "We collected several of the fallen machines littering the sites of your planet-side engagements, for example. As well as the corpses of bio weapons. Not to mention the nano machines we've extracted from Keelhaul. Will it be enough to track down the perpetrators? Who can say... I only know that the MOTHs will be called upon to fight once again. Sooner, rather than later. "

Though Keelhaul resided in a separate chamber, he had been provided with a pair of aReal glasses, so even though he had no Implant, Rade and the others were able to communicate with him.

"You look like a professor with those glasses," Manic told Keelhaul one time.

"A professor?" TJ scoffed. "If the village idiot wore glasses, he'd look like Keelhaul."

"You know, something's been bothering me, Keelhaul," Skullcracker said.

"Yeah, what's that?" Keelhaul asked.

"What you told us about your sister," Skullcracker continued. "Was it true? Did she really die like that?"

Keelhaul lowered his gaze. "She did. Though I didn't call myself Keelhaul to remind myself of what I had done to her, but to remind myself that I had to live my life to the fullest, to repay my debt to her. I still believe it should have been me who had died, not her. I was the one who made the dare. I promised her spirit I would live my life to the fullest, and that I wouldn't let her death be for nothing. So Keelhaul was kind of a way for me to honor her."

"Sounds a bit morbid, if you ask me," TJ said.

"Or in bad taste, at the very least," Manic added. He switched to a Czech accent. "I keelhauled my sister, so now I'm going to call myself Keelhaul. Because I'm so very good at it."

"Come on people," Rade said. "Let's go easy on him, all right? The death of his sister obviously caused a lot of pain."

"We'd go easy on him if he chose a better callsign," TJ complained. "It would make sense if he'd dragged an enemy underneath a boat or something. But I have to agree with Manic, it doesn't work when you've keelhauled your own damn sister."

Keelhaul sighed. "You'll never understand."

"I suppose we won't," Manic said.

"What was your old callsign?" Skullcracker asked.

Keelhaul shrugged. "I don't want to say."

"Come on, you can tell us," Manic said. "We risked our lives to board an alien ship to get you out, after all. It's the least you can do."

Keelhaul opened his lips, then shook his head. "I can't..."

TJ threw up his arms. "That's gratitude for you."

Keelhaul hesitated a moment longer, then: "Bootlicker."

"Your nickname was Bootlicker?" Manic said in disbelief. "No, I don't believe it. Boss, is it true?"

As LPO, Rade had access to Keelhaul's complete record. He couldn't recall seeing that callsign, however, so he refreshed the entry on his Implant. "It seems his old callsign was indeed Bootlicker."

"Well I'll be dipped in fecal-based products," TJ exclaimed.

"Apparently Team Eight uses different rules when it comes to callsigns," Rade said.

"I took the name in good humor," Keelhaul said. "It's all part of the camaraderie of the Teams."

"I suppose so," Rade said. "While I don't necessarily approve, who am I to judge how another Team is run?"

"I'm just glad I'm on Team Seven," Skullcracker muttered.

Roughly a week later Rade and those with him were released. Keelhaul was cleared a few days after, and scheduled to receive a new Implant.

As one of the first orders of business, Rade contacted Lieutenant Commander Braggs in regards to Vicks.

"Sorry Mr. Galaal," Braggs told him. "Her location, and her condition, are classified."

"Don't you think the platoon has the right to know what happened to her?" Rade said. "Given that we were the ones who risked our lives to rescue her?"

"Preaching to the choir, Mr. Galaal," the lieutenant commander answered. "Captain's orders."

"Can't you talk to the captain?" Rade asked.

"Already have," Braggs replied. "He won't budge on the issue."

When Rade told Tahoe, his friend was devastated.

"I can't believe not even Braggs will help us," Tahoe said. "After everything we've done."

Rade rested a hand on his friend's arms. "We'll find out what happened to her."

Rade went to Chief Facehopper next. "I don't suppose the LC has told you Lieutenant Vicks' condition?"

"No, Braggs hasn't told me a thing," the chief replied. "Sorry." Before Rade left, Facehopper added: "Leave it alone, Rage."

"What?" Rade said, all innocent-like. "I haven't done anything."

"Not yet," the chief replied. "But I can see it in your eyes. You're planning something."

Rade pursed his lips. "Not at all."

Rade scheduled a clandestine meeting with TJ and Bender. He had them assemble in a corner of the galley, in a blind spot where the ship's AI had no cameras for lip reading. As the robot cooks clattered their pans and whirred their blenders, he applied a noise canceller about the three of them and spoke.

"Have you disabled recording in your Implants?" he asked.

"What the frick!" Bender said. "You think we're amateurs? We, the two people who taught you how to hack your own Implant to do the same?" He stared at Rade in what seemed utter outrage, then smiled sheepishly. "Yeah I forgot. I'm shutting it down now, boss."

"All right, good," Rade said. "Listen. You guys are the best hackers in my platoon. If anyone can find out where they're keeping Lieutenant Vicks, it's you guys."

And so they did. Compartment 2-75-9-C.

Rade, Tahoe and Manic visited the two masters-at-arms on duty outside 2-75-9-C the next morning.

The first MA stepped forward. "This is a restricted area."

"Wait a second," the second MA said. "I think these guys are MOTHs!" He seemed overawed by their presence. Good.

After some friendly banter, Rade stared the first MA directly in the eye and said: "The woman you're guarding inside is a good friend of ours. We'd like to see her. Will you let us pass?"

"I'm sorry, petty officer Galaal, I can't do that," the MA told him.

Rade nodded. "I didn't expect you would."

The two MAs stiffened, as if expecting trouble.

Rade stared at the man for a moment longer, then he glanced at Tahoe and Manic. "Let's go."

He and Manic turned around but Tahoe still lingered by the entrance.

"Tahoe," Rade said.

Tahoe didn't reply. Rade was worried he was going to do something they would all regret.

"Cyclone," Rade repeated.

Finally Tahoe obeyed.

"So what are we going to do?" Tahoe said when they were out of hearing range.

"I have an idea," Rade told him.

He called upon the chief later that day. "My men are getting antsy. I'd like some duty assignments at the earliest possible opportunity."

"You're talking menial shipboard assignments, mate?" Facehopper asked. "Like assisting the MAs with security?"

"That's exactly what I mean," Rade said. "We've taken on patrols and watches as necessary in the past..."

Facehopper shrugged. "I'll see if anything opens up."

Rade wasn't about to leave the openings to fate. With the help of Bender and TJ, he worked out the guard rotation of that particular MA division, and hatched a plan to incapacitate them all.

"How do we know they won't replace them with robot MAs?" Manic asked when Rade imparted his plan.

"They'll want human beings on watch for this operation," Rade said. "Trust me."

He had Manic and Fret visit the various shifts when they were off duty in the mess hall. While Fret distracted the men, Manic swapped their drinks; Tahoe and Bomb stood in strategic locations, shielding Manic from the watching eyes of the mess hall cameras.

Bender and Skullcracker were called in to serve the first watch shift in front of 2-75-9-C the next morning, as most of the MAs from the respective division had reported in sick, it seemed.

Rade and Tahoe approached at 0700. They were jogging, pretending to be engaged in PT. They paused just before the bend that led to the destination compartment, and leaned against the bulkhead as if to catch their collective breaths.

A sparrow chirped—a notification tone that played over his Implant. That meant TJ had successfully substituted a looping video feed for the passageway, as well as the adjacent passageway and the area immediately in front of 2-75-9-C, so that the ship's AI would be none the wiser to what would happen next. TJ had promised to add some randomization elements to the loop, to fool the watchful, algorithmically sensitive eye of the AI.

Rade and Tahoe shut down the audio and video logging of their respective Implants and approached.

The two MOTHs on guard duty, Bender and Skullcracker, stepped aside so that Rade and Tahoe could enter the compartment.

A man dressed in a white lab coat in front of a glass isolation chamber looked up. As expected, he was the only one on duty at that hour.

"You shouldn't be in here," the scientist said.

Rade gazed at the container. Vicks lay on a bed inside it, along with various monitoring equipment.

"I'm part of the platoon that rescued her from the enemy," Rade said. "I protected her with my life. I have every right to be here."

Tahoe went to the container and rested a longing palm on the glass.

"The ship's AI is recording everything that's taking place here," the scientist said. "You'll be arrested."

"My men have momentarily locked-out the AI," Rade said. "Everything you say and do here is off the record."

The scientist cocked an eyebrow. "You have skilled men, then."

"The best," Rade said. "Now, I have some questions, if you don't mind."

His eyes defocused, as if he were accessing an Implant or contact lens aReal. "It seems you are telling the truth, Mr. Galaal. Fine, then. What is it you wish to know?"

Rade studied Vicks. "Well, first of all, what's the prognosis?"

The scientist joined Tahoe at the glass. "Nano-machines swarm inside her head."

"Nano-machines?"

"Yes," the scientist replied. "The same machines we found in the Implant of your MOTH friend. Except she has not been so lucky: she has no Implant, you see. She wears the contact lens equivalents. So she had nothing to draw the machines away from her brain tissue. Though I suppose it's also possible your MOTH friend would have suffered the same fate, if you hadn't gotten to him in time.

"The things are systematically destroying her neurons, using the constituent molecules to construct new versions of themselves, replacing her brain cells, forming their own neural net. Her brain is slowly moving from organic-based, to machine-based. The interesting thing is, the new nano parts exactly mimic the specialized neurons they replace, taking over the same functions. The hippocampus becomes the hippocampus. The thalamus the thalamus. In memory cells, the same engrams are appearing in the replacements. It's as if her entire consciousness is slowly transferring over to the new machine neural net. When she wakes up, she might not even know that she has changed—that she no longer has a living brain. It's quite extraordinary, really."

"Come on, Tahoe, let's go," Rade said. "There's nothing more we can do here." He turned toward the scientist. "We'll be back when she awakens."

"But how will you know?" the scientist asked.

"We'll know," Rade said. "In the meantime, would you mind deleting our little conversation from the logs of your aReal?"

The scientist frowned. "This is very unprofessional behavior on your part." He glanced at Tahoe, and when he saw the pained expression the MOTH wore, the scientist's face softened. "It's done."

A few days later Bender informed him she had awakened. Once more they arranged for a certain MA division to fall ill, and members of Alpha Platoon were assigned as their replacements.

"You probably shouldn't go," Rade told Tahoe before they left their berthing area to pay a visit.

"Why not?" Tahoe asked.

"It's not Vicks, not anymore," Rade said. "Her brain has been completely replaced by nano machines."

"I thought those machines mimicked her axons and dendrites precisely?" Tahoe said. "Transferring her consciousness neuron by neuron?"

"That's what the doctor believes," Rade said. "But not me. You can't transfer consciousness like that. I'm pretty certain the Vicks we knew is dead. While she might have the same memories, and perhaps even the same personality, she won't be the same person. Definitely not human, not anymore."

"I'll decide that for myself."

Rade sighed. "All right."

When Rade and Tahoe arrived, they found the scientist seated in front of the glass chamber, engaged in conversation with her.

He stood up when they entered. "I was wondering when you would arrive." He beckoned toward the chamber. "She's been asking for you. She's all yours."

Rade had seen the video recording Tahoe had shared during his debriefing of the survivor from the *John A. McDonald*—the man he had met on the surface while rescuing the lieutenant. Vicks had those same dead eyes.

"Hello, Tahoe," she said.

Tahoe approached and rested a hand on the glass. She didn't mimic the gesture.

"I can't tell you how good it is to see you," she said.

"It's good to see you as well," Tahoe said.

"No, you don't understand," Vicks said. "I can really *see* now. Everything around us, I perceive for what it actually is. None of this is real. Quantum properties. Bundles. Spin states. The higher dimensions. You have no idea. It's quite extraordinary. I finally understand the cosmos. And who we are. We're all just embodiments of the universe. The universe doesn't realize it exists, except through us, and the existential loops that develop in our minds. If you could see what I'm seeing... it goes beyond augmented reality. Far beyond it. I perceive the reality that exists beyond this one. The real reality."

Tahoe sighed sadly. He lowered his hand and gave Rade a forlorn look.

Vicks stood up and approached the glass. "I have a link to them, you know."

"To who?" Tahoe asked.

"The creators. I can shut them out when I choose, but I prefer to let them in. The knowledge they possess... I can imagine the experience feels similar to an AI linking to a cloud computing resource. The understanding... the intelligence... for once in my life, I truly feel complete. I'll never be alone again. I finally understand what it means to be more than the sum of one's parts."

"Goodbye, Rebecca," Tahoe said sadly.

"Goodbye, Tahoe," she said. She flashed him a hint of a seductive smile. It never reached her eyes.

"I trust you will delete the relevant entries from your log files?" Rade asked the scientist before leaving.

The man inclined his head. "Already done. I won't be seeing you again, will I?"

"Somehow, I doubt it."

Rade and Tahoe departed. As they rounded the bend, they switched to a pretend jog so that TJ could restore the live video feed.

The pair passed two young men in tight-fitting black outfits marching in the opposite direction. Petty officers first class, according to the chevrons on their sleeve insignias. Intelligence specialists, Rade guessed, judging from the characteristic metal suitcases they carried, no doubt filled with the tools of their profession: scalpels, dental forceps, stun rods. Fleet interrogators, or "tactical interviewers," as they liked to be called.

He pulled up their public profiles on his Implant. He was almost expecting the rating field to be classified, but he supposed that would draw attention. The first individual was an IS-3924, or Operational Intelligence Analyst. The second an IS-3913, or Navy Tactical Counter-Intelligence and Human Intelligence Specialist.

Yeah. Interrogators.

Rade and Tahoe paused to watch the pair round the bend behind them. A moment later they heard the hatch to 2-75-9-C shut with an ominous thud.

Rade glanced at Tahoe. "You going to be okay?"

Tahoe shook his head. "Like you said, it's not her anymore."

They resumed their jog.

twenty-seven

The months passed. The Builder vessel completed the construction of the return Gate without incident. No further attacks came. The telemetry probes mapped out every nook and cranny of the system, not to mention the planet 11-Aquarii III, but if further signs of the strange robots or bioweapons were discovered, the knowledge wasn't shared with Alpha Platoon.

Two destroyers remained behind in the system while the survivors of Task Group 68.2 traveled to UC space. Alpha Platoon eventually returned to Earth, and Rade and the others were given leave. They returned to the base refreshed and recharged.

The months passed in a blur of PT and training. The downtime between deployments always proved a restive period, but the current atmosphere proved particularly trying: the mood on the entire base was electrically charged. Everyone knew another deployment was coming, and soon. And it was going to be a big one. Rumors were flying that the fleet was gathering an invasion force of some kind. Alpha Platoon didn't want to be left out.

Finally Lieutenant Commander Braggs summoned both platoons under his command for a briefing. The members of Alpha and Bravo gathered in the conference room. The energy among the men was one of nervous excitement.

"You're looking well-rested," Braggs told Alpha. "Good. Because you're going to need your strength in the days to come. Phi Hepti, a Franco-Italian system, has been attacked. We've received footage of the invaders, and their ships match the dodecahedral design we saw in 11-Aquarii. The FIs have reached out to their allies, and the UC has answered the call. Unfortunately, Phi Hepti IV has already been lost. The following orbital footage was taken two weeks ago."

An image of the planet overlaid Rade's vision: a bright, green, healthy terraformed world. A swath of gray near the middle indicated the human settlement.

"This is the same footage from last week," the lieutenant commander said.

A new image appeared. The green bands had been replaced with brown, and the gray settlement was pocked with black craters.

"They've taken over the entire system as far as we can tell," Braggs said. "They've destroyed the comm nodes and all other FI infrastructure. They attack anything that come through the Gates. The footage you're seeing was obtained from an FI freighter that barely escaped."

"Do we know what they want?" Lui asked. "Why they attacked the colony?"

The lieutenant commander clenched his jaw. "The Special Collection Service has spent the past few months interrogating a certain individual with known ties to the enemy."

Rade glanced at Tahoe. They both knew who that certain individual was.

"According to this person, Phi Hepti IV was merely a stepping stone," the LC continued. "They've taken the colony as their own, and populated it with their robots and bioengineered abominations. They want the UC to give them five more terraformed colonies in adjacent systems, as well as recognize them as an official space-faring nation. Of course, the UC is going to do no such thing."

"It sounds almost like they're space nomads or something," Mauler said. "Without homeworlds or colonies of their own, and they want to join the big boys club by skipping a few steps and taking ours."

"Were the residents evacuated in time?" Rade asked, fearing a whole colony converted like Lieutenant Vicks.

Braggs nodded. "There were only fifty thousand of them. Most escaped through the far Gate before the invasion force arrived. Maybe a thousand were left behind."

Rade exhaled in relief. Still, a thousand people with minds destroyed by nano machines...

"We're going to be part of the repatriation force," the lieutenant commander continued. "See, the Franco-Italians, they want to preserve the surviving infrastructure of the colony, and spare the lives of as many of those civilians who were left behind as possible.

So we can't just nuke the settlement outright. Unfortunately, we're expecting some heavy street to street fighting: although only a week has passed, apparently the enemy has already amassed a significant military presence. We're going to have to retake the settlement on a block by block basis."

"Shit," Bender said. "By the time we're done, there won't be much of the city left anyway. Might as well bomb it from orbit."

"You're forgetting the civilians," the LC replied.

"Yeah?" Bender said. "I bet half of those civilians have already been converted into enemy robots like a certain former scientist of the *Rhodes*."

The LC's brow furrowed. "How do you know about that?"

Bender shrugged. "News travels on the grapevine. And we saw what nearly happened to Keelhaul, after all."

All eyes in the conference room fell on Keelhaul, who shrugged. "I'm fine now."

"In any case," the lieutenant commander continued. "We have our orders. There will be no bombing from orbit. You'll be teaming up with the Marines on this one. Once we reach the planet, we're going to launch a coordinated, beachhead type assault. You'll be escorting Marine Companies C and D of the 2nd Assault Battalion. Your participation will be entirely mech-based. Each and every one of you will be given a shiny new toy."

"What kind of new toy?" Fret asked suspiciously.

"I've arranged for thirty-two new Zeus class mechs to be transferred aboard the supercarrier *Intrepid*," the LC said. "Do I ever do you wrong?"

"Wait a second," Tahoe asked. "Zeus class? Those haven't ever been tested in the field, have they?"

The lieutenant commander shrugged. "They've passed the controlled tests with flying colors. Trust me, you're going to love these mechs. Why the disappointed looks? I thought you'd all be happy."

"We are happy," Bomb said. "We're here to fight. We just like tech that we know works, is all."

"I think you'll be more than pleased," Braggs replied. "Facehopper has updated the simulators with the latest Zeus package. Get some practice in—you're all due to report for deployment next Monday. See you on the *Intrepid*."

The two platoons took shuttles into orbit the next week and rendezvoused with the supercarrier and its task group. The weeks passed slowly as the task group navigated between the different systems, taking Gate after Gate. Eventually, six weeks later, the fleet rendezvoused with the major battle group in Delta Ceti, and prepared for the final Gate crossing to the neighboring system, Phi Hepti.

Lying on his bunk in the berthing area, Rade stared at the Gate through the forward feed Lieutenant Commander Braggs had granted him. Bender and TJ had been unable to hack into to the systems of the supercarrier, so the platoon was at the mercy of the lieutenant commander and whatever feeds he deigned to stream.

Rade had never seen so many battle ships queued up in one place like that before. The fighting was going to be intense on the other side, no doubt. Rumors had it that the entire enemy fleet was stationed beyond the Gate, waiting to attack every ship that passed inside. Once through, if the *Intrepid* survived the initial engagement, it would take at least three days to reach the colony, even if it made a direct run for the planet.

Three days before the platoon would see any action.

The *Intrepid's* turn at the Gate came. Rade involuntarily held his breath as the supercarrier approached.

The video feed abruptly clicked off.

"What the—!" That was Bender.

"Braggs can't do this to us," Manic complained.

Rade immediately tapped in Facehopper. "Chief, we lost the feed."

"I know," Facehopper replied. "The LC decided it was better for us if he turned it off."

"Is it that bad on the other side?" Rade asked.

"Apparently so."

The moments ticked away. The *Intrepid* had no doubt traversed the Gate by then.

Rade felt a slight rumbling underneath him. The hull began to moan in the distance, and he knew they were already under attack.

"Hang tight, people," Rade said. "Our turn is coming. Real soon now."

twenty-eight

Crushing G forces assailed Rade as the inertial dampeners of the *U.S.S. Intrepid* struggled to compensate for a sudden directional change. The feeling quickly subsided, but the bulkheads of the berthing area rumbled, and the deep moaning of the hull momentarily intensified.

The others in the berthing compartment said not a word. There was nothing *to* say. The only thing the MOTHs of Alpha Platoon could do during the attack was wait it out and hope the captain and crew of the supercarrier carried them through the moment of crisis. The platoon members remained stock-still on their bunks, dealing with the feelings of fear, helplessness, and impotency in their own way.

Bender and TJ acted all casual, wearing their best poker faces, the drone operators refusing to show fear. Manic was sweating, the port-wine stain a particularly bright red that day as he quietly prayed to himself. Tahoe had his eyes closed, and he too seemed to be praying to those spirits he claimed not to believe in, though his lips barely moved. The remainder of the platoon distracted themselves in one of the virtual reality war games that was popular at the moment, their defocused eyes and their jerky arm movements giving away the fact they resided entirely inside of their Implants.

The rumbling abruptly flared up as the deck resounded with some distant boom. Manic flinched, and Tahoe opened his eyes.

Something had struck the hull nearby, Rade guessed; probably had torn a hole clean through.

Tahoe closed his eyes once more as the shaking subsided.

Rade tried to pull up the damage reports on his Implant, but he didn't have the authorization. He'd never know how close he and his team had come to dying.

The current state of affairs wasn't entirely unfamiliar to them. A similar scenario had played out shortly after the *Intrepid* had passed through the Gate into the Phi Hepti system three days ago, where a large enemy fleet had awaited in ambush. The rumbling of the deck and the inertial compensator lag hadn't been nearly so bad then.

After that battle, Rade learned that the *Intrepid* had been one of the luckier vessels: it had received only minor damage during the initial engagement. Though the enemy outnumbered them slightly, the UC battle group had prevailed, apparently because of the weaknesses Task Group 68.2 had gleaned from their previous encounter, employed to devastating effect: the opposing fleet quickly fled to the far side of the system, leaving an open path to Phi Hepti IV.

The UC battle group had split into three battle units. The first remained by the Gate to guard it. The second pursued the enemy. The third proceeded to the planet. The majority of the starships sent toward the undefended planet were troop carriers, full of the Marines who would liberate the colony, two companies of which Rade and his platoon of MOTHs would be escorting.

The *Intrepid* had spent the last three days journeying toward the planet with the latter battle unit. According to advance telemetry, the planet was relatively undefended. The two enemy vessels stationed near Phi Hepti IV had fled, and on approach the battle unit shot down what appeared to be orbital defense platforms. Rade and his platoon were due to report to the drop bay in an hour.

But then a klaxon had sounded, and the detached voice of the ship's AI had come over the main circuit to warn of an impending attack—the planet wasn't as defenseless as initially believed. Though the means of attack weren't mentioned, Rade guessed the enemy utilized some form of surface to space bombardment: missiles, lasers, railguns, mortars, or a combination thereof. Either that, or some new weapon the UC had never seen before.

And so Rade sat there tensely in the berthing area, waiting for the order to report to the drop bay.

An order that would never come.

The starship continued to rumble for some time. One particularly loud moaning of steel came from above, and the platoon members glanced upward nervously. Those who were playing virtual reality war games shut them down.

"Anything from the chief?" Lui asked.

Rade shook his head. "Haven't received any orders to make for the drop bay, yet."

Another loud rumbling came from above.

"Geez," Mauler said. "They're really strafing our hull good."

"You think the enemy has fighters?" Grappler asked.

"Well, whatever they have," Trace said. "It can't be good."

Rade tried to wear his most reassuring expression. "Stay calm, people. Whatever—"

He was interrupted by a terrible screeching sound. The lights flicked off; an instant later the emergency HLEDs kicked in. The whole world then turned sideways, and everyone was thrown against the far bulkhead, along with any other loose items: clothing fell from lockers; spare aReal goggles and noise cancellers slid from tables. The lockers themselves, along with the steel bed frames beside them, were bolted to the deck, thankfully. The mattresses were similarly strapped down. Unfortunately, Rade was battered by Manic's portable refrigerator.

"Damn it. I told you to secure that fridge, Manic!" Feeling nauseous, Rade painfully kicked the appliance off his leg, and to his surprise it floated to the far side of the compartment. He felt what could only be a reactionary force, pressing his body firmly into the bulkhead.

As Rade floated into the air, he realized the nausea he felt wasn't because he had been hit by the fridge.

"Artificial gravity is out," Trace said.

"No, really?" Bender said.

"What the hell!" Bomb peeled off a pair of skivvies that had landed in his face. "Who's ginch is this?!" His nose wrinkled in disgust and he threw it away as if it were a grenade. "Got skidmarks in it!" The brown stains of the "skidmarks" were fairly obvious inside the underwear as it floated across the compartment.

"Chief!" Rade transmitted over the comm. "What the hell is going on out there?"

Facehopper didn't answer.

"Chief?" Rade tried again

"Got some bad news," Facehopper replied. "The *Intrepid* has been cut clean in half."

To Be Continued...

Acknowledgments

THANK YOU to my knowledgeable beta readers and advanced reviewers who helped smooth out the rough edges of the prerelease manuscript: Noel, Anton, Spencer, Norman, Corey, Erol, Terje, David, Jeremy, Charles, Walter, Lisa, Ramon, Chris, Scott, Michael, Chris, Bob, Jim, Maureen, Zane, Chuck, Shayne, Anna, Dave, Roger, Nick, Gerry, Charles, Annie, Patrick, Mike, Jeff, Lisa, Lezza, Jason, Bryant, Janna, Tom, Jerry, Chris, Jim, Brandon, Kathy, Norm, Jonathan, Derek, Shawn, Judi, Eric, Rick, Bryan, Barry, Sherman, Jim, Bob, Ralph, Darren, Michael, Chris, Michael, Julie, Glenn, Rickie, Rhonda, Neil, Doug, Claude, Ski, Joe, Paul, Larry, John, Norma, Jeff, David, Brennan, Phyllis, Robert, Darren, Daniel, Montzalee, Robert, Dave, Diane, Peter, Skip, Louise, Dave, Michael, David, Merry, David, Brent, Erin, Paul, Cesar, Jeremy, Hans, Nicole, Dan, Garland, Trudi, Sharon, Dave, Pat, Nathan, Max, Martin, Greg, David, Myles, Nancy, Ed, David, Karen, Becky, Jacob, Ben, Don, Carl, Gene, Bob, Luke, Teri, Robine, Gerald, Lee, Rich, Ken, Daniel, Chris, Al, Andy, Tim, Robert, Fred, David, Mitch, Don, Tony, Dian, Tony, John, Sandy, James, David, Pat, Gary, Jean, Bryan, William, Roy, Dave, Vincent, Tim, Richard, Kevin, George, Andrew, John, Richard, Robin, Sue, Mark, Jerry, Rodger, Rob, Byron, Ty, Mike, Gerry, Steve, Benjamin, Anna, Keith, Jeff, Josh, Herb, Bev, Simon, John, David, Greg, Larry, Timothy, Tony, Ian, Niraj, Maureen, Jim, Len, Bryan, Todd, Maria, Angela, Gerhard, Renee, Pete, Hemantkumar, Tim, Joseph, Will, David, Suzanne, Steve, Derek, Valerie, Laurence, James, Andy, Mark, Tarzy, Christina, Rick, Mike, Paula, Tim, Jim, Gal, Anthony, Ron, Dietrich, Mindy, Ben, Steve, Allen, Paddy & Penny, Troy, Marti, Herb, Jim, David, Alan, Leslie, Chuck, Dan, Perry, Chris,

Rich, Rod, Trevor, Rick, Michael, Tim, Mark, Alex, John, William, Doug, Tony, David, Sam, Derek, John, Jay, Tom, Bryant, Larry, Anjanette, Gary, Travis, Jennifer, Henry, Nicole, Drew, Michelle, Bob, Gregg, Billy, Jack, Lance, Sandra, Libby, Jonathan, Karl, Thomas, Todd, Dave, Dale, Michael, Frank, Josh, Thom, Melissa, Marilynn, Bob, Bruce, Clay, Gary, Sarge, Andrew, Deborah, Bryan, Amy, Steve, and Curtis.

Without you all, this novel would have typos, continuity errors, and excessive lapses in realism. Thank you for helping me make *Hoplite* the best military science fiction novel it could possibly be, and thank you for leaving the early reviews that help new readers find my books.

And of course I'd be remiss if I didn't thank my mother, father, and brothers, whose untiring wisdom and thought-provoking insights have always guided me through the untamed warrens of life.

— Isaac Hooke

www.isaachooke.com

Lightning Source UK Ltd.
Milton Keynes UK
UKOW02n0840301116

288828UK00002B/71/P